The Nested Charmer

The Nested Charmer

A Matryoshka's Hidden Legacy

Jessica May Broyles

JMB Publishing

DEDICATION

To my loving husband, George, for encouraging me to reach new heights and for always believing in me. To my golden-doodle, Charlie who stayed by my side throughout the writing process.

Time is too slow for those who wait, too swift for those who fear, too long for those who grieve, too short for those who rejoice, but for those who love, time is eternity.

Henry Van Dyke

Prologue

The Secret

Alex **placed brightly** painted wooden soldiers on the windowsill without paying attention to the crowd of people below. Vera sang to him while gathering necessary items he needed to travel, not knowing when or if they'd return.

(Translated into English)
A clumsy little bear was walking in the forest
He was gathering pine cones and singing songs
A pine cone fell directly onto his forehead.
The little bear got angry and stamped his foot!

A stray bullet ricocheted off the window frame and nicked the glass. When it shattered, Vera stifled a scream. Alex fell back, shrieking, and climbed into her arms. She rocked him and brushed blond hair from his pale forehead.

"Shh." Vera held him close in her lap. Alex found the uncommon noises beyond the three-story Golitsyn home overwhelming, and his father's urgency that morning left him confused. The estate's housekeepers and caretakers refused to appear for work in fear of becoming grouped as supporters of the monarchy or aristocracy. Thus, the family found themselves in charge of collecting indispensable attire on their own as quickly as possible. Many of the city's poor huddled around bonfires and spoke in low tones full of nervous suspicion waiting for the inevitable. It was the fall of the year 1917, and the revolution was coming to Moscow.

Vera gently unleashed the child's arms from her neck and directed him to sit while she peeked out the window. A burly fellow pointed a pistol heavenward and squeezed off bullets until the chamber was empty, then reloaded and repeated.

"There's no reason to be afraid. Come see for yourself." She reached for him behind her. "It's a drunken old man playing with his toys." Returning her attention to the child, she saw his pajamas flying behind him as he hurried out the door. "Alex, come back!" He ignored her and scampered across the hall to his Da's room, who was leaning against the wall studying a map.

Earlier, in preparation for the task of packing, Vera wound her long dark hair into a tight bun to keep it off her face. Now a strand escaped and curled onto her forehead. She brushed it aside and finished filling Alex's trunk. Once complete, she dragged it into the foyer, so his father could carry it to the waiting coach.

Mr. Golitsyn paced the hall all afternoon and stopped at each doorway to monitor the family's progress. As the hours ticked by, he became more agitated and continuously reminded everyone to hurry. "We must be on the road before dark," he'd said. What he didn't say was; The forest is full of revolutionists who won't take kindly to wealthy Christian Aristocrats, especially those who sneak off before being interrogated, robbed, and locked up.

At the end of the street, flames engulfed one of the smaller estates. Muscovites watched the fire service attempt to douse the burning building with fire-fighting carriages. The shallow water tanks and short hoses proved mostly ineffective in completing the task.

Vera pulled a massive chest from beneath the bed in her room and flipped up the domed lid. She rummaged through her wardrobe, ignoring the clatter of activity in the hall behind her. The nervous prattle made her anxious. Alex's babushka appeared at the door and gazed upon the teen hastily tossing garments into the trunk.

"You have grown to be a competent young lady," the babushka said.

Caught unaware, Vera slipped and fell on her bottom with a thud onto the varnished floor. Her long skirt billowed and exposed her undergarments. Twisting to see the grandmother staring at her, she sighed and clumsily got to her feet. The same flyaway curl bounced onto her forehead, and she brushed it back into place. She smoothed down her hem to calm her nerves before turning to face Alex's grandmother.

"Mrs. Golitsyn, I didn't hear you come in."

On a typical day, Vera read stories to Alex in the library, and the babushka sat in a corner appearing interested, but then shuffled out during the best parts. When Vera read about past events in Russia, the grandmother interrupted continually by reciting stories of when she was a little girl. A time when Moscow cared more about its people, not how much money was in the coffers.

Many a night, the senior Mrs. Golitsyn ranted as she bumped along the second-floor hall. When Vera heard the cane bouncing along the corridor, she waited until the noise was right outside her closed bedroom door before running to hide underneath the blankets of her featherbed. Mr. Golitsyn, the grandmother's son, mimicked her mumblings and limping gait at breakfast. His wife always admonished him for fear Alex would copy the tomfoolery while Vera ate oatmeal and giggled beneath her hand.

Now the grandmother seemed very determined as she stood in Vera's doorway.

"You've endured tragedies, and yet you are so strong." Her eyes twinkled.

"Me?" One hand flew to her chest. "But, I'm not brave at all."

Until the Golitsyn family took her in, Vera was frightened of everything. Part of that fear came from never staying in a place longer than a few weeks during her young life. Her family traveled with several others, always making camp just outside a town or village. When their welcome wore thin, they packed and left in the middle of the night. Their escapes usually happened when there was a threat of violence.

Vera banded with some of the older kids the day the villagers murdered her family. Returning to camp laden with stolen bread and sausages, they found their tents and belongings burned to the ground. When Mr. and Mrs. Golitsyn found her, she had lived in the Catholic orphanage for three years. Now with the revolution looming, Vera feared she would lose her new home and family.

The grandmother turned to look down the hall, then stepped inside the room and lowered her voice. "You're a smart girl," she mused. "But, there's something else about you I can't quite put my finger on." She looked toward the ceiling as if trying to capture a thought, then refocused on the girl. A trace of a smile passed across her lips. "You know things." Alex's grandma continued, "In today's world, it's good to know things most others don't."

Vera sometimes possessed an insight into future events. She knew when a storm brewed on the horizon on a sunny day or if the estate would receive guests without notice. Sometimes Vera had dreams of things beyond her understanding. Nothing serious, or so she thought until Mr. Golitsyn returned home with a newspaper. It spoke of skirmishes miles from the city and said the fighting would stay outside Moscow, but the whispers on the street made him nervous. After much rumination, he called Vera into his study. To him, her intuition was nothing more than lounge tricks, but in the end, he wanted to know.

"Are we in danger?" His eyes locked on hers.

She broke her gaze from his stare and glanced down at her wringing hands. Then, she looked up. With a face drained of hue and lips trembling, she nodded. He stood and called the rest of the family to join them to explain as best he could. They would depart by the end of the day.

Now Vera looked through her bedroom window. With the sun low on the horizon, "Madame, shouldn't you be preparing to leave?" She attempted to pass the older woman and move into the hall, but the babushka blocked her path. "Let me help you with your trunk." Vera glanced at the woman's features, and her breath caught in her throat. Mrs. Golitsyn's face had twisted into an angry scowl.

"I refuse to run from the home of my birth like an animal."

"But it's too dangerous to stay. I, I've heard whispers. The Bolsheviks are planning to attack the city."

"My mind is made up." She hobbled out of Vera's room. "Come with me. I have something to show you." Mrs. Golitsyn shuffled down the hallway, but instead of following, Vera hesitated.

Common sense told her to ignore the woman. She gazed back at the opened trunk but, after a few seconds, threw up her hands. I know I will regret this, she thought. Her jaw tightened.

Vera followed the babushka through the darkened foyer and up the staircase into a vast living area. A massive armoire with two ornate doors stood poised against one wall. The babushka opened it and rummaged through while humming a lullaby. Beautiful fabrics from around the world landed haphazardly onto the Egyptian rug.

Alex's father's voice echoed somewhere downstairs in an attempt to mollify his son's fears. "You know." His voice was soothing. "Your Da would never allow anyone to hurt you? Come, you will help me get your trunk into the carriage."

Vera felt sweat trickle down the back of her neck. She crossed her arms and tapped her foot silently onto the plush carpet. I must be insane to be up here, she thought.

After struggling with several quilts and blankets, the grandmother stopped humming.

"Aha!" She pulled something from the back, beneath a pile of winter coats. "Here it is." She held up a blue velvet bag. Caressing it to her chest, she faced the girl.

"Come, sit beside me." A divan at the end of a massive four-post bed awaited. Holding out her hand, she beckoned Vera to sit with her.

"But, we need to leave, Mrs. Golitsyn." Vera stayed rooted to the floor.

"This will only take a minute. I promise."

Vera grudgingly joined her on the divan. The grandmother loosened the cord from the bag, and when the soft material fell away, a nesting doll revealed itself. She cradled it in her hands. Then, she held it out. Vera leaned back.

"You must take this with you. But you have to carry it

secretly."

"What?" Vera's mouth fell open. "I don't understand. It's just an old matryoshka."

"This is not just any matryoshka." Her eyes shone brightly. "You will see."

"But why not give it to your son, Mr. Golitsyn?" Vera pleaded. "Shouldn't he be the one to care for it?"

"Never tell him you have it." The older woman sighed. Her voice turned raspy as if forcing the words from her throat. "He knows nothing of what this is or of its power." She pushed the doll into the girl's hands. "No, it must be you."

Alex's mother's shrill voice echoed from the floor below, "Vera! Are you ready? We must leave immediately." The sound of heavy luggage banged along the main hall.

"Coming!" Then to the old woman, "You aren't making sense." She tried to give the matryoshka back. "Why don't you hold on to it? Come with us!"

"No, I cannot." She folded her hands into her lap. "You must protect it," her expression was solemn. "Now go. Before you are left behind."

Vera reluctantly hid the doll within her luggage. When the family carriage escaped into the darkened streets, she heard Mrs. Golitsyn's last words in her head. "Above all else, you must keep it safe and hidden."

A group of fortune-hunters pretending to be revolutionists ransacked the estate and searched for the special matryoshka. Mrs. Golitsyn looked out her bedroom window and rocked in her chair. They assumed the older woman was too feeble to have any valuable information. She hummed her lullaby and never spoke of the doll again.

The Golitsyn family passed through Siberia and China

during the cold winter months. In the spring, they booked passage and sailed to America. They settled in San Francisco. Young Alex grew up and moved to Los Angeles to learn all about movie-making. He became a producer after the development of film and created many of the first action movies. Vera turned eighteen and became an independent woman. She set out on her own with the doll, telling no one she had it.

CHAPTER ONE

The Get-Away

The more she fought, the deeper Audrey sank into the dark abyss. Her lungs screamed to breathe. She struggled to rise to the surface, but a shadowy figure pressed her shoulders down. With arms flailing and lungs desperate for air, she reached for his face. Her fingernails bore into soft skin and peeled it away from his cheek. The black circle of his mouth screamed, echoing in her head, and she fought to escape. Breaking free from his grip, she pushed through the surface and emerged from the depths of the dark Atlantic.

She covered her eyes with her fists and cried silently. "It's not real; it's only a dream." After her breathing and heartbeat returned to normal, she sat up to clear her head. "I can't do this anymore." She swallowed a sob and reassured herself, "I'm in my bed." Feeling something sticky, she held up her hands and found dried blood trailing down her arms. There were cuts in her palms where her nails dug in.

The Aeroflot Airbus A320, destined for Moscow, sat on the Miami International airport runway crowded with men and women in business attire with families interspersed. Everyone was settling in for the long flight.

Audrey sat by the window, transfixed by how the crew loaded luggage from large drivable carts into the belly of the aircraft in the darkness. They worked without hesitation and reminded her of how ants scurried between thin panes of glass in the giant ant farm at the Palm Glade zoo. When she was a little girl, she and her dad visited the cave-like tunnel where exotic spiders and snakes dwelled. She sat on his shoulders while using her finger to trace the ants' paths working tirelessly for the queen, who laid eggs for the colony. Observing the flight crew functioning together made her realize how calculated and meticulous the process was. Cold and deliberate without thought or emotion. She needed to be that way now more than ever.

The bright interior cabin highlighted her reflection in the window, and she blew out a sigh. With gray streaks through otherwise dark hair, she noticed similarities between herself and her Grandma Josie when she was the same age. To calm her nerves, she silently recited the Lord's Prayer and observed the passengers now boarding.

Were any of them showing an interest in her? Could one be watching and waiting for the right moment? She pursed her lips and glanced toward the rear of the plane, then looked toward the front. She scrutinized each passenger coming down the aisle. I wonder if the KGB can take an American into custody in the U.S. I'm certainly making it easy for them. She shook her head.

The passengers went about the business of loading their carry-on bags into the overhead bins, taking seats, and strapping on safety belts. Most didn't look as though they were fully awake. The man seated in front of her reclined almost into her lap, and after a few minutes, snored loudly. The thought of coming out of hiding terrified her, but she had to take the chance. *Father Matthews knows I'm on my way,* she thought. *Moscow is a big city like New York. I'm perfectly safe going there.*

⌘

Two days before her trip was like every other day over the last forty years. Audrey grappled daily with loneliness, but she felt safe in her tiny apartment until a man began to follow her. At first, she thought it was just her overactive imagination, but she knew every resident in her quaint community on sight. Most left her alone, and she kept to herself. Strangers in the small Ohio town made her nervous.

A tall, thin older gentleman with black hair and a white mustache stood outside the post office. He wasn't doing anything in particular, but he seemed out of place. When she approached the entrance, he turned away and disappeared around the side of the building. *That's odd,* she thought. Sometimes out-of-towners became confused in the downtown area. Most of the buildings had an old-time feel and similar exteriors of rustic red brick.

The next day, the same man sat in a parked car one row over when she came out of the grocery store. He watched her load her bags into the back of her old, dependable Chevy station wagon. Pretending not to notice, she pulled out of the parking lot, but he followed, staying a few cars back. After making a series of left and right turns with him close behind, it became apparent. Somehow, they had found her.

Her heart hammered in her chest. She no longer needed to wonder whether they forgot about her or what she would do if they ever caught up to her. How would she react? Would she freeze up or run? Could she fight? White knuckling the steering wheel, her mind raced. She hoped to lose him in traffic, but he matched her every move and was eventually right behind her. He no longer took care to be discreet.

Her tires skidded into a parking space in front of the library. She scrambled out, slamming the door behind her. Looking back at the highway, she stumbled over her feet but mentally said a prayer and kept her balance. Think, Audrey! He will kill you if given a chance.

When she burst inside, a clerk staffing the front desk looked up. A group of youngsters sat on the floor to the right and listened to the librarian read a story. Beyond the reading circle were the books—row after row of fiction, non-fiction, children's literature, and magazines. To the left were several computers. Silently, she whisked past the children and slipped into the mystery section.

Audrey moved further back into the books. I should have been more prepared. I always knew they'd eventually find me, she thought. Slipping between the shelves, she kept the front of the library in her line of sight while listening to the librarian's sing-song voice and the children's youthful laughter. The bell above the main entrance chimed, and he entered. His dark eyes scanned the length and depth of the building's interior.

"Can I help you with something?" The clerk asked.

His mustache twitched in silent reply; then, he glided past the desk.

When he turned down the science fiction aisle, Audrey got a good look at him. He hadn't changed much with one exception. He was older. Much older.

Audrey crept three rows over to non-fiction and tiptoed back toward the front. She didn't see him but sensed him move toward the back. Once she passed the reading circle, she hurried between the computer tables and to the door. The clerk called, "Have a good day!"

Audrey hopped into her car and sped from the parking lot with tires squealing. The man shot out and into the street. He grabbed for the passenger side handle but missed by inches.

At her apartment, she slammed the door and bolted the lock. Her back slid against the only barrier between her and the outside world until her bottom reached the floor. When she caught her breath, the tears flowed, and her shoulders shook violently.

Six months prior, she'd convinced herself that they'd forgotten about her or even decided she wasn't worth the trouble. Now, she knew they'd never stop looking. Her mind tumbled into a dark place. They would hunt her down and kill her. How did they find me? She wondered. Haven't I been careful? Then, her thoughts took her even lower. When they catch me, how would they dispose of my body? She scowled at the thought as tears continued. Her eyes were swollen and raw when she shed her last tear.

I need to stop this. Even though it looks terrible, I have choices. I can surrender, or I can do something. Audrey wrapped her arms around her legs and laid her forehead on her knees. She closed her eyes, and to calm her nerves, she rocked. It started as a little at first, then more forcefully, until her back bounced lightly against the door. She wasn't ready to give up on herself just yet.

When she eventually calmed, she called the manager at her grandmother's bank in Miami, Florida, and set up an appointment to discuss Grandma Josie's estate. After years without a word from anyone, he was happy to finalize the house and property's finances. She booked a flight to Miami, then telephoned Father Matthews, leaving a message to inform him of the change in her itinerary. She would visit him much sooner than their agreed-upon date but excluded the details from her recording. After finishing with the bank, Audrey booked one more flight for the following morning to Moscow, Russia.

⌘

A flight attendant breezed down the aisle, opening and closing the overhead bins. Her crisp uniform jacket lapel revealed her embroidered name as 'Teresa.' Audrey admired her long blond hair tied smartly in a ponytail. Conversations in muffled Russian and English echoed throughout the cabin while the passengers settled into their spaces.

Checking with the flight desk before she boarded, Audrey knew the two seats next to hers were unoccupied as of 6:00 A.M. Let's hope they stay that way, she thought. With a pen lodged between her fingers, she reflected on the events of the last three days and how she'd summarize them in the journal lying in her lap. How could she explain her recent actions without sounding like a crazy woman?

Thinking back, they seemed rash. Dangerous even, but this trip was a soul-altering decision. Tired of hiding and being afraid, Audrey made up her mind. Life is going to change for the better, she thought. Behind her, a young mother softly sang a famous Russian lullaby to her toddler lying in her lap with a thumb in his mouth. He clutched a plush Mickey Mouse toy.

(Translated into English)
Tili tili bom
Close your eyes now
Someone's walking outside the house
And knocks on the door

Tili tili bom
The night birds are chirping
He is inside the house
To visit those who can't sleep
He walks
He is coming
Closer

Tiny hairs on the back of Audrey's neck bristled, and a sense of dread passed over her. The lullaby was the same one she heard when she was a kid. Why a mother would want to frighten her children into going to sleep, she never understood.

The lyrics were interrupted by a much louder voice coming from the front of the plane. Audrey shook off the eerie feeling and looked to see the cause of the commotion. A woman of about twenty-five years of age with long dark wavy hair moved down the aisle toward her. I have a bad feeling about this, she thought. Audrey glanced at her watch. Shouldn't we be taxiing down the runway by now?

⌘

"Excuse me, sorry. Excuse me. Sorry I'm late, my dog, the bad boy, ate my alarm clock," the woman explained to no one and everyone. Managing to bump every third seat, she hastily made her way through the cabin with a backpack and a guitar case.

She stopped next to Audrey and observed the row number. Her eyes moved to the ticket crumpled in her fist along with a water bottle. She popped up the overhead bin only to find it full. Teresa appeared beside her and snapped it shut.

"I'm sorry, but you'll need to check your luggage, that's too large for our bins, and we are full this morning," Teresa's British accent, distinctive as she attempted to usher the woman back to the front of the plane.

"But I can't check my guitar!" The woman planted her feet and refused to budge. Her eyes flashed, boring into Teresa's unwavering stare.

"I'm afraid the overheads are full, so you don't have much choice."

"The last time I checked my luggage, I had to wait a week to get it. Can you imagine going a week without underwear?" She giggled and looked for laughter from the other passengers. Someone snickered a few rows down. The woman winked at Teresa.

Most of the passengers stopped what they were doing and regarded the drama playing out in the aisle with interest. The sleeping child behind Audrey stirred, then whimpered. He fought his mother's urges to stay down and sat up, rubbing his eyes. Teresa tsked, shook her head, and crossed her arms. The woman shrugged her shoulders.

"How about this? Let me take it upfront to stow in our oversized bin." Teresa held out her hand. "I promise it will be safe there." Her rehearsed customary smile appeared while she waited for the woman to release custody of the precious cargo.

"I'll be able to get it on my way off the plane?"

"Of course."

"Nobody will take it?"

"I'll personally safeguard it."

"Well, okay, but I'll sue this airline if anything happens to it!" Her voice became louder. She bent close to Teresa and said, "That's not just a warning."

"I expect nothing less." Teresa took command of the case, and the woman leaned into her seat to make way.

"Zoomers," Teresa mumbled under her breath and marched

toward the front of the plane.

"Oh, and I'll need a drink as soon as you have a minute," the young woman called. Teresa's hasty retreat stopped for a moment, and her shoulders straightened. The woman stowed her backpack underneath the seat preceding hers and collapsed into her own with a gratifying sigh.

She wore faded jeans with holes on each knee and a thin cotton blouse unbuttoned enough to draw the eye without revealing anything. Audrey noticed the young woman's olive skin and elegant features. Her eyes were amber and hinted of European descent, possibly Italian. The woman extended a hand across the middle space toward Audrey and adjusted herself to be face-to-face.

She spoke loud and slow, mouthing her pronunciation clearly, "Do you speak English?"

Audrey arched an eyebrow, then glanced out the window. Dawn was breaking. She closed her journal and stowed it into the pocket of her carry-on luggage. It occurred to her to respond in French, but in the end, let it go.

"Most of the time," Audrey said with a stiff smile. Her eyes moved to the out-stretched open palm. She relented and shook it.

"Isabella Rizzo, singer for Smoking Gun," The woman bowed her head and mimicked the pulling out of an imaginary dress hem at her sides in a clumsy curtsy. "But everyone calls me Izzy." She was petite, maybe a hundred ten pounds.

Audrey sighed. She just wanted to sit alone without having to carry on a conversation with some stranger she'd never meet again, but Izzy's eyes twinkled, and Audrey's attitude softened.

"What kind of music do you play?" she asked and adjusted her posture to appear interested.

"You never heard of us? I'm shocked!" Izzy laughed. "We

mostly play Alternative, but sometimes we crank it up with nineties punk. We have to be careful with that in Moscow. Don't want to get tossed in jail for public indecency." Her smile radiated.

"Sorry, I can't lie. I haven't heard a lot of new music these days. Are you famous?"

"Ha! Not really. We play in little cafes around Moscow and St. Petersburg. Tiny crowds, but we have a following."

"Ever play in the United States?"

"We're working on it." She leaned toward Audrey and whispered. "Just met with a music agent, and he kind of likes our stuff. He's willing to put together some gigs and promised to contact us."

"It sounds exciting."

The plane inched out of the terminal, and Izzy's eyes cut to the window. She grabbed both ends of her seatbelt, snapped them together loudly, then pulled the slack tight across her hips. Her fingers resembled claws clutching the armrests. Her face turned ashen.

"Where is that stewardess with the drink cart?" Izzy looked down the aisle in both directions.

"You're not nervous about flying, are you?"

"I hate flying."

Audrey pressed herself against the window to stay clear of what could come next. "Tell me you aren't going to be sick. We haven't even left the ground."

"I hope not." She dug through the pocket of the center seatback when the one in front of her turned up empty. "Sometimes, I can't catch my breath when I'm nervous, so I have to breathe into something." Her eyebrows arched. "It helps." She returned her attention to scavenging the mesh pocket. "Aha!" She pulled out a folded bag, held it up, and then leaned forward and breathed into it methodically.

Audrey sat up taller and looked for Teresa. When she didn't see her or any other flight attendant, she tentatively put her hand on Izzy's back and rubbed ever so lightly.

"I have some gum if you need it. Is there anything I can do?"

"Can you get the stewardess? If I get wasted, I'll be okay."

The plane taxied to its place in line on the runway while the flight attendants pantomimed the preflight instructions that reverberated throughout the cabin.

"I don't think you'll get anything until after we're in the air. Try to relax."

"Okay, just talk to me. The back rubbing is good too," Izzy said between breaths.

"What do you want me to talk about?"

"I don't know. Tell me about yourself." Again, she breathed into the bag. "Why you're flying," 'Breathe.' "to Moscow." 'Breathe.'

Audrey pulled her hand back, and Izzy stopped. They looked at each other for a moment while neither moved.

"Or not," Izzy said. She returned to the bag.

"It's okay." She sighed and bit her lip. "It's a long story, but we have a long flight ahead of us. Maybe it would be good to tell someone finally." Her forehead wrinkled. Can I trust this woman? Absently, she rubbed Izzy's back harder.

"Ow!" Izzy stopped breathing and pulled away with her mouth agape. "Please! Gently."

"Sorry. It's just very personal, but I'll never see you again, right?"

"That's very true."

Audrey watched Izzy take a few more breaths. Okay, here goes, she thought. She adjusted herself to get comfortable and began the story, "It all started on my honeymoon." She stopped and shook her head. "Forget it."

"What? You promised me a story." Izzy's disappointment was evident. "Come on. You aren't some sort of spy or secret agent, are you?"

Audrey giggled. "Well, of course not." She glanced away. I can't tell her the real truth, she thought. Maybe I'll share my story up until things went wrong. She sat straighter and began again.

"It started many years before that.

"One night, my dad took me to the county fair. It was something he wanted to do before he left. We ate junk food and rode all the rides. I watched him throw baseballs at bottles. He played baseball as a kid, so he was good at it. Like the New York Yankees pitcher, he let go, and the bottles toppled. He won another stuffed animal for me, so I tried to be excited. But I wasn't. Not really. My eyes burned, and I wanted to cry, but I wiped the tears away before he noticed."

"So, your dad was leaving? Were your parents divorcing? I know that happens in America."

"If you'll be patient, I'll tell you." Audrey glared at her.

⌘

The plane heading to Moscow took off and reached cruising altitude. Flight attendants made their way down the aisle selling headsets, movies, and alcohol. Teresa stopped to ask Izzy what drink she'd like.

"I'll take a double of the strongest thing you've got." Izzy placed the air sickness bag into Teresa's hand.

Teresa paused for a moment, her expression tight, then tucked the bag into her jacket pocket.

"How about Stoli?"

"That's works!" Izzy's smile radiated. "With cranberry. I'll make it my breakfast." Izzy leaned her head back against the headrest and closed her eyes.

The captain came on the overhead speaker, "Good morning, this is your captain speaking. We are currently 52 miles from Freeport in The Bahamas with a cruising altitude of 35,000 feet. We should be landing in Moscow on Tuesday at approximately 6:42 A.M. Moscow time. It looks like we will be heading into some rain, so please keep your seatbelts fastened while sitting. You are free to move around the cabin if necessary."

Audrey looked out the window, and images of the beautiful islands filled her head. She remembered her honeymoon. It started as the best week of her existence, but everything in her life changed drastically. The dark ocean below reminded her of the recurring nightmare she'd had over the years. She turned away from the window to find Izzy white-knuckling the armrests. Her eyes were focused on the beverage cart, about twenty rows up. The flight attendants appeared calm, taking the time to serve every passenger.

"Relax," Audrey patted Izzy's hand. "You'll be fine."

Izzy got her Stoli and cranberry. She drank it down quickly and ordered another before Teresa could serve anyone else on the row.

"Just the vodka this time."

"Should I leave some extra bottles?" Teresa asked with a cynical edge. Her chin tilted upward, and her nostrils flared.

"You know what? That's a great idea." Izzy returned the cup. "Fill it up with ice."

Teresa sold her four more bottles, then filled the cup with ice and gave it to her.

"What would you like, Hon?" Teresa asked Audrey.

"Water, please."

Teresa handed her bottled water.

"Give her a cup of ice too. She's going to tell me a story, and I have a feeling she'll need something to loosen her up." Izzy winked at Audrey.

"I'm fine. I don't need any."

"Nonsense." Izzy took the second cup of ice before Teresa could pass it across. Teresa served the passengers across the aisle. She eyed Izzy and frowned, then moved her cart along to the next row.

Izzy filled the cup with vodka for Audrey and poured another for herself. "Cheers!" She tapped her drink to Audrey's then tossed the vodka down her throat.

Audrey gazed at the miniature cup of straight liquor gripped in her hand. She wasn't much of a drinker. Never the way her mother was. She took a small sip then held it in her lap.

"Don't you think you should take it easy?"

Izzy wiped her mouth with the back of her wrist and slapped her cup onto her tray table. She poured another drink. The empty bottles stood in a semi-circle like little soldiers protecting her from all her high-altitude demons. She leaned in and whispered with a slight slur, "I have a cast-iron stomach." Her breath smelled like cranberries. "Don't worry. Your secrets will be safe with me. Because!" Her voice was loud. She raised an index finger into the air. "I'll be asleep before you know it." She snuggled into the cushioned back, grinning.

The gentleman across the aisle glared at Izzy and shook his head. Leaning forward, he caught Audrey's attention and offered a deep sigh with a lopsided grin. Audrey shrugged her shoulders and smiled back.

Izzy screwed the caps on the empty bottles and tucked them into the seat pocket in front of her. Giggling at some inside joke that was only for her, she placed the last full bottle next to her hip and pushed the seat back as far as possible. The plane shook with more turbulence, and her hands balled into fists. Her mouth settled into a tight line, and her eyes closed. When the aircraft stabled, her face softened.

"Well? I'm still waiting," she said and yawned.

"You should rest."

"Come on. You promised me a story." Her speech slurred even more.

"You're drunk!" Audrey shook her head. "If I tell you a story, would you promise to get a nap, and for heaven's sake, lower your voice?" Audrey looked at the man across the aisle. He appeared comfortable leaning back with headphones on. Lucky him, she thought. His travel mates seem content to let him be.

"I'll be quiet." Izzy smiled, with eyes closed, she hummed an unfamiliar tune, but Audrey knew she was waiting.

Maybe my life would have turned out differently if I was more like this girl, Audrey thought. She pushed the seat between them back and reclined her own. "I'm going to start this story when I met my best friend." She faced Izzy and leaned back. "Okay, one boring story coming up."

CHAPTER TWO

Bewildered

Shadows danced on the kitchen ceiling above the dim light globe, and whispers carried into the darkened living room. Audrey, in her thin pajamas, ducked behind the white elephant umbrella stand. Her mom first noticed the unique find in a second-hand store when they took their first trip to town. She begged Audrey's dad to buy it as a housewarming gift, but he scoffed at the idea. That piece of ceramic costs more than two paychecks, he told her. He said stuff like that all the time. He'd act tough and say they couldn't afford it only to bring it home to surprise her. The stand's smooth finish felt cold against Audrey's skin, and she shivered.

Her parents thought she fell asleep hours before but kept their voices low not to awaken her. After rousing with a strong urge to pee, she ran to the bathroom. She shouldn't have had that glass of water before bedtime but begged her dad for it, and he relented. Stealthily tiptoeing into the living room, the whispers sounded like arguing. She wondered if they were fighting about her as they often did.

"But Don, you promised me the last time. I don't understand why you think you have to do this?" Her mom's voice was shaky.

"Because we're losing the damn war Claire, and I need to be there to help. You know, some guys have been over there more than four times. This trip would only be my third, and I promise, cross my heart, it will be the last. The guys need me."

"Did someone tell you this? Or did you come up with it on your own?"

"They aren't going to say it, but I know. The Marines are putting guys out there with no experience."

"I'm afraid you'll go and never make it back!" Claire released a sob. Audrey listened, and tears flowed down her cheeks. When she couldn't stay quiet any longer, she stood up and ran into the kitchen.

"Daddy, don't go! We need you more than the guys do." She laid her head on his lap and wrapped her arms around his waist. He wasn't wearing a shirt, which showed his biceps decorated with tattoos.

On his left arm, an artist etched the words Semper Fidelis in blue. Just below that, an eagle with wings spread soaring over the earth sat atop an anchor. When he returned home from his last tour, he brought a new tattoo on his right. It was a big, red heart with Claire and Audrey's names written in cursive with a blue ribbon running around it.

Don stiffened and looked down at his daughter with his arms raised in frozen confusion. He lowered them and patted her back. "Hey, Honey. It won't be for very long. A couple of months, and I'll be home before you miss me." He pulled her up to look her in the eye, but she kept her face lowered. She threw her arms around his neck this time and cried into his shoulder. His mouth fell open. "What brought this on?" His eyes pleaded with Claire, who sat silently watching.

Claire sighed and shook her head. "Tsk." Throwing her arms up in surrender, she retreated to the sink to wash dishes.

"But you promised." Her breathing turned into hitches, and she hiccupped.

"Come on, girl. You're ten years old. You're too big to cry," he said and rubbed her back. His gentleness soothed her until she only sniffled a little with the occasional hiccup.

"Hold your breath, Audrey!"

Audrey took in a large gulp of air, and with her cheeks fully expanded, she tried not to breathe. After about thirty seconds, she blew it out.

"Mommy doesn't want you to go either." She turned to look at her mother and hiccupped again. Claire ignored her daughter and continued to attend to the dishes. A large ceramic bowl clanked into the drainboard.

Gripping his daughter's elbows, he spun her around. She lost her balance and fell into a powerful hug, then squealed when he tickled her ribs. He tousled her hair and peered over her head at his wife. She turned off the water and glared back at him.

"Come here." He reached for her.

"You know you're spoiling her." She wiped her hands with a dishtowel and complied. He pulled her into a three-way bear hug.

"You do know I love you two more than anything in this whole wide world, right? I would never do anything to hurt you."

"So, when do you leave *this* time?" Claire's chin tilted upward.

Audrey hiccupped. He grabbed her and tickled her armpits

until she slid to the floor in a heap of laughter.

"Not for two weeks. We can spend what's left of the summer vacation doing all kinds of fun stuff." He thought for a moment, then said. "Hey, I have an idea. I read in the newspaper the fair will be in town tomorrow. What do you think?" Claire returned to her chair and dried her hands while Audrey jumped up, her hazel eyes brightening.

"Can we?" She asked, looking at her mom.

"Don't we have that get-together thing to go to tomorrow?"

"Sure, but we can go for a couple of hours and leave early."

Audrey's shoulders sagged. She didn't like going to ship's parties because it was just a bunch of people drinking alcohol and getting loud. Her bottom lip poked out.

"Look, I gotta show up," he said to his daughter. "Or they'll be calling wondering where I am. Bring your swimsuit, and you can play in the lake."

"And you." He looked at his wife. "As always, you will be the most beautiful woman there." He reached over and grabbed Claire's hand.

"If you say so." Claire absently pulled a few stray strands of hair behind her left ear with her right hand.

"I do!" He kissed her palm.

"Audrey," Claire said. "You'll play with some of the other kids, right?" She went back to the sink and finished washing dishes. "You spend too much time alone and not enough being social. It's not normal." She wagged her finger at her daughter. "When you go to high school, you'll want some friends. If you're by yourself all the time, people will make fun of you."

"But I don't know anybody here." Audrey's eyes pleaded for her dad to defend her but realized help would not materialize. He knew not to disagree with Claire when Audrey was listening, but they both had different ideas about raising her.

Audrey hiccupped once more.

"You need to get to bed, but first, I'll take care of that nasty habit of yours." He turned her up-side-down and shuffled into the living room with his hands around her ankles. He swung her in a circle until her laughter turned into screams. Audrey laid stretched out on the carpet until her head stopped spinning. At least, her hiccups didn't return that night.

⌘

The next day when they arrived at the park, the aroma of steaks and burgers sizzling on the grill hung in the air. Audrey emerged from her dad's Ford Fairlane and noticed the food line wound along the picnic area's perimeter. A crowd of adults assembled at the back of a van where music blared. Another group played volleyball in a sandy pit. Everyone wore bathing suits or shorts to combat the heat.

Audrey found an empty picnic table away from the music and sat down while her parents chit-chatted with adults. She scanned the crowd. This party is just like all the others, she thought. Nothing but adults acting like kids, but not a lot of real kids around. Although, one girl about her same age stood in line for ice cream. The rest were little and sat in playpens or toddled about with their parents chasing them. I just need to get through a couple of hours of this, she thought.

The guys liked her mom. Audrey knew this by the way they laughed when she was around. Several of her dad's Marine buddies vied for her attention, and Audrey was old enough to know her mother was beautiful. Her short blond hair curled around her ears, showing off the large opal earrings her dad brought home from Vietnam the year before. Her bronzed skin shimmered in the hot sun. With a broad smile and distinct giggle, she quickly became the center of attention. After a while,

Audrey's dad walked over to sit at the table beside his daughter.

"You doing okay?"

"I'm fine. You?"

"I'm great." He squeezed the back of her neck, and her shoulders jerked up to her ears from the pressure. "The line's getting shorter." He pointed to the food tables. "Go get something to eat. I don't think your mother will be cooking tonight." He forced a smile.

"I'm not hungry."

"They have ice cream."

"Maybe later."

They both watched Audrey's mom playfully slap the arm of a muscular man named Marty, her dad's best friend since Recruit Training. He had attached himself to Claire the moment they arrived.

"I'm going to need to save your mom now. I'll be back in a minute." He went over and took Claire's hand and whispered in her ear. She nodded and looked over at Audrey.

After a few minutes, her dad returned to the table. They watched Claire chase Marty and throw water on his back. She screamed when he returned the favor.

"Does it bother you at all?" Audrey asked.

"They're just having fun, letting off a little steam. I'd trust both of those two with your life."

"My life, Dad? Don't you mean, you'd trust them with your life?"

"Heck, no! Have you seen your mother drive?" He tickled her and guffawed loudly. She giggled too, squirming away. He had a great laugh that always made her feel warm inside.

"Touché." Audrey smiled. "You save Mom again, and I'll hide over there." Her head nodded to a large oak tree a few yards from their table. She grabbed her <u>Archie and Friends</u> comic book and sat down. Opening it to the first page, she immediately dropped into Archie's world and tuned out the party.

A while later, Claire sashayed across the grass with a drink in one hand and a cigarette between the other's fingers. The ice made a tinkling sound in the amber liquid as she stopped and steadied herself before continuing to the picnic table in her bare feet. She wore a halter top, tied at the back of her neck, and it came down to above her navel. A pair of very short cut-off jeans sat loosely on her thin hips. Audrey loved the gold bracelet with the different animal charms her mother wore. Her dad brought it home along with the opals. Claire walked by a group of men at another table, and they whistled at her. Audrey's dad gathered her onto his lap and kissed her on the neck. She laughed and pulled away. Noticing her daughter alone under the oak, she walked over and sat down next to her. Audrey didn't acknowledge her mother but instead continued to read.

"Why aren't you playing with the kids. I told you to wear your swimsuit. Did you?" Claire pulled at her daughter's tank top to reveal a bright green suit beneath.

"Mom!" Audrey jerked away and tugged her shirt down. Her eyes darted to the crowd.

"Why don't you go in the water and have some fun?" Claire gently squeezed Audrey's arm.

Audrey shrugged. "I don't feel like it." She pushed her mother's hand away. Claire flinched. Her body stiffened, but she sat silently, watching her daughter read the comic book. Then she scanned the crowd of adults mingling around the drink table.

"You should at least try to make a friend." She raised her chin, and her eyes cut back to Audrey. "We plan to live here now because your daddy's getting out. He'll get a job when he comes back. No matter how much you beg, we aren't going back to Virginia." She blew smoke up toward the sky, then crushed her cigarette into the ground. "I'll see if I can get some of the kids to come over to meet you."

"Please don't, Mother. I want to read right now, okay?" She glanced up to see her mother staring at her, and her eyes quickly returned to the comic book.

"Suit yourself." Claire hopped up and sauntered over to her husband, who talked to a group of men standing around the beer keg. "I could use a refill. Who's the bartender around here?"

⌘

Audrey set her comic book on the picnic table and walked over to the lake. If her mother couldn't see her, maybe she wouldn't be bothered by her aloneness. She looked out into the water at the shore, where a couple of young boys played on a blow-up raft. They wrestled with each other to be king of the float. Stupid boys, she thought. She sat down at the shore's edge to watch. I wish we never moved here. I don't want to make friends anyway. I do just fine by myself. After a few minutes, she noticed a shadow grow in front of her.

"I don't need any help, Mom. Okay?" Shading her eyes with her hand, she gazed up behind her. The girl from the ice cream line held two plates of watermelon.

"You're new here, right?" She asked. "Your mom said I should introduce myself, so here." She handed one to Audrey.

"Uh, thanks." Audrey set the plate next to her on the ground and looked out at the lake again. The boys still fought and laughed uncontrollably. How embarrassing to have my mother ask a kid to play with me, she thought.

"I'm Jenny." The girl sat next to her. Jenny shaded her eyes with her hand and turned to face Audrey. "Are you thinking about going swimming?"

Audrey wanted to run back to the table and grab her comic

book. I can sit in the car until the picnic is over, she thought. She looked out at the boys and wondered how she would get out of this without embarrassing herself.

Without taking a breath, she blurted out, "My name is Audrey. We moved back here from Virginia, where all my friends live. I don't have any friends here. I'm going into the fourth grade. My grandma lives here, and my parents went to high school together here. I'm not going to get in the water. It looks cold." She sighed, picked up the watermelon, took a bite, and then returned it to the plate.

Jenny stared at her without speaking. Her mouth dropped open. Audrey glanced over, but her eyes quickly returned to the water. Her face and neck felt hot.

"Uh, nice to meet you." Jenny grabbed Audrey's right hand and shook it. "I'm in fourth grade, too, so we'll probably see each other a lot." She smiled broadly.

Audrey looked down at the watermelon and thought about what the girl said. After a moment she gathered her courage.

"Sorry about my mom making you come down to meet me. She wants me to have friends so that I'll like living here."

"Your mom didn't make me; she asked my mom, and she made me." Jenny grinned. "But that's okay. I already like you."

"You think we'll be able to eat lunch at school together?" Audrey asked.

"Sure. We'll probably even be in the same class. It's a small school."

"I changed my mind. Let's go steal that raft." Audrey put down the watermelon rind, stood up, and pulled off her tank top and shorts. She kicked her sandals into the grass.

Jenny shielded her eyes with her hand and looked up at her. "Well, okay!" She stood and did the same. They both jumped in, screaming about the cold, and chased the boys away who gave up the raft without a fight. The girls leaned on it together and kicked around the roped-off area. They tried to keep it afloat but kept falling in because they couldn't stop laughing.

When they rejoined the party, people were leaving. Jenny's mom called her to help pack up because they needed to go too. After loading the car, Jenny started to get in but instead ran over to her new friend. She grabbed Audrey's arm and wrote her phone number on it with a pen from her shorts pocket.

"Don't wash it until you have it memorized, and call me. Maybe we can ride bikes or something before school starts."

"I will." Audrey hugged her arm to her chest as Jenny's family drove away. She spun around and giggled. Maybe things won't be so bad here after all.

"Let's go!" her dad yelled through the Fairlane's opened passenger side window. Her mother's head leaned on the door frame. She guessed her mom had a terrible headache.

When they got home, Audrey sat down in the living room to wait for her dad to get ready. Pictures of the war silently flashed across the television screen, and she wondered how anyone could hate enough to kill so many people.

"Okay, she's asleep. It's now or never." Her dad joined her in the living room. He saw what she was watching and switched it off.

"It's now!" Audrey ran out the door and hopped into the front seat before he could grab his car keys and wallet.

⌘

Audrey stopped telling the story when Izzy began to snore lightly. She envied the young woman's relaxed posture and the way her body snuggled into the cushion. *One day soon, if all goes well, I'll claim my bit of peaceful rest. My guess is she'll* spend the remainder of the flight sleeping off the alcohol. Now maybe I can relax a little before we land. I'll need all my wits and courage to do what I'm about to do.

Izzy turned toward Audrey in her seat and mumbled something unintelligible. The small bottle of Vodka fell to the floor with a thud. Audrey reached down and grabbed it before it rolled away. When she came up, she found Izzy's eyes opened, staring at her. Audrey handed it over and leaned back to look out the window. Nothing but water in every direction.

"What'd I miss?" Izzy asked.

"Not a thing. Go back to sleep."

Izzy sat up and stretched her arms toward the ceiling. She grabbed a water bottle from her bag and took a huge swig. To clear the cobwebs, she shook her head and rolled her shoulders.

"I'm awake. Sorry, but your childhood put me to sleep. No offense."

"Not a problem," Audrey said with a pinched expression. "It just means I'm succeeding in calming your irrational phobia."

"My what?" Izzy glared at her.

"You must know that more people die in car accidents than in airplanes."

"Yes, I've heard." Izzy's jaw twitched. "Getting back to your childhood, didn't you ever do anything you weren't supposed to?" Her eyes twinkled. "You know, like steal something? Or get your teachers mad enough to make you stay after school?"

"You want to hear the story or not?" Her cheeks felt hot. "I can stop right now and take a nap. Like you."

"No, no. Please, go on. I'm good now." Izzy sat up.

"You sure? You don't feel sick or anything?"

"I'm fine. Continue!"

Audrey's mind returned to the fateful night when she and her dad left Claire at home to sleep off her headache while they slipped off to the fair.

⌘

The night air radiated with the electric buzz of excitement, and Audrey skipped to the gate pulling her dad to hurry him along. The roller coaster whooshed down the tracks, and screams mixed with laughter reached their ears while the scent of popcorn and funnel cakes made her stomach growl. The Ferris wheel blinked red, white, and blue lights, and people waved from its highest point while it lumbered in a vast circle.

Father and daughter made their way to the game booths after a whirlwind tour of all the rides—a not-so-wholesome dinner included hot dogs, Cracker Jacks, and cotton candy. Her dad threw baseballs at wooden milk bottles. Winding up his arm like the New York Yankees pitcher, he let go, and the milk bottles toppled over with a loud clatter. Audrey squealed and clapped her hands. The thought of him leaving for another trip made her eyes burn, but she wiped the tears away before noticing.

"I heard that part already," Izzy said.

"So, you were listening," Audrey smirked.

"Okay, so what happened after that?"

Audrey shook her head and crossed her arms. "You sure you want to know?"

Izzy tsked. "I'll let you know when I've heard enough. Please finish the story!"

Audrey laughed. "Okay, pay attention."

"You're the big winner!" The man shouted. He reached over and grabbed a small monkey off the wall and handed it to

Audrey. It had gold cymbals attached to each hand that banged together when she squeezed its sides.

"We should start heading back in case your mom wakes up and wonders where we are."

"Do we have to?" Audrey didn't want the night to end and felt a lump in her belly. "You're leaving soon." She dreaded the thought of being alone again with her mother.

"Hey, what'd we talk about?" He held her shoulders and looked into her eyes. "Huh?"

"I know, but."

"But nothing. No excuses. We still have the rest of the summer to do things. We'll go to the beach, and I'll teach you how to swim." He turned her to face the direction of the exit and gave her a gentle nudge.

On their way out, Audrey noticed a sign just to the right of the exit gate. She grabbed her dad's hand and pulled it hard to get his attention.

"Hey, Dad! It says, 'Learn about your future from Mystic Vamonda, the Fortune Teller.' You want to?" Audrey pointed to the sign. Beneath the wording, an arrow directed them toward a large white tent that sat alone away from the fair. A dim light shone through the tent wall.

"You're kidding, right? You want your fortune told?"

"I don't know. What about you?" Audrey attempted nonchalance.

"Not me. I'll pay for you, but I don't want to know my fortune."

"Don't you want to know if I'll have a sister?" It was a running joke between them. She wanted a baby sister, but her mom was against it. No more dirty diapers and potty-training, her mother admonished, especially when Audrey's dad was still making trips to Vietnam and leaving her to do it all.

"I'd like to know that too."

"If you stopped going on your trips, Mom says maybe."

"Okay, you ask the fortune teller that question, and we'll know for sure."

Walking around to the front of the tent, Don put his hand out to stop her. She looked up at him, but he cocked his head to one side and listened. A man was yelling at someone in an angry tone.

"I'll be back, and I expect your old lady to return what isn't hers. I know you have it, so be ready to hand it over if you know what's good for you." The thick accent sounded foreign.

Don pulled Audrey into his arms just when the man rounded the corner. He came inches from propelling right into her. With clenched fists, he composed himself and hastily stomped off.

⌘

"Welcome! You are here to learn your fortune?" Audrey and her Dad turned to see a small woman with flowing gray hair and dangly silver earrings. She, too, had a foreign accent.

Don looked once more at the angry man storming off toward the rides, then returned his attention to the older woman. "You tell me since you're supposed to be the fortune-teller." He elbowed Audrey.

"Dad!" Audrey punched his arm.

"Is okay. I hear this a lot from customers." Her eyes sparkled blue, and a large black cat rubbed against her leg beneath her skirt.

"Awe!" Audrey's eyes grew huge. "Did you see the cat, Dad?" She crouched to pet him, and his nose poked out from beneath the hem. He rubbed his head along her outstretched palm vigorously. With eyes closed, he purred. "He's beautiful."

"Come inside, and let's see what the future will bring for you." The fortune-teller stepped aside and ushered them in. She reminded Audrey of gypsies she'd seen on T.V. Her whole demeanor hinted of mystery and secrets.

"She's doing it." Audrey's dad pointed both his index fingers down toward her head while walking close behind. "To be honest, I don't believe in all the mumbo-jumbo, but she likes it." He rested his palms on Audrey's shoulders.

"Excellent! Such a young lady must have an exciting future ahead of her. Maybe you change your mind after she tells you about what she finds?"

"Doubtful. I believe in God, country, and the Marines."

"Ah, a military man. We will see." She observed him as if penetrating his brain. He shook his head but smiled. She guided Audrey to a chair at a table covered with a white tablecloth. At the center of the table was a white lit candle.

"Wow," Audrey said. Her eyes wandered to the depths of the tent, and the hairs on her arms stood up. Lit by kerosene lamps, the room was full of ancient artifacts. Along one side, a sturdy wooden box resembled a treasure chest. Statues of varying sizes stood positioned around the room. Some made of stone, others of wood. Ancient kings stood proudly dressed in robes. Large animals, mostly wolves and wild cats, prowled silently. They all resided in the shadows. "This place is so cool." Audrey couldn't take her eyes off the beautiful effects. Most she'd never seen before, even on television.

"I am glad you like," Mystic Vamonda said. "A lifetime of travel is here."

A great coffin with the face of an Egyptian Queen sat in one corner, a large cross made of brass stood in another, and a stone gargoyle in a third. Large ornamental rugs hung from the walls. Fans painted black with a lacquered finish, and gold inlay depicted flowers and tigers.

"Are you ready," she asked. Lights from distant rides penetrated the tent wall behind her, while a shadow moved silently outside in the darkness.

"What, no crystal ball?" Don asked. He stood behind Audrey's chair at the table and pulled his wallet from his rear pocket. He watched the shadow make its way around the outside of the tent.

"Pay after." The fortune-teller sat across from Audrey. She smiled at him and set her hands on the table patiently. The bright blue scarf tied in the back covered the top of her head and matched her eyes. She wore a white peasant blouse, tucked neatly into her long silk skirt that billowed out, making a crinkly sound when she moved.

The shadow from the outside appeared at the entrance as a tall, thin man. He peered warily through his thick glasses at both father and daughter before addressing the fortune teller.

"Sorry, Mother. I didn't know you were still taking customers." To Don, "Let me get you a chair, and you can wait by the door."

He went around the room and turned down all of the lanterns, so the light emitted from the table candle alone. He grabbed a canvas foldout chair from the corner next to the opening and set it outside the door.

Don sat and leaned back. The summer would be over soon, and he worried about his daughter, who clung to him when he was home. Lately, Claire seemed preoccupied, even irritable. He wanted to be available for his family, but it was more important for the country to win the war once and for all. There will be time to make things right when I'm home again, he thought.

In the distance, crowds of people laughed, and music from the carousel rang out. He lit a cigarette and inhaled deeply. The night air felt chilly with the scent of confederate jasmine. He breathed in the aroma, and his muscles relaxed. Leaning his head back to scan the star-filled night, he spied a meteor streaking through the heavens. Now, that's a good sign. I must be making the right decision.

⌘

"Okay, let's begin." Mystic Vamonda reached across the table and took Audrey's hands. She closed her eyes, lowered her head, then breathed in and out rhythmically for several minutes. The tent took on an eerie feel with shadows wisping silently among the deeper reaches. Audrey's throat became dry, and she swallowed hard. The mystic continued breathing with her head down so that Audrey couldn't see her face, only the top of her scarf.

By the door, her dad sat with the man who turned out the lights. She deciphered a few words about rain but mostly heard mumbling. Audrey knew her dad always talked to adults about the weather.

She returned her attention to the clairvoyant. Maybe I don't want my fortune told. This lady is kind of weird. With her mind changed, she slipped her hands back to her side of the table. The woman's head jerked up, and her eyes looked at the ceiling. Again, she took Audrey's hands and held firmly. A gust of wind came through the door and caused the candle to flicker violently. The temperature dropped, and Audrey shivered. The old lady rocked back and forth, moaning softly at first. Then louder. Finally, she began to speak in a low tone.

"You are a shy girl who doesn't make a lot of friends, but when you do, they are yours for life." Her breathing slowed, and she squeezed Audrey's hands gently. "I see great love in your future." The rocking became infectious, and Audrey felt herself join in. "A handsome man will come into your life and make you very happy."

The gypsy moaned and rocked without speaking for what seemed like forever. Then, "You will realize sad truths about someone you love, but this won't come easily. You will fight it." Mystic Vamonda stopped rocking. "This person will break your heart, and it will happen more than once." She moaned again, and her piercing blue eyes searched the tent ceiling. "Such sadness." She breathed in sharply. Searching for words, Vamonda stopped a moment as if deciding something in her mind. "Honesty. Yes, honesty will mean everything to you. And family. You'll wish to have children. Many children."

Mystic Vamonda looked into Audrey's eyes, and her face changed. "But." She cocked her head and pulled back. She let go of Audrey's hands as if they were on fire. Using her own to cover her mouth, she stifled a sob. Wild-eyed and shaking, she stood slowly and leaned on the table. Audrey's mouth dropped open, and her eyes widened.

"I'm sorry, child. That's all. Your fortune is free." Her eyes resembled sapphires in the candlelight, and her head jerked away so Audrey wouldn't see the tears. Stumbling to the back of the tent, she opened the flap, passed through, and closed it behind her.

Audrey sat alone and watched the candle's flame flicker. She wondered why Mystic Vamonda left so abruptly. Did she finish? Her eyes darted around the tent. Is she coming back? Audrey didn't understand most of what was said, but she knew something happened. Whatever it was, it upset the fortune teller. The man who called her his Mother appeared at the table. His eyes flicked to the back of the tent. He seemed confused but said nothing. He quickly turned up the kerosene lanterns, then retraced his mother's steps out the back.

Okay, that must mean my fortune is over, Audrey thought. She slipped out of the chair and peered once again at the vast interior of the tent. I can't wait to tell Jenny about this place, she thought. It's so creepy, but it's cool. Careful not to disturb what lurked in the shadows, she tiptoed to where her father sat.

"Let's go, Dad." He seemed lost in thought, but she pulled him to his feet and dragged him to the exit. When they reached the gate, she turned to glance back at the tent and saw Mystic Vamonda walking across the darkened field toward the carnival rides. Her cat scurried close behind, occasionally stopping to sniff the air and flick his tail but never straying far.

⌘

"Well? Are you going to tell me what she said or what?" Her dad shifted the car into reverse and drove out of the parking lot.

Audrey's shoulders raised to her ears. "I don't know. Nothing much." She looked out at the darkened storefronts as they drove toward home. "She did say I'm going to find a handsome guy and have lots of love."

"He better not come around anytime soon. You're still too young for any of that."

"Daddy! She meant in the future."

"Oh?" He winked at her. "I bet that old bat says that to all the pretty young girls." Audrey's ears burned, and her face grew warm. She never thought of herself as pretty. He's saying that because I'm his daughter, she thought.

"I think she was creepy."

"She was a strange bird. No wonder it didn't cost anything." He lit a cigarette with the car lighter and drove in silence for a few miles. He took a drag, causing the lit end to glow red in the darkness. The smoke escaped through his open window. "She didn't tell you much of anything, huh? What else did she say? Nothing about a baby sister?"

"Nope. Mostly, she said things about being honest and how I'm shy and stuff. Oh, and how I want to have lots of kids."

"No way!"

"Yes, way!" She giggled. "Lots and lots of babies! I'll be the old woman who lives in a shoe."

"You're going to grow up to be a doctor or a lawyer and not worry about getting married to someone who wants you to stay barefoot and raise a bunch of brats." He threw his cigarette out the window. "That's why I didn't want to do it. Fortune tellers are all a bunch of fakes and brain-washers!"

Audrey rolled her eyes. Her dad was about to go off on one of his tirades. "I thought she was going to say something else, but she didn't. She left without telling me." Then, "At least it was free." Her eyes cut across to see his response.

"And I like free. Hey, listen. Let's take a quick detour before we go home." He pulled to the curb and stopped. "I was going to pick it up tomorrow, but it can't wait. My pal Marty is holding on to something for me that your mom will love." He did a three-point-turn with the car to head in the opposite direction. "I was afraid to bring it home too soon because she knows all my hiding places."

"Is it jewelry?"

"How'd you guess?"

"Because you're always getting her jewelry." They rode in silence. Then, "Why do you bring mom so many beautiful things when you come back from the war? Is it because you miss her, or because you don't want her to be mad at you?" Audrey avoided her father's gaze by looking out the window.

"Man, you ask a lot of questions. How did you get to be so curious?" He chose to deflect his answer. "And smart. You take after your mother because you sure didn't get your brains from me."

"Oh, Daddy!" She smiled sheepishly. "You should bring me jewelry too. I could never be mad at you."

Her father tilted his head back and let out a fake mad scientist laugh. Audrey crossed her arms, and her mouth turned down.

"When you're older, maybe, but right now, you'd either lose it or break it." He laughed for real, this time in his familiar way. "How about this, you get your ears pierced while I'm gone, and I'll pick you up some earrings. I can get you some turtles or something. What do you think?"

"I'll make that deal. If Mommy lets me." She looked out at the neighborhood as they rolled through. Her grandma Josie lived a couple of blocks away.

"Oh, she'll let you. I'll insist."

Audrey rolled her eyes. Her mother never allowed anyone to insist she do anything. Especially her dad.

"Hey, Dad, does Mommy like kids?" She aimed for casualness but failed miserably.

"Well, of course, she likes kids." His hand was warm when he grabbed hers. He shook it for emphasis. "Why are you asking something like that?" His eyes searched her face for a moment, then returned to the road. Her heart pounded in her ears, and the stomach ache she felt earlier intensified.

"I don't know." Her brow bunched. "I hate it when you go away. She always acts like I'm a pain."

"What? No." Her dad pulled the car over to the curb once again and turned to Audrey. "She just gets so busy sometimes with the upkeep of the house and all." He gently brushed a stray hair from her face. "She cried when you were born. Did you know that?"

"Why?" She tilted her head and looked up at her father.

"Well, because she was so happy that you finally decided to join us. You weren't in any hurry, kiddo. She took one look at you with your dark hair and said, you look like a little Audrey. You know that's a famous actress, right?"

"An actress? Who is she?" Her shoulders inched to her ears, and her eyes widened.

"Audrey Hepburn. Very famous." Her dad beamed as he recalled the memory. Audrey's face held a blank expression. He continued. "She's a very classy actress and starred in some great movies. Your mom loves Breakfast at Tiffany's and Roman Holiday." He thought for a moment. "Oh, and if you like scary stories, there's a new movie called Wait Until Dark. It's still playing at the drive-in, so we should go see it."

"I guess that's cool." She bit her lip.

"Of course, it's cool!" He grinned.

"You know she doesn't like me watching scary shows." Audrey frowned.

"She'll let you watch this one. We can all go next weekend. Don't worry. I'll talk to her." He caught his daughter rolling her eyes again and lightly squeezed her arm. "The move back to Palm Glade took a lot out of her. You know she loves you, right?"

Audrey looked down at her lap. "I wish you could stay home and let Mommy go fight with the guys."

"That'll be the day." He pulled the car back onto the road. "Believe me. War is no place for your mom. She'd have the whole platoon switching sides just to get away from her." He laughed again, but his smile didn't quite reach his eyes.

When they pulled into the darkened driveway, Audrey's dad said, "Hmm. I bet he went to the club, but I can still get the necklace. I know where it is. You want to come in?"

"Sure. What's it look like?"

"You'll see. It's solid gold and has a large heart. But you have to keep it a secret."

"What's it worth to ya?" She laughed and hopped out of the car, then ran up to the porch to wait for her dad. "Since I won't be getting a sister anytime soon, how about a dog?"

"You could bribe me into getting you a puppy." He pulled up the welcome mat, and Audrey grabbed the key. She made a fist with her empty hand, held it above her head, and then pulled it down in front of her face. "Score!"

"Hold on a minute. I need to get something." He ran back to the car, reached inside, and pulled out a box of cigars he'd picked up for Marty while in Tampa.

She inserted the key into the lock, turned the knob, and opened the door. Mommy's going to be so surprised when Daddy gives it to her, Audrey thought. She'll even forgive us for going to the fair without her. At least until she finds out we're getting a puppy, she giggled. I'll tell her the puppy can stay in my room, and I'll feed it, and take it for walks, and everything.

Audrey entered and peered into a darkened living room that opened up into the kitchen just beyond. When her eyes adjusted, she saw her mom's head pop out from behind the refrigerator door. Audrey's mind tried to make sense of what her eyes were telling her.

Bent over peering into the refrigerator, Claire had wrapped herself in a striped sheet, grasped beneath her arms, and held up with one hand. She peeked over the door to see who came in.

Don stepped through the doorway while fumbling to open the cigar box and stopped short of running into his daughter. "Oops! Girl, I almost ran over you." He glanced up into Claire's eyes, then snapped his head back behind him to the lit front porch before returning his attention to the scene playing out in front of him. Somewhere beyond the bedroom, a toilet flushed.

"There should be some ice cream in the freezer. Bring two spoons," Marty said as he left the bathroom. "Honey? Did you hear what I said?" He walked into the living room in his skivvies and saw Audrey and Don standing in the foyer. His head seemed to turn in slow motion to Claire at the refrigerator. She dropped a carton of vanilla ice cream onto the floor with a resounding thud.

"What the hell is going on here?" Don said.

"Oh, my God! Audrey!" Claire placed her hand over her mouth to stop herself from screaming.

Audrey wanted to be anywhere other than where she was at that moment. She backed into her dad, turned, and ran past him out the door. She tripped over a planter and fell, hitting her head on the porch post.

⌘

The nurse at the emergency room front desk took Audrey into a side office. Her crisp white uniform whispered as she walked. Inserting a glass thermometer into Audrey's mouth, she kept it in place by holding the girl's chin. She looked closely at the battered face by turning it slightly to the left, then right.

"Girl, I hope the other kid looks worse than you." Her tongue clicked, and her head shook slowly. "You should consider yourself lucky. It looks like it could've been much worse." Audrey sighed, and the nurse released her grip. She pulled out the thermometer, took a look, then shook it. "Okay, head on down to the last door on your right. The doc is waiting."

Audrey stepped out of the nurse's station and whispered to her dad, "I'm sure lucky I went face-first into that porch post."

"Hey, that post never did anything to you. Now go and let

the doctor fix you up." He shooed her down the hall. "I'll be right here."

When Audrey fell and connected with the wooden post, she came within two inches of hitting her eye on a rusty nail. The doctor cleaned the swelling lump on her forehead and used four stitches to close the cut on her cheek. He also gave her a tetanus shot but joked throughout the process, cheering her up. She laughed through the pain and couldn't decide which hurt worse, the lump, the stitches, or the shot.

Casually, he asked her what happened. Although it wasn't the first time she had to cover for her mother, the question caught her unprepared, just the same.

"I was running, and I tripped."

Doc's eyes searched her face for more information, but her eyes escaped his steady gaze and studied the floor. Her jaw worked, then settled without another word.

The waiting room, lit by fluorescent lights, smelled of rubbing alcohol. Audrey's dad leaned forward in one of the many purple plastic chairs hooked in a line. His chin sat in his hands, and his elbows rested on his knees. God, I hope it's not anything major, he thought. What if they have to do surgery? He looked out the glass front of the emergency room for a sign of his wife in the parking lot. Come on, Claire, where are you? She promised Audrey she would follow them to the hospital to calm her down. Claire, what's happened to us? He thought, and his head returned to his hands.

Doc Whittler finished with Audrey, and they strolled together to the waiting room. He continued to joke, making her laugh. Her dad saw them approaching and stood.

Audrey's eyes searched the lobby for her mother, and her brave smile disappeared. The lump on her forehead stood out swollen and red on her furrowed brow.

"Hi, I'm Doctor Whittler. You must be Audrey's dad." The doctor held out his hand. He, too, scanned the room for another parent.

"Yes, I'm her father." Don grabbed the doc's hand and shook it vigorously.

The room was empty except for an elderly couple sitting by the large glass front. The woman's head leaned against the man's shoulder. Her eyes were closed. He held her hand and whispered in her ear.

"Slow night. Lucky for you." Doctor Whittler said to Audrey. He could see her dad was nervous, and his many years of experience told him a slow approach would produce more positive results with jittery parents.

Her dad's eyes were bloodshot. Whiskers on his cheeks and chin gave his face the same dim glow Audrey recognized from their 'Sleep-In' Sundays when he made pancakes for her and her mom.

"She doesn't have a concussion, but she may have a headache for a few days." Dr. Whittler looked past them to the older couple sitting by the entrance. The woman snored deeply, her head now in her husband's lap. "I'll be with you in a few minutes." He called to them.

"Take your time, Doc." The gentleman whispered hoarsely. "I'd rather she gets a little shut-eye while she can."

"So anyway, I think she'll live." Dr. Whittler returned his attention to Audrey and her dad.

Don looked up at the ceiling and released a heavy sigh. "Thank God!" He grabbed Dr. Whittler's hand and shook it much harder this time. With eyes glittering, he turned his focus to the floor, and his fingers swiped at his short hair.

"Keep her in your sights for the next 24 hours, and if she's not acting her usual self, bring her back in."

"Like how, not usual?" Don observed Audrey paying close attention to the conversation. He glanced away, pretending not to notice. He didn't want her to worry.

"If she's irritable or sleeping a lot. Vomiting."

Don smiled and stared at his daughter. "What if she's irritating?" He poked her shoulder. "She can be pretty insufferable at times."

"Hey! I can't even have a proper trip to the emergency room without you kidding around." She punched his arm.

"I'd like her to come in next Tuesday and see the attending physician to make sure the stitches are healing. She may end up with a scar. It was a deep cut." Dr. Whittler's expression turned serious. "So, she tripped?"

Audrey peeked up at her dad for a sign that didn't come, then stepped heel to toe on the shiny tiles, pretending not to listen. Don looked directly into Dr. Whittler's eyes and laid his hand on Audrey's shoulder.

"Yeah, she was running and tripped."

Dr. Whittler studied them both for a moment. "Well, she's one lucky girl."

"Yes, she is. Thanks for everything, Doc. I'll sure keep an eye on her." He turned to Audrey. "Let's get you home, young lady. Your mother is worried sick." He bent down and peered at Audrey's cheek and forehead. She closed her eyes and tried not to move her face too much. "Does it hurt?" He touched the knot. The doc had painted it red with Mercurochrome. The black thread on her cheek crossed four times with a neat bow at the top and glistened with Vaseline.

"Ouch!" Audrey sucked in her breath.

"Oops, sorry. I told you, you are hard-headed."

Audrey tried to laugh, but it hurt too much. Her eyes watered a bit from the sting.

"You do good work, Doc. Thanks for all your help."

"Here's a prescription for the pain." Dr. Whittler pulled a script pad from his pocket. He tore off the top sheet and handed it to Audrey's father.

"She may need something now, so if you can't get it filled tonight, here are a couple of samples." He pulled an envelope out of his other pocket and handed that over as well. "One before bedtime and then as needed for the pain. No more than four a day." Dr. Whittler looked straight at Audrey.

An ambulance pulled up to the front entrance with lights flashing.

⌘

"Excuse me," Dr. Whittler said, gently squeezing Audrey's shoulder. He walked over to the check-in counter, opened a side door, and rolled out a gurney. He hurried through the glass entrance to assist the paramedics in bringing in an injured patient. Audrey and her dad backed out of the way and watched from the window.

The attendant in the passenger seat hopped out of the vehicle and swiftly moved to the back. His uniform hung on his thin frame. Doc Whittler met him with the rolling bed.

"What do we have here, Jake?" Dr. Whittler asked.

Jake shook his head to move his thick blond hair away from his face.

"No need to rush, Doc. This one didn't make it." He opened the back and pulled out a stretcher. The wheeled legs beneath popped out smoothly and hit the pavement. Dr. Whittler's eyebrows knitted. He helped Jake transfer the covered body to the gurney while the driver stayed in the vehicle and wrote on a clipboard.

"Do we have an injury report and time of death?" Dr. Whittler asked.

"Dale's writing it up now." Jake returned the stretcher to the vehicle and closed the doors. "We caught the call at the station house. Dispatch said a woman was screaming something about a crazy guy who perched himself at the top of the Ferris Wheel out on highway 440. You know, out at the fairgrounds?" He pushed his hair out of his eyes again. "Anyway, we thought we were going to be talking down a drunk who took a dare or something." He spread his arms out away from his sides with palms out. "But it's the darndest thing. As it turns out, we were too late." His hands fell to his sides, and his eyes looked at the pavement.

"Okay. And?" Dr. Whittler's hands went to his hips.

"And. Witnesses said he took a swan dive and landed on the concrete. Right in the middle of a huge crowd of people." He shook his head. "It's a wonder he didn't land on anybody." Jake's eyes flashed, and he leaned toward the doctor. "Broke his back in multiple places." He looked down and kicked a piece of gravel into the grass. "But, that's not what killed him."

Dr. Whittle's eyes focused intently on Jake's expression. "Well, what killed him then? In your medical opinion."

"Cats."

"Say again?" Dr. Whittler's attention focused keenly on Jake's face. He cocked his head to the side in case he didn't hear him correctly.

Dale, the driver, joined them with the clipboard in his hand. He presented it to Dr. Whittler for his signature, but the doc waited to hear more from Jake. Without changing his focus, he held up his palm before Dale could ask again. Dale was short, around five feet, eight inches, with a muscular build.

Jake shrugged. He grabbed the top of the sheet, pulled it

back to the chin, and showed a male's head in his late twenties or early thirties. The man's expression appeared to be calm as if asleep. Jake finished uncovering him to the waist. The man's throat was gone. In its place was a gaping dark hole where his larynx once sat. Dried blood covered the front of the man's shirt. Dr. Whittler's mouth dropped open.

"Unfortunately, we have nothing to go on except witness accounts," Jake said. "But from what we surmised, when this gentleman landed, a herd of cats attacked him. You know, those wild cats that hang around looking for a free meal? Some carnies finally pulled them off, but this is what's left of the poor guy."

"Jesus." Dr. Whittler was unable to tear his eyes away from the corpse.

Dale tapped him on his arm with the clipboard, and Doc's gaze turned to him slowly. He accepted it along with the pen Dale handed him, but his eyes returned to the body. Dale waited patiently, then cleared his throat. He and Jake shared a glance. Dr. Whittler turned his attention to the release forms and signed them with an unsteady hand.

"I don't believe Jesus had anything to do with this. More like the Devil himself," Dale said. He shivered, then crossed his arms and looked out into the darkened parking lot. "Feels like the temperature dropped some." He rubbed his hands along his biceps and waited for the rest of the forms to be signed.

Jake covered the body again and returned to the passenger side of the rescue vehicle. He grabbed a plastic bag with the contents of what they found on the victim.

"There might be some trouble reaching the next-of-kin," Jake said. He laid the bag on the dead man's chest. "He has a Russian passport."

"So, he isn't from around here," Dr. Whittler said. "Lovely."

"Probably worked with the carnival group at the fair. They

hire a lot of immigrants," Dale said. His sleeves rolled high showed goose-pimpled skin. "Oh, and look here," he stood close to the doctor to show him the top form. He pointed to his tightly written notes at the bottom. "Matryoshka."

Dr. Whittler looked at him and waited for an explanation. "And? That is, what?"

Dale's shoulders inched up, and he turned his palms heavenward. "Beats me. One of the witnesses said that's what the guy yelled just before he took his fateful dive."

Don guided his daughter to stand behind him, then backed away from the entrance so that Dr. Whittler could wheel the gurney inside. Another siren howled in the distance, and he turned to look before the automatic doors closed completely.

"Sounds like business is picking up." The doc addressed Audrey and her dad with a wan smile. "I think it's going to be one of those full moon nights." He sighed. "You take care of yourself, young lady." He winked at Audrey. "Remember to come in next week to have that noggin' looked at." Audrey gave him a thumbs-up.

They watched Dr. Whittler, now assisted by the nurse, roll the bed to one of the doors that led to the rest of the hospital.

"That was him," Audrey whispered to her dad.

"What was him?"

"The man they had on the stretcher. I saw him when the ambulance man showed Dr. Whittler his face. He's the guy who almost ran into us when we went to the fortune teller's tent. You remember, the one who runs the Ferris Wheel?"

⌘

In the parking lot, the fog had attached itself to the empty streets. Audrey looked out the window with the overhead lamp still on, and her reflection stared back at her. The lump made the shape of her face appear distorted. Her dad rooted himself in thought, and she decided not to ask him why her mother never showed. The lamp went out. As they drove, a few car lights approached, and through the slapping of the windshield wipers, they resembled ghosts floating by.

When they pulled into the driveway, their house was just as they left it. Claire's Tiffany lamp shone dimly through thin curtains in the living room, but her Chevy Nova was not in its spot. Don let the car idle for a minute, then turned the key. The engine rumbled a second or two more, then quieted. A lonesome dog barked somewhere in the distance. Audrey's dad kept his eyes forward, not wanting to face his daughter at that moment. A chill crept in from outside. Then he looked over at her.

"How are you feeling? Head hurt?"

"A little." She found it hard to speak.

"Go in, put on your pajamas, then take one of these pills, Dr. Whittler gave you." Her dad handed her the envelope.

Audrey opened the car door but looked back at him before getting out.

"Is Mommy coming home?"

A breath caught in his chest, and he found it hard to leave his daughter this way. Seeing her confusion broke his heart. "Well, of course, she is. She's got some things to take care of first. Now go on in. She'll be here in the morning when you wake up. I promise."

"Are you coming in?"

"I'll be home soon. Don't worry. I called your Grandma Josie, and she should be here any minute to stay with you until your mom gets home."

"Where are you going?" Tears fell onto Audrey's cheeks, and her throat clamped shut.

"Come here." He reached over and wrapped her in his arms.

"You and mommy aren't going to fight, are you?" Audrey whispered through her father's shirt.

"No. We won't fight. Everything will be alright."

He kissed the top of her head, then released her. "Now, go on."

When she reached the front door, she turned and waved to him. Her grandmother pulled up and parked on the side of the road. Josie went to the door where Audrey stood, and Don watched her hug his daughter, then inspect her face. They went inside and closed the door. Wiping tears from his eyes, he cleared his throat. Audrey opened the curtain and watched him back the car out of the driveway. It was the last time she saw her father alive.

⌘

After Don dropped his daughter off in 1968, he made arrangements to return to Vietnam immediately, deciding it would be best for his family. Claire needed some space to figure out what to do about their marriage and if she wanted to stay a family. He rejoined his platoon within the following week and focused on beating back the Viet Cong once and for all.

After several sleepless nights of introspection and lonesomeness, he cured himself of any doubt. The crazy fling Claire and Marty had was just a one-time occurrence. Everyone makes mistakes, he thought. If I'd been home more, maybe none of it would've happened. Claire and Audrey both should hear it from me in my own words, he thought. So, he wrote two letters—a steamy one for Claire complete with her favorite aftershave aroma, and one addressed to Audrey containing a knock, knock joke. It said, 'Knock, knock. Who's there? A wagging tail. A wagging tail who? A new puppy for your birthday!' He mainly wrote about how much he loved each of them and promised things would be different when he returned. He hinted to Claire that it would be the perfect time to have another kid. He had it all figured out and was determined to make them a happy family once more.

On a dewy morning after being in the bush for a month, Don walked point well ahead of his platoon. They heard chatter the evening before of enemy forces sighted in the area. After a couple of miles of nothing, they radioed in that the stretch they covered was clear. Before heading back, he strolled casually out to witness a stunning panoramic view of the valley as the sun appeared over the horizon.

"Hey guys, get up here and take a look. This site is a real vision and makes getting up at the butt crack of dawn worthwhile." He tossed his cigarette, took two more strides to get a better glimpse of the river below, peeking through the trees, and stepped on a land mine.

They said his death was quick and painless. Audrey saw the black car with the American flag pull into the driveway, so she hid in her room and listened through the door. She had been spending a lot of time there since her dad left. A week after his death, Claire and Audrey received the letters he wrote.

At the funeral, Claire was more angry than sad and made a scene by refusing to accept the American Flag covering his coffin. She blamed Don for returning to Vietnam, but she also blamed the Marines for their failure to keep him safe. The Honor Guard presented the flag to Audrey while she sat next to Grandma Josie. When the Color Guard began the Twenty-one Gun Salute, Claire walked to her car and drove away. Audrey never got that scene out of her head. Claire continued to blame the Marines and cursed Don for months. In her mind, he left her alone to raise a kid. When the Survivor Benefits Checks began rolling in, she started drinking. A lot.

One stormy night, Audrey waited for her mother to come home from work. It was raining hard, complete with strong winds, lightning, and thunder. Grandma Josie came over and took Audrey to her house because Claire ended up in the hospital. She totaled the Nova by running it into a tree, luckily only suffering cuts and bruises. After that, Claire complained about chronic back pain and lost her job because she often wouldn't or couldn't get out of bed.

Grandma Josie convinced her to go to the doctor about the back pain, and he prescribed a painkiller. Audrey stopped calling her, 'Mom,' then because it seemed to her that she was now the mom and Claire the kid. Grandma Josie begged Claire to bring Audrey and stay at her house for a while. They needed time to work through their grief. Claire refused, preferring to remain at home where nobody would dictate what she could and couldn't do. Audrey felt comfortable at her Grandma Josie's house, so she stayed there more and more while Claire picked her up less. From then on, it was Grandma Josie who pretty much raised her.

CHAPTER THREE

Savage Blossom

Sixteen-year-old **Audrey** gritted her teeth and squeezed the brake handle of her ten-speed. The thin tires rolled over the concrete driveway where sand had collected due to months of neglect. Audrey didn't want to be there but promised her grandma she would stop in.

The house used to be beautiful, with a manicured lawn and rows of trimmed hibiscus, the exterior now needed a fresh coat of paint to cover the mildew creeping up its walls. Weeds flourished between the cracks along the driveway and stone path. The air, humid with the sun peeking just above the roof, caused Audrey's tie-dyed tank top to feel damp. Her dark hair worn in a ponytail hung limply to her back, and her bangs clung to her brow. Gathering newspapers lying on top of a fire ant hill, she breathed a heavy sigh. Dew and grass stickers clung to her sock-less red tennis shoes. From her front pocket, she extracted the key to what once was her home. She tentatively closed the door behind her and leaned against it, not sure what she might encounter. A mixture of beer, cigarette smoke, and body odor reached her olfaction.

She never knew what to expect from Claire, terrified she'd one day find her dead.

"Claire. You here?" Her voice echoed off the walls.

No answer.

The house showed evidence of a party the night before with empty beer cans and full ashtrays scattered around the living room. An old Red Sox ball cap hung from the trunk of the ceramic elephant umbrella stand. Dirty dishes sat piled high in the kitchen sink. The beige living room carpet once kept in spotless condition, flourished with large purple stains. Her dad's favorite recliner, now disabled, sat askew and scarred by dropped cigarettes.

Audrey called out again and heard scuffling from one of the rooms somewhere down the hall, so she wandered in that direction. Quietly, she turned the knob of the first door, and it opened into her bedroom. Stuffed animals covered the bed, and Davy Jones, above in his red jacket from India, smiled back at her. A black-light poster of a dark stallion hung on the wall over the dresser. When Jenny came over, they'd lie on pillows and listened to records.

Audrey closed the door. Making her way down the hall, she came to a bathroom with the door slightly ajar. Please don't be dead. I don't want to find a corpse, especially in the bathtub. She couldn't stop her mind from racing. The first thing she saw beyond the door was a dingy white tennis shoe pointing toward the ceiling. Her mother's glassy blue eyes stared unfocused in the same direction. Audrey felt her heart slam against her chest, and blood pulsed in her ears. She kneeled beside her mother's foot and shook it. No response. Just as she moved to check her wrist for a pulse, Claire sat up, leaned over the toilet, and threw up. Audrey rocked back on her haunches and fell into the hall. She covered her nose and mouth with the inside of her elbow.

"Ah, Claire! What's going on?" Acrid vomit now scented the air.

With her face inside the bowl, Claire began to heave. Her shoulder-length hair hung limp around her face. When her stomach settled, she shot Audrey a blood-red glare. She tucked a few stringy blond strands behind her left ear with her right hand, then fell back to the floor on her side. Her body curled into a ball, and her arms covered her head.

"What do you want, Audrey?" She mumbled with her eyes closed.

"Did you have a party last night?" She helped her mother back to a sitting position, then tried to get her on her feet.

"Ow! Don't pull me!" Claire jerked away and laid back down.

Audrey stood up and put her hands on her hips. "Come on, Claire. You should go to bed."

"Leave me alone! I can do what I want when I want." Her face contorted into an ugly scowl. "You and your Grandma have no say in it!"

She attempted to get up on her own but fell against the towel rack. Audrey helped keep her mother standing upright, but Claire pushed her away again and stumbled out of the bathroom. She leaned on the wall and made her way into the bedroom at the end of the hall. The bed was unmade with the comforter and pillows on the floor, but she fell into it anyway. Audrey followed and watched her mom lay on her stomach and struggle to get comfortable.

"Hey! Little Miss Priss, hand me that pillow." Claire pointed to one of the pillows on the floor. Audrey complied. She slipped off her mother's tennis shoes and set them on the floor next to the bed.

"I'm starting at Palm Glade High School next week." She pulled the comforter from the floor to cover her mother. Audrey went to Palm Glade Junior High for seventh through ninth grade, which resided across from the high school. She felt more than ready to start tenth grade.

"Get me a beer, would ya?"

"Did you hear what I said? I'm starting high school this year," Audrey tried again.

"Okay?" Claire opened her bloodshot eyes and glowered at her daughter. "What do you want me to say? Don't get pregnant?" Claire punched the pillow and laid her head back down.

"I thought you'd like to know. You used to tell me about all the fun you had in high school. Remember? How you and Daddy fell in love?"

Claire raised her head and pierced Audrey with her stare. "Damn it! I don't want to hear any more about that, you understand? Now, go get me a beer!" She made that ugly scowl and returned her head to the pillow. Over the years, she made a point of never wanting to discuss Audrey's dad. Audrey's bottom lip quivered, and she looked away to quell tears starting to form. Claire's eyes closed.

Red-faced, Audrey turned to leave. "Get your own beer," she mumbled. Her hands clenched into fists, and her feet felt like lead weights.

Claire's eyes opened, and her lips curled back. She twisted her body around and glared. "Listen here. Don't you EVER talk back to me!" Audrey found the strength to drag her feet out of her mother's bedroom and down the hall. Something she never did before. "Come back here. You spoiled brat!"

When the weights lifted, Audrey shot out of the house, slamming the front door behind her. The hinges rattled, and the impact boomed like a cannon. Mounting her bike, she screamed a sharp guttural cry. Her tears streaked her cheeks as she tore out of the driveway and onto the street. A man in a pickup truck came within inches of slamming into her. Caught by surprise, he jerked the steering wheel sharply to the right and skidded off the road.

⌘

Audrey needed to calm her nerves after the encounter with her mother. She learned early in life what a nasty person Claire was when she drank and vowed to stay clear of her during those times. Living with Claire was a lot like riding a roller coaster. There were times when she worked hard at staying sober and would keep the same job, sometimes for months. Then without notice, something would click in her mind, and she'd get depressed and end up at a bar or marine buddy's house.

Instead of going straight back to Grandma Josie's house, Audrey rode around her old neighborhood's streets. The homes appeared peaceful in the early morning stillness. Most occupants had yet to start their Saturday chores. A lawnmower came to life a couple of streets over, and as Audrey rode beneath a shady oak and rounded the bend, she came face-to-face with her best friend's old house. It looked empty, so she stopped. The last tenants had moved on. The windows stood dark, but Audrey recalled all the fun she and Jenny had when listening to records on the back porch and attempting to copy the latest dance moves from American Bandstand. They spent many nights at Jenny's house and did almost everything together until Jenny's dad lost his job, and he moved their family back up north.

Audrey looked down at her feet, planted on each side of her bike. There on the sidewalk was her name in the concrete inside a heart. Jenny's had a star around hers, like a star on the Hollywood Walk of Fame. She stepped off, lowered the kickstand, and sat next to the names. She traced the lines with her finger and thought about how it came to be.

After eating Popsicles, the girls used the sticks to write in the wet concrete. Jenny's mom yelled through the kitchen window as she washed the dinner dishes.

"I see you, girls. Don't you know you can get arrested for defacing public property?"

Jenny and Audrey giggled and pretended to pull dandelions from the soft grass next to the freshly poured sidewalk. The sign and string barrier bordering it alerted people to keep off.

"Let's just write our first names," Jenny said. "That way, they won't be able to figure out who did it."

After Jenny and her family moved, the two kept in touch by writing to each other. Jenny wrote about her new school and how her parents were fighting. Audrey responded with how boring their old school was and how Claire was such a mess. They stayed friends over the years and dreamed of one day getting a place together to leave all their problems behind.

⌘

When Audrey walked her bike up Grandma Josie's driveway, she felt better. After wheeling it into the garage, she strolled around to the back of the English Tudor style home. There, beneath the shade of giant oaks, and among the many rows of colorful roses was Grandma Josie in her over-sized straw hat. She hummed an undiscernible tune to herself with her attention focused on a small bush full of blossoms the same shade of orange as tangerines. She took great pride in her roses and even entered some of them into the Palm Glade Garden Club competition each year, often walking away with either first or second place.

Audrey's mouth turned into a wicked smile as she tiptoed up behind her grandmother and quietly slipped her arms around her waist. Grandma Josie sucked in her breath, then crossed her own arms in front of her. She took Audrey's elbows into her hands and squeezed. Audrey leaned over her much shorter grandmother and placed a kiss on her plump cheek.

"You smell good. Is that a new, old toilet?" Audrey plopped down into the gardening wagon next to a bag of potting soil and swung her feet in the air. The toes of her tennis shoes just short of touching the ground.

"That's 'Eau de Toilette,' smarty pants. You smell my honeysuckle lotion."

Josie's focus returned to the rose bush. She took a magazine from her gardening apron's pocket, folded it to a particular page, and held it next to the plant. She shook her head and clucked her tongue. "Mm, mm, mm. Not good."

"What's not good?" Audrey climbed out of the wagon to look at the picture of a rose bush.

"Black spots. It's what I was afraid of." Josie returned the magazine to her pocket. "It says it could be a type of fungus. I'll pick up some neem oil the next time I go to town."

Audrey walked along the row and inspected the other bushes. "Are there more, or is that the only one?"

"That's all I've found so far." Grandma Josie moved on to the next one with a pair of hand clippers. "So, how did it go with your mom?"

Audrey strolled a few paces before answering. "Fine," she lied and held the bloom of a blood-red rose in her cupped palm. She tucked a loose strand of hair behind her left ear with her right hand, then leaned in to breathe the rich fragrance.

"What did she say?" Grandma Josie turned to look at Audrey and noticed the familiar hand gesture with her hair. She frowned. Audrey only did that out of nervousness.

Claire had not been responsive to any of Grandma Josie's phone calls. Sometimes Claire got so depressed that Audrey knew her Grandmother thought she might take all of her pain pills at once, even though she'd never admit it.

"Was she excited about you going to high school this year?"

"Not really." Audrey ran her fingers along one of the red rose bush's long stems. "Ouch!" She snagged the top of her middle finger and quickly withdrew her hand. She stuck her knuckle in her mouth and tasted blood. After glimpsing the damage, she shook it.

"You know your mother loves you."

"She's got a funny way of showing it."

"She's got a lot of issues right now."

Audrey remembered how her dad used to say the same things. She stopped to face her grandmother. "I think she had a party last night. I saw a lot of beer cans, and surprise, surprise! She was sick again." She turned to the next bush. "Do you think she's got cancer or something?" She tried to sound nonchalant but was never good at acting.

Grandma Josie peered at Audrey over her glasses, her forehead wrinkling. "I bet she had too many beers."

"I guess, but if she did get cancer, I bet she'd never tell me."

"Your mom has a lot of pride, but she'd tell you. Don't worry. She's not sick. Help me take this stuff to the shed."

Grandma Josie smiled as they loaded gardening tools into the wagon, but Audrey could tell she wasn't happy to learn Claire started drinking again. Audrey swung the hoe and rake over her shoulder, then walked toward the shed at the property's edge while Grandma Josie pulled the wagon alongside.

"You still haven't told me how registration went." Josie opened the shed door.

Audrey hung the tools on the wall, and they walked back to the house.

"The school is huge! So, I'm afraid I'll be late for class. I heard if you're late three times, you have to stay after school, and the principal gives you a whack with his paddle."

"You'll figure out how to make it on time." Josie grinned with a twinkle in her eye.

"At least I don't have to go as far as the band kids. They go from one end of the school to the other, and all in five minutes." Audrey held her hands out wide to help illustrate the school's size. "With their instruments!"

"Well, I don't worry about you. You never get into trouble at school."

"That's because all my other schools were smaller, Grandma. You should try to walk a mile in five minutes."

"A mile! I don't think it's quite that far." Josie laughed. "Did you see anyone you know?"

"For sure! All the sophomores registered at the same time, so I got to see almost all the kids from PGJH." Audrey's voice raised an octave. "Oh, and you know what? They had some of the seniors helping us find our classes."

"Ah. Did some dreamy guy show you around?" Josie teased.

"Nope. It was a girl." Audrey shook her head. "But she told us who the most popular boys are."

"Is that so?" Grandma Josie kicked off her boots on the back porch and opened the glass sliding door. They both stepped into the air-conditioned kitchen.

"And you already found a boy you like, I'm guessing."

"Well, of course! This one guy named Eric showed another

group around the school, and he's cute. I want to find a way to meet him, even though he's a senior."

"Uh, oh." Grandma Josie knew when her granddaughter put her mind to something, it was hard to get her to change it.

"Uh, oh, nothing. You watch! One day he's gonna be mine." She giggled, turned her nose up, and batted her eyelashes.

"My little Prima Dona." Grandma Josie's mouth formed into a one-sided grim.

CHAPTER FOUR

Chagrin

When school started, Grandma Josie encouraged her granddaughter to join a club or sport. She believed it was essential to stay connected to school activities to get good grades and meet like-minded students. Audrey wasn't interested until learning Eric was on the swim team. Every day she fretted about how she should join and reminded herself to bring the information home.

Eric held the Glade's best time for the butterfly and had several medals to show for his efforts. Audrey grew up with limited knowledge of the water. She mostly stuck to jumping around under the sprinkler and playing in the shallow end of the city pool. Except for when she and Jenny met at the lake. How hard can it be? She thought. All I need is the right swimsuit.

After talking Grandma Josie into it, they spent all weekend shopping for the perfect bikini. She settled on one with yellow polka-dots and admired herself in the boutique mirror. "If this doesn't get Eric to look at me, nothing will," she said. Grandma Josie raised an eyebrow but kept her comments to herself. The next day after school, Audrey brought home the sign-up packet and pranced around the kitchen, waving it in her hand. Grandma Josie snatched it from her and sat down at the table to read the requirements.

"Audrey, this is expensive."

"I know, but I want to join, and you said I should pick something to meet people."

"I did, but this isn't something you can quit when it gets a little difficult. You have to stick with it."

"I will. I promise."

"You're sure? Even if the boy you like doesn't pay the least bit of attention to you?"

"Yes, Grandma!" Audrey rolled her eyes.

"Okay, where do I sign?" Grandma Josie scanned the forms. "Here it is. There, I signed it, so no backing out now."

"I can't wait to start. Who knows, maybe I'll be able to save you from drowning one day." She continued to pirouette around the table.

"You're not fooling me; I know exactly why you want to do this, but that's okay. If you work hard, you might become a good swimmer. Maybe save your own life one day." Grandma Josie continued to read the form. "Uh, oh. News flash. It says here you will wear the team swimsuit."

"Wait. What?" Audrey stopped spinning and went to look over her grandmother's shoulder. She read the bold type aloud, "No bikinis allowed." Her forehead wrinkled.

Izzy snickered under her breath and shook her head. Audrey glanced at her before going on with the story. The two locked eyes and Izzy stifled her giggle. Audrey frowned and looked down at her hands.

"Oh, come on! I'm sorry, but you didn't know they wouldn't allow you to wear a bikini on the swim team?"

"Did I mention that I just started high school and never participated in any sports before?"

"Not even as a spectator?"

Audrey frowned. "My mom never had time for extra-curricular activities." She looked out the window.

Izzy leaned forward to capture Audrey's attention. "Maybe you should consider yourself lucky. I never had a choice. When I swam, I had to wear an ugly one-piece bathing suit and a bathing cap."

Audrey looked back at her. "The team started wearing caps after I graduated. They were the school colors and looked pretty, especially bobbing through the water."

"See! Ours were the ugly white ones that pulled your hair out every time you put them on."

"So, is my story still boring?"

"It's getting better. Your mother was a piece of work."

"Nobody's ever described her quite like that before." Audrey laughed for the first time in what seemed forever, and it felt good. Izzy appeared taken off guard. Audrey sighed and looked into Izzy's eyes. "You don't know the half of it."

⌘

On the first day of practice, she, along with the other two new sophomore swimmers, made their way to the poolside. Her eyes darted around the crowded pool area, and she tugged at the bottom of her unflattering one-piece suit. She felt exposed. Like everyone was watching her and thinking, she's not a swimmer or even an athlete. The pool deck sizzled in the Florida sun.

She noticed Eric standing next to the diving board, chatting with several upper-class team members. His brawny shoulders glistened with water that dripped from his hair. Three girls in team swimsuits joined him, and one slid Eric's arm around her shoulder. They all started laughing at once and appeared to be enjoying something funny. One of the girls looked over her shoulder at Audrey, and the other two new swimmers then turned back and said something to the group. The hilarity continued. The rest of the swim team swam laps while the three new team members watched at the edge of the pool, resembling lost ducklings.

Coach Jameson wore a white sailor cap with the brim turned down and a pair of aviator sunglasses. Her nose stood out red and white with sunburn and zinc. She visually patrolled the pool from her perch and leaned on the lifeguard chair armrest. She reminded Audrey of a queen reigning over her subjects. When Jameson's eyes settled on the new swimmers, she sat taller and pointed her megaphone in their direction.

"Newbies! What are you waiting for, Christmas? Jump in and start swimming laps."

Audrey knew the other two sophomores from PGJH. Both extremely dedicated to their sports. Thomas participated in both basketball and soccer, while Rebecca played softball. Never a member of anything, Audrey felt a flutter in her stomach, and sweat beaded across her forehead.

Thomas watched the other swimmers for a minute, then looked at Audrey and Rebecca. He shrugged his shoulders and dove into the water. When he returned to the surface, he swam to the opposite end.

"He practiced with the swim team over the summer," Rebecca said. Her light, brown hair hung limply in a ponytail over her thin chest. She and Audrey sat down at the edge and dropped their legs into the pool. Audrey's skin chilled when her feet entered, but the sensation felt good with the sun radiating on her shoulders.

"Man, that's cold." She reached forward to splash water on her legs. She sneaked a peep at Eric when he dove off the board and decided he was perfect in every way. Her imagination found herself playing with him in the water. She'd splash him, and he'd swim after her. She'd try to get away, but not too hard. They'd both giggle while he held her in his arms. Then he would put his soft lips on hers. Then,

"Are you looking at Eric Reynolds?" Rebecca asked.

Audrey returned to the real world. "No, why do you say that?" Her face turned scarlet.

"Yes, you were. Eric's the captain of the swim team. And that girl? Over there, sitting in the stands with the red hair? See her?" Rebecca cocked her head in that direction without looking. "That's his girlfriend."

Audrey sneaked a peep, pretending to look at Rebecca's hair. It never occurred to her that he would have a girlfriend. The girl ran up and kissed him on the cheek, then returned to the stands. She was tall and pretty. She didn't have on a swimsuit but sat watching the swimmers with a bunch of senior girls. Eric climbed the ladder and walked out to the edge of the board. He strolled back, then turned and faced the pool again with a look of deep concentration. Standing tall, Eric breathed in deeply, then ran and jumped high into the air. His body spread out wide and, on his way down, he tucked his knees to his chest and wrapped his arms around them. He landed a perfect ten cannonball. His splash reached most of the girls in the stands, and they immediately jumped to their feet and screamed. Laughing as he climbed out of the pool, he walked over to the girls, where they rewarded him with more shouts and giggles.

Audrey laughed too.

"What's her name?"

"Tabitha Street, and she's only one of the most popular girls in this school."

"That figures." Audrey looked down into the clear water. The black lane lines at the bottom appeared to move like a mirage in the desert. I should drop this whole crazy idea, she thought. Who am I kidding? I can't even float. Audrey watched swimmers flip at the pool's edge and return in the direction from which they came to do the same all over again.

"He's a senior anyway. Seniors don't go steady with sophomores." Rebecca stood up and brushed the back of her swimsuit with her hands. "The only way to get used to it is to go in all at once. See you on the other side!" With that, Rebecca jumped into the water. When she surfaced, she dog-paddled toward the opposite end.

⌘

"Hey, you, Honey. Let's go." The coach was no longer in her chair but instead walking around the pool. Audrey's head jerked around, and her eyes slipped over to Eric as he took a seat next to Tabitha. He looked up in their direction along with every other person who wasn't swimming laps. Coach Jameson stood over Audrey with her hands on her hips.

Audrey's face turned ashen. Uh oh. Do something, she thought. Without an appreciation for the consequences, she stood like Rebecca before her, closed her eyes, and jumped.

Everything quieted once she went beneath the surface. Talking and laughter above the water became muted, and the splash of the swim strokes dulled. The chill made her body numb. She touched the pool floor with one foot and pushed off, returning to the surface. When she broke through, her throat was as tight as a fist, and her lungs felt like cement blocks. Without a deep breath before she jumped, she quickly depleted her lungs of oxygen. She panicked and struggled for air. Her feet couldn't find the pool floor, and her splashing and sputtering didn't help. She slipped back under, sinking to the bottom where she sat. Once she stopped fighting it, her body calmed. Her long dark hair, loose from its ponytail, swirled around her face. It felt peaceful. I could stay here forever, she thought. Grow gills and become a fish.

Then, something clamped around her chest and yanked her to the surface. She found herself lying on the deck, struggling to breathe. Coach Jameson slapped, and rubbed her back, then leaned her on her side. That's when she threw up a bunch of water and coughed like she was choking. After what seemed like forever, her breathing started to even out.

Audrey's throat and sinus cavities felt raw and tasted like chlorine, but she started to feel normal again. She glanced around. The team stood motionless, their faces a sea of concern. Some spoke to each other in concerned whispers. Even those doing laps watched from their lanes. Her eyes returned to the pool deck, and she hid her face behind her dripping hair.

"Everyone, go back to swimming." Coach Jameson shouted. "You still owe me 50 laps before you leave today." Soaked from head to toe, Coach appeared visibly shaken. Her hat floated in the water. Team members moved back into the lanes and resumed their smooth, methodical strokes.

"You okay, girl?" Coach Jameson's brown eyes searched Audrey's face.

"I couldn't catch my breath."

"That can happen if you aren't used to going from 94 to 65 degrees in an instant." The coach helped her stand up.

"How about you go on home now, Darlin'. You can try again

tomorrow if you're up to it."

"But I'm okay. I can stay and do laps." Audrey's face felt hot, and tears formed in her eyes.

"Nope, sorry. I have a rule. If you swallow more than a cup of water, you're out of the pool for 24 hours. Have your grandmother call me if you have problems tonight." She sat down on a pool bench. "Better yet, tell her I'll be calling after practice to see how you're doing."

Audrey scooped up her towel and shuffled toward the back gate where her bike stood in the rack. The parents and students in the stands watched her leave and whispered to each other. Audrey kept her face pointed to the deck. Eric stood by the pool's edge and looked down into the water. He didn't turn to watch her walk past the stands like everyone else. When the gate clanged shut, he dove into the water to retrieve Coach Jameson's hat and took it to her.

"Is that new girl okay? She looked pretty upset," Eric said.

"Yeah, she's fine. Embarrassed as all get out. Why don't you go with her and make sure she gets home? I'm afraid she may have swallowed too much water." Coach dried herself off with a towel and shook the water out of her short gray hair. She took her hat from him and put it back on her head.

"Sure, Coach."

He grabbed his t-shirt and ran to catch up. Audrey, already at the end of the block, prepared to mount and begin her ride home.

"Her name is Audrey," Coach Jameson shouted at him before he went through the gate.

"Where are you going?" Tabitha said.

"I'll call you later!"

Audrey's eyes glistened, although she tried hard not to cry. What a stupid idea that was, she thought. I'm never stepping foot into any water again unless it's a bathtub. By the time she got to the crosswalk, she'd made up her mind. I'm never going back to that school either. I'll quit and get a job.

"Hold up." She heard someone call from behind.

She turned to see Eric trotting toward her. His blond hair, still wet, hung in loose curls. His tanned skin appeared mostly dry except for his swim trunks. Droplets fell onto his bare feet when he reached her. He pulled his team shirt over his toned torso.

"Coach asked me to walk you home."

"I'm fine." She turned away from him and continued crossing the street. She wanted more than anything to find someplace to hide and scanned bushes for a place to disappear.

"I know you're fine, but Coach Jameson still wants me to walk with you." He stopped in her path, and their eyes met. "She means well, but she's very protective of her swimmers. Especially the newbies." Eric's smile was big, and his blue eyes twinkled.

⌘

Audrey filled the sink with soapy water and washed the supper dishes. She tried not to listen to Grandma Josie's phone conversation with Coach Jameson but couldn't help herself. It seemed not only the whole school heard about her almost drowning, but everyone in the town of Palm Glade knew as well. When Grandma Josie hung up, Audrey laid out her idea to quit school. When that didn't pan out, she resorted to Plan B.

"Audrey, you haven't even given it a chance." Grandma Josie dried the dishes while Audrey finished washing.

"I'm not a fish. Otherwise, I would've been born with gills, Grandma. That's what Daddy would've said."

"To be honest, I bet your dad would've had something to say about you joining the swim team just to meet a boy in the first place. If he were here, he'd probably make you stick with it now that you started."

"Eric's a senior, and seniors don't go with sophomores. Anyway, he has a girlfriend." Shaking her head, she pulled the plug at the bottom of the sink. Her eyes followed the water down the drain. Then she dried her hands. Ready to forget the whole ordeal, she hastily walked out of the kitchen, lost in thought. He walked me home only because the coach asked him to, she thought.

"I think you will regret this, but if it bothers you that much, I can't stop you," Josie called after her.

"I'm sorry. I'll see if I can get a refund." Audrey ran up the stairs. She was relieved when her grandmother didn't say, 'I told you so,' although it still made her feel guilty.

⌘

The next day when the last bell rang out in her biology lab, Audrey hurried to her locker and then to the pool office. She wanted to get in and out before too many swimmers recognized her. The swimsuit was clean and folded neatly on top of the notebooks she carried in her arms. Team members passed her going into the changing rooms. A few giggles echoed through the locker room door, indeed, at her expense. But at least nobody said anything to her.

Coach Jameson's office door was closed, so Audrey knocked, then heard someone walking toward her. She glanced around, and her face bloomed red. She turned back to the door, hoping he wouldn't recognize her.

"Hey, Audrey, glad to see you came back. You want to share

a lap lane?" Eric reached for the boys' locker room door handle and stopped a moment to look at her. She studied her sandals while her heart pounded in her ears.

Her eyes darted up to his, then flicked back to the concrete. Say something, dummy, she thought. "Uh, oh, hey," she mumbled—a huge lump formed at the top of her throat.

"Meet me by the far end, and we'll go over some different strokes." He disappeared into the boys' changing area.

Coach Jameson came out of her office with her clipboard and keys in hand. "How're you feeling, girlie?"

Audrey adjusted her books to give her feet some needed shade from the sun's rays. Her long hair clung to her back now. The faint scent of chlorine floated on a gentle breeze.

"I'm okay." She shrugged. Sweat collected at the back of her neck

"You ready to get started?" Coach Jameson locked her door and stepped over to the girls' changing room.

"That's why I need to talk to you."

Coach Jameson ignored Audrey and said, "One of our seniors said he'd work with you until you felt more comfortable in the water."

A female swimmer slipped around them and disappeared into the locker room.

"But, I can't." Her chest felt tight. "Swim." She breathed in a sob, and her eyes glittered. She looked away.

Coach Jamison wrapped her arm around Audrey's shoulders and squeezed gently. "It's okay. Everybody needs to learn sometime, so don't decide yet. Let's see how today goes." She loosened her embrace. "You know the one who walked you home yesterday? Eric. He's one of our best swimmers, and I asked him to help teach you a few things."

Coach Jameson opened the girl's locker room door and

stepped inside. The door silently closed behind her. A moment later, it opened again, and she poked her head out. "Let's not be late for practice." She guided Audrey inside. "I'll see you out there."

Eric worked with Audrey all afternoon. He told corny jokes and made her laugh at herself. After showing her how to move her arms and legs at the edge of the pool, Audrey watched him glide across the water with purposeful strokes. His arms were tanned, and his muscles toned.

Maybe I'll quit after today, she thought. Eric grabbed her hands and gently pulled her in. The water was freezing, but she didn't care. She'd warm up quick enough. He handed her a floating block, and they both kicked side-by-side in the same lane for several laps. Other swimmers gave them curious looks, but she ignored them. Even though the coach assigned Eric to her, she loved the attention. Who knows? Maybe I'll learn how to swim before I quit. She returned every afternoon with a plan to say it was her last.

⌘

One afternoon at the end of practice, when Audrey had been on the team for a few weeks, the coach picked up her megaphone.

"Alright, that's a wrap for today. Let's go, everyone out of the water." The sun was well on its way toward the horizon when her voice echoed throughout the pool area. Coach Jameson stood at the edge and watched the swimmers climb out. Water poured off them, splashing onto the deck and into the locker rooms.

"Get changed without any lollygagging. I have a coaches' meeting about our first swim meet, and I'm already late." She tossed the gate key to Eric. "Make sure to lock up as soon as everyone's out."

"I'll take care of it, Coach."

Audrey was one of the last to climb out. She strolled over to the locker room door and waited for Coach Jameson to drive out of the parking lot. Then she ran and jumped back into the water.

"Hey, what're you doing? Coach says we need to leave." He put his hands on his hips and shook his head.

Coach Jameson said Audrey had a shot at doing well in the breaststroke and that she should focus on getting comfortable with it. With only a week to prepare for her first competition, she wanted to be ready. Grandma Josie, of course, planned to be there to cheer her on. Maybe even her mother would come.

The rest of the students left the locker rooms and headed out the gate. Eric watched the last student pass through, then returned to the pool's edge. Audrey moved effortlessly through the water to the far end. He noticed how much she had learned in the short amount of time she'd been on the team. Her head bobbed up and down as her arms pulled her body forward, and her long legs kicked out forcefully behind her. Instead of telling her to get out again, he changed tactics and dove into the water. He swam to the bottom then surfaced in front of her. She opened her eyes with her next stroke, and Eric's face floated inches from hers. She jerked back.

"What are you doing?" She treaded water, her expression a picture of confusion.

"I thought you said you were quitting." He grinned.

"Maybe tomorrow." She smiled and splashed water into his face.

"So, you aren't ready to get out?" He wiggled his eyebrows, and his face turned into a wide grin. He tapped her shoulder lightly and said, "Tag, you're it!" He reached wide behind him and raced back toward the other end of the pool. Audrey's eyes blinked a couple of times while watching him swim away. Over the weeks of practice, she learned how playful he could be.

Eric climbed out of the pool, ready to run, then turned to look for her. Instead of swimming after him, she took a deep breath and sank to the bottom. He dove in again and met her there. They both sat crossed-legged on the pool floor for a moment. Her face appeared serene, and her hair, held in a ponytail, swirled around her shoulders. Eric held up his palms, and she grabbed them, lacing her fingers between his. They kicked off and surfaced together. She pulled away from him and swam to the edge.

"You're it!" She pushed herself up to climb out, but he caught her by the waist. She giggled and fell backward into his arms.

When her laughter subsided, she looked into his eyes and saw something in his expression that she never noticed before. His hand caressed her cheek, causing her pulse to quicken. His lips softly brushed against hers. Her mouth parted, and he kissed it gently. Her flesh exploded with chills, and her brain felt dizzy. She wanted him to do it again and reached her arm around his neck.

The gate clanged, and they both turned to see a swimmer walk in. He strolled over to the bleachers without noticing them, grabbed a towel, and went back through the gate. Audrey pushed away from the embrace and climbed out of the pool. Grabbing her towel, she hurried into the locker room.

Oh my God, she thought. What just happened? After she squirmed into her shorts and yanked her tank top over her swimsuit, she slipped out of the locker room. Eric watched her approach while waiting at the gate to lock up. He had changed into his club shirt and dry shorts. Audrey peered past him into the parking lot where her grandmother's car sat idling. How long had she been there? Did she see what we were doing? Her neck flushed, and it crept to her cheeks. She winced as she passed beneath his arm.

She peeked at his face, and he returned her gaze. His eyes softened, and he cocked his head playfully. She glanced away and fumbled with her towel before hopping into the passenger seat. It hit the payment, and she reached down to grab it. Eric waved to Grandma Josie, and she maneuvered the car out onto the quiet street. She waved back. Once the vehicle picked up speed, Audrey turned to watch him drift down the darkened sidewalk.

⌘

A few days later, when Audrey was at her locker, Tabitha appeared behind her, with two senior friends. They wore cheerleader uniforms and had ribbons weaved through their hair. Painted on their faces were the school colors, garnet, and gold. Freckles covered Tabitha's face and arms, and an auburn braid trailed along her back complete with a garnet bow. Audrey felt them glaring at her but pretended to look for something lost in the back of her locker. Tabitha whispered to the girls, and they walked away, but not before giving Audrey hard looks.

A geometry text tumbled from the opened compartment onto the floor, and the thud echoed down the hall, creating unwanted attention. Although the morning temperature was chilly, sweat gathered beneath the armholes of Audrey's sleeveless blouse. She scrambled to pick up the hefty volume and fumbled the two binders already in her arms.

"You're Audrey, right?" Tabitha asked and sat on her haunches to assist her with the books and folders.

"Um. Yeah." They stood up together.

"Well, I'm Tabitha." Her chin jutted out, and she looked directly into Audrey's eyes.

"I know who you are." Audrey shuffled back, obviously shaken and feeling like a mouse caught in a trap.

Tabitha gave her a sideways glance. "So, I hear you've been swimming with Eric in the pool."

Audrey's mouth went dry, and she licked her lips. "Well. He's been teaching me to swim." Her eyes darted away from Tabitha's face. "We just swim. Nothing else." How did she find out? Audrey wondered. That kid who came back for his towel must have blabbed.

"Hey, Tabby!" Another cheerleader called from an open door across the hall. "I need your physics notes from yesterday."

"Okay, sure. I'll stop by after the game, and you can copy what I have, but you'll owe me!" Tabitha smiled at her friend.

Audrey closed her locker and stood motionless. She looked to the end of the hall for her next class then slipped away in that direction, hoping Tabitha would leave her alone.

"Audrey, wait." Tabitha caught up with her. "It's okay. Everyone thinks Eric and I are going steady because we've known each other for so long."

Audrey stopped and searched Tabitha's face for the joke. "So, what are you saying? He's not your boyfriend?"

"He's more like a brother. No way is he, my boyfriend." Tabitha laughed. "I know too many of his bad habits and little secrets."

Audrey placed her free hand on her chest. "Wow, I thought you two were an item." The hint of a smile reached her lips as the two continued down the hall.

"He talks a lot about you."

"He cracks jokes in the pool all the time, but he does that with everyone." Audrey's mind raced. "What's he saying?"

"Just stuff, but I can always tell when he likes someone because he never shuts up. Anyway, I wanted you to know we aren't going steady. In case you were wondering."

"Okay." Audrey shrugged her shoulders and feigned indifference. They walked on in silence. Then, "So, you think he likes me? I'm just asking because the coach made him work with me."

Tabitha stopped in front of her classroom, and Audrey waited to hear more. "If there's anyone I know, it's Eric. Are you going with anyone?" Tabitha asked.

"Who me?" Audrey's voice squeaked.

"Yes, you silly. The goof doesn't know I'm asking, so please don't say anything. He'll kill me."

"Okay."

"Listen, if you don't like him, don't lead him on. He's such a romantic. It would hurt him if you did."

"Oh no, I'd never!" Audrey paused. "I thought seniors never went with sophomores."

Tabitha laughed. "He doesn't care if you're a sophomore. If he likes you, he likes you."

"Oh." Audrey's mind returned to what happened in the pool, and her face flushed.

"I don't know if you've heard anything about him, but he had it rough growing up. His mom died when he was a kid, so his dad raised him and Michael, his older brother."

"No. He's never said anything."

"Maybe he'll tell you if you start going steady. He's a straight-up guy, and talented too."

"Yeah, I've seen him swim."

"Not just that, he's a whiz at mechanical stuff."

Mrs. Waters, Tabitha's Economics teacher, hurried past on her way to the teacher's lounge. She looked directly at the girls and tapped her watch. The bell would ring soon.

"Well, I gotta go. See you around," Tabitha said. One of her friends grabbed her by the elbow and dragged her into the classroom. A couple of students hurried into other rooms before the doors closed.

Audrey's brain tried to make sense of the new information. She came to her senses when the late bell rang out. She slunk into her second-hour class and tiptoed to her desk. The teacher busied herself, writing the geometry assignment on the board. Safe! Audrey thought. Mrs. Sands droned on for the rest of the period about squares and triangles, but Audrey wasn't listening. When the end of class thankfully arrived, she called Audrey up to her desk and handed her a tardy detention slip. Typically, this would cause worry, but all Audrey could think of was her conversation with Tabitha.

Tabitha and Eric first met in kindergarten. When she heard about his mom having cancer, instead of shying away, she made a point of being his friend. Whenever he was sad, she cheered him up by telling him stories her dad told her. Mostly about herself, but Eric didn't mind.

"I come from the planet Sparkle, where the popular kids are the ones with the most freckles," she said. "Every freckle on me is a baby star waiting to be born. Or, "I'm a princess because I am the most exceptional violin player. Only real princesses can play so beautifully." Her dad told her as much, and according to Tabitha, he knew everything. She, of course, practiced her violin every day.

Afterward, she and Eric rode bikes around the neighborhood. Eric's bike was one his dad put together for him from odd parts he collected from the auto garage. It needed a paint job, but it maneuvered as smoothly as Tabitha's shiny new bike. Eric attached playing cards to their wheels. They loved how the cards flapped against the spokes and made their bikes sound almost like car engines. He patched their tires when they went flat and adjusted their chains when they got loose.

During the summer months, they ate picnic sandwiches that Tabitha made and skipped stones in the pond behind her house. She dreamed of performing at Carnegie Hall and pretended she was on stage. Eric applauded and whistled when she finished playing her violin air contralto. He'd yell, "Bravo!" Tabitha and Eric got along so well that friends and family predicted they would marry someday.

⌘

To most everyone's surprise, Eric and Audrey started going steady. One day after swim practice, they walked to Claire's house. Claire's moods varied from day-to-day. Sometimes when Audrey brought friends over, Claire said embarrassing stuff. It had been months since Claire had a drink, so Audrey decided to take a chance.

They sat around the living-room, and Claire asked questions about how Eric was doing in school and showed an interest in his family. She even smiled and told jokes—this thrilled Audrey. Claire could be charming when she wanted. After a while, Eric left for work. Audrey stayed and sat with her mother on the couch and waited to hear what she thought.

"He's dreamy, Audrey, but too cute for my taste. Those dimples are adorable, though."

"What?" She searched for understanding in Claire's face. "Don't you like him?"

"Sure, I like him. He's cute. But maybe a little too handsome?" She smirked. "He'll probably cheat on you as soon as he gets bored." She smiled and squeezed Audrey's hand.

"Eric's not like that!" Audrey pulled away from her.

"You know I don't like to talk about your dad, but I'll say this one thing. I could've picked someone a lot more handsome; I'm not saying your daddy wasn't handsome." She faced Audrey. "But I went with him even though I could've done better because I knew he loved me above all else, and he would never cheat on me."

Audrey's mouth dropped open, but no words came to her. She absently rubbed the scar on her cheek, and her thoughts went to the night she and her dad surprised Claire at Marty's. "Why would you think that about Eric? You just met him."

"You wanted to know what I thought, so I told you."

Audrey shook her head and picked at her shorts. Inside, her blood boiled. Her eyes started to burn, but she didn't want to cry.

"Audrey, honey, I'm teasing." Claire giggled. "Eric's great, but you're so pretty and smart. I know you can do better. You should marry a rich lawyer."

"Daddy wanted me to be a rich lawyer, not marry one." Audrey busied herself gathering her books and gym bag. She'd heard enough.

"See! Your father and I would've agreed. You shouldn't be thinking about marrying anyone right now anyway. You're too young."

Audrey stopped and glared at her mother. Her mouth was tight. "I never said I was marrying him." Then her eyes softened. "I just thought."

Claire's smile turned ugly. "You just thought?" She mocked. "What?" She leaned closer. "I know how these things work." With hands balled into tight fists, she said. "You may be friends now, but you should listen to me. He'll take you out behind the bleachers, and the next thing we know, you'll be having to marry him." Claire stood, ready to bolt for the bedroom. Audrey rose, grabbed her mother's hands, and held them to her chest.

"Let's not fight. Okay?" The last thing she wanted was to make her mother mad, knowing where it could lead.

Claire pulled back and turned away from her daughter. "Don't you think you should be heading to your grandma's? She'll be calling looking for you, so you better get going." She sat once again, crossing her legs. Her foot bounced vigorously beneath the coffee table.

Audrey bit her bottom lip and waited for a beat. "She knows I'm here." She returned to the couch next to Claire and searched her face. Not able to hold her daughter's gaze, Claire looked away. With one arm around her tiny waist, she held up her other with palm up. Her fingers curled toward her and studied her nails.

Audrey sighed and began collecting her things once again. "Coach Jameson is going to let me compete in our first swim meet." She glanced up casually at her mother's expression. "She says I have a chance of doing well in the breaststroke." Then hastily. "Do you think you can come?"

Claire's foot stopped bouncing, and she looked at Audrey. "Breaststroke? What kind of silly swimming is that? Aren't they supposed to be teaching you how to swim the right way?" She shook her head. "All this crazy stuff they're filling your brain with at school isn't going help you one bit in the real world." Her foot started bouncing again. "You need to be able to save yourself when you get in over your head." She looked back at her nails. "Which you often do," she mumbled.

"What's that?" Audrey said, not quite hearing the last part.

Claire shook her head. "Nothing."

"Anyway, if you come, I can have a seat saved for you right up front since you're a parent." She looked inside her gym bag and pulled out a flyer which contained the swim meet schedule and held it out.

Claire hopped up and strolled into the kitchen. "I'll check with work to see if they can manage a day without me." She opened the refrigerator door and bent over to look inside. Audrey followed her to the kitchen and leaned on the door-frame. Claire's face popped up with eyebrows raised as if to say, "Well, what are you waiting for?"

Audrey took her cue and headed out the front door, but not before she dropped the flier onto the coffee table.

⌘

Eric asked Audrey to the homecoming dance. Grandma Josie thought it would be a good idea to include Claire, who begrudgingly agreed to allow Audrey to go. She only asked to be the one to take her shopping for a dress.

After going to several boutiques, Claire complained about how much time her daughter took to decide. Audrey wanted to find a dress perfect in every way. Claire told her if she didn't pick something at the next shop, she would have to go to the dance wearing whatever was in her closet. Hastily, Audrey found three and took them into the changing room.

"Don't take forever! It's just a dress, for Christ's sake!" Claire sat close to the mirrors to wait for the modeling to begin. The first one, Audrey believed, showed off too many curves.

"That's not bad." Claire mused to herself, then said, "Boy, you sure have grown up fast."

Audrey looked at herself in the mirror. The purple dress hugged her hips with a deep plunge neckline and very short hem.

"I like the color, but it feels like my boobs are going to pop out of the top," She pulled the top part up high enough to cover her cleavage, but this made the hem appear even shorter and her legs overexposed.

"All the boys will be lining up to dance with you." Claire winked. "Get it." She leaned back with her arms splayed across the back of the bench.

"But I'm not going to be dancing with all the boys. Just Eric. It's too tight." She went back into the changing room.

"Suit yourself. I like it. It looks killer on you." Claire was bored and ready to leave.

Next, Audrey came out wearing a sleeveless black dress that went down to her knees. It was also a little tight, but it had a pretty pink rose connected to the belt.

They looked at each other, and both said, "Nah." She went back into the changing room.

The last one was a blue dress with shiny sequins and sheer sleeves. It was low cut at the cleavage, but chiffon covered it with the same blue shade as the sleeves. It didn't have a snug fit like the other two, and Audrey liked the way it felt against her skin.

"What do you think about this one?" she asked.

"I liked the other one better."

"The purple one was too tight, but this one feels much better, and it isn't too short."

"I don't like all those glittery things. You'll look like a lit-up Christmas tree."

Audrey peered at herself in the mirror. The hem came up a couple of inches above her knees. She turned to look at herself from behind. The dress flared a little at the bottom, so she spun around, and it billowed out.

"But I love it! Can we buy it?"

"I still like the purple one." Claire noticed Audrey's hopeful expression. "But sure, why not. If it's the one you want."

"Thank you, Claire! You're the best!"

"Do I at least get a hug?" Claire stood, ready to leave.

Audrey ran up and wrapped her arms around her mother and squeezed. She was so excited that she picked her up from the floor and spun around.

"My back! Ow! Audrey!"

Audrey put her down immediately.

"Oh, no! I'm so sorry, mother. Are you hurt?" Audrey stepped back, afraid to touch her.

"I can't move my back. Call an ambulance!" Claire dropped to the floor and laid down.

The sales clerk briskly walked over. "Is everything alright?" Noticing Claire on the floor, she hurried back to the sales counter and called the hospital. Audrey knelt next to her mother and rubbed her shoulder. She didn't know what else to do. "I'm so sorry."

"Will you be buying the dress?" The clerk asked when she returned. She eyed Audrey sitting on the floor, still wearing it. Audrey looked down at herself and realized it was getting wrinkled and maybe even dirty.

"Oh! I'll change out. I'm sorry." She hung the dress neatly back on the hanger and handed it to the sales clerk.

"Shall I hold it for you?" The clerk asked. Audrey looked down at her mother's anguished expression.

Audrey shook her head. "No, that's alright." Then knelt next to Claire.

Once they arrived at the hospital, the doctor came in and examined her. He gave her a cortisone shot and explained the jolt from Audrey's embrace caused Claire's back to go into spasms. He prescribed Valium. It was guaranteed to relax her muscles so it wouldn't happen again.

Grandma Josie came and picked them up. She took Claire

home and put her to bed. Then she and Audrey returned to the boutique and bought the dress. From that day forward, Claire blamed Audrey every time her back hurt, which required her to take more of the medication. The doctor told her never to mix the pills with alcohol, but Claire began to do just that. Not long after, she started going missing for days.

⌘

At the end of her first season, the Palm Glade High School swim team voted Audrey, the best candidate for the Most Improved Swimmer medal. It was the first time she'd won anything, especially in sports.

Claire never made it to any of Audrey's swim meets. She said her boss was a real ogre and never allowed her any time off. It didn't matter. Audrey just wanted her mother to be proud of her. She parked her bike in Claire's driveway and knocked several times. Without an answer, she used her key to get in. Her mother wasn't home. Before she closed the door to leave, she noticed a photo album lying open on the couch. She sat down to take a look.

It was full of pictures from her mom and dad's wedding, and she could tell her dad adored Claire just by the way he looked at her. The photo of her mom smashing a piece of wedding cake into her dad's face revealed a bulge in her stomach area. Would they be married now if he was still alive? She doubted it. Her foot kicked something under the coffee table. Reaching for it, she pulled up an empty whiskey bottle. "Oh, crap!"

Audrey sped out of the neighborhood on her bike. Semi-trucks and cars passed her on the busy highway and honked. She ignored them and leaned forward off the seat to gain speed. Past the skating rink, dry cleaners, and convenience store, she pedaled on the highest gear to achieve the most velocity. Her labored breath came to her in heavy bursts, but she didn't allow herself the luxury of slowing down.

Tucked between an abandoned warehouse and an empty lot was Bernie's Highway Inn. Her tires skidded when she turned onto the gravel driveway. In the parking lot sat a single car and two motorcycles. She jogged her bike up to the red brick building and leaned it against the wall beneath a flashing Budweiser sign.

The scuffed black door held firm for a moment but then relented to the pressure of her push against its sun-heated surface. The rain that morning must have caused the aged wood to swell, making it stick. She stepped into a cold dark world. Instinctively, she crossed her arms over her chest to protect herself. An air conditioner rattled somewhere above her head, and 'Kiss an Angel Good Morning' by Charlie Pride played on the jukebox on the left wall. Her eyes adjusted, and the room came into focus.

Round tables with empty chairs scattered haphazardly sat deserted, and the floor needed a good sweeping. Audrey's tennis shoes stuck to the cheap linoleum and made a scrunching echo with each step. Odors lingered of full ashtrays and used plastic beer cups containing varied amounts of warm beer from the night before. Cigarette smoke hovered close to the ceiling. She stifled a gag and approached the bar.

⌘

Bernie poured beer for a single customer who sat on a stool. With elbows on the bar, the patron propped up his hands to cradle his head. Thinning locks revealed a red, cracked scalp. His body trembled with what Audrey thought to be alcohol withdrawal. Her dad used to say, "He's looking to get a taste of the hair of the dog that bit him." She witnessed the symptoms many times while living with her mother.

Unlike the rest of the bar, Bernie appeared fresh with a striped nostalgia bartender shirt and vest crisply ironed, and his turned-up handlebar mustache, freshly waxed. His and Audrey's eyes connected with shared knowledge, and he nodded toward the back where a billiard game was in session. With a sigh, she moved in that direction.

A huge bearded man leaned over the pool table and took a shot. His braided ponytail covered the snake embroidered on the back of his black leather vest. A portly woman stood behind him. Her hair was short and gray at the temples. She, too, wore a black vest with the same emblem and squealed with delight when he sank the eight ball. He scowled and dropped his cue stick onto the green felt surface.

"Rack'em darlin! Me and my friend are playing now," the biker woman said. Rather than comply, he shook his head and strolled back toward the bar. The woman giggled hoarsely and drifted to a small table in the corner. With a skeptical grin, she watched the teen approach. Audrey returned the woman's stare. There, on a stool, was Claire with her back leaning against the wall. Between the fingers of one hand smoldered a cigarette with an inch-long cinder hovering over an ashtray. The biker woman nudged Claire's shoulder enough to rattle her bloodshot eyes open. She sat up, and the ash dropped into a multitude of cigarette butts.

"I'm awake!" Claire leaned her head against the wall and peered at her daughter. "Audrey. My darling daughter."

"Claire, let's go." Audrey reached for her mother's hand, but Claire pulled away.

"Awe, come on, Audrey. Can't you see I'm having fun with

my friends?"

The biker woman laughed at Claire, then started a coughing fit. She flapped her hand at the cigarette smoke.

"You've been drinking." Audrey glared at her mother.

"Who is this pup?" The woman stood and pulled her hefty jeans up around her waist. "I didn't know they allowed young'uns in places like this."

"My daughter thinks she's my mother the way she nags me all the time." Claire lit another cigarette from the one in her fingers and continued to balance unsteadily on the stool.

"Well, that just won't do." The biker woman stepped in front of Audrey with a menacing glare but became distracted when she noticed the Most Improved Swimmer medal hanging from the girl's neck.

"What's this?" She held it in her hand and flipped it over to see both sides. "Let's see it."

"It's a medal for swimming." Audrey pulled the ribbon over her head and handed it over.

"You see this?" The biker woman held it out for Claire to view, returning her seat. Claire barely acknowledged it, nodding with eyes half-closed. Audrey noticed and realized she'd made a mistake to think her mother would care.

The biker guy walked up. "I got you both a beer to help with your game." His right-hand double-fisted the frothy mugs while he sipped from the one in his left. Then he set them in front of the ladies.

"Hey, Earl! Take a look at this." The woman tossed the medallion up to him, and he reached high to catch it. He looked at it for a few seconds, then cocked his head to one side. "So?" He tossed it back.

"It looks like gold. Maybe it's worth somethin'?" She tossed it to him again. Audrey tried to grab it, but he held it high out of reach, spilling beer on the floor.

"Give it back to her," Claire said. "Audrey, go home to your grandma." She looked sternly at her daughter, not as wasted as she appeared minutes before.

The biker couple continued to toss the medal to each other, but Audrey stopped grabbing for it. Instead, she glared at her mother and crossed her arms.

"I thought we were playing Eight Ball," Claire said. "Who's turn is it?" She stood and brushed past Audrey toward the pool table to rack the balls.

The biker woman laughed again and tossed the medallion to Audrey. Instead of catching it, she let it hit her chest, then fall the floor with a dull clang. Without another word, Audrey walked out. Claire watched her leave, then picked up the medal and slipped it into her pocket.

⌘

Grandma Josie was crazy about Eric and treated him like family. When he called that afternoon, Audrey told him about what happened at the bar. After they hung up, Audrey walked into the kitchen and found her grandmother at the sink looking out the window, lost in thought. When Josie noticed her granddaughter's presence, she shook it off and busied herself with the dirty dishes.

"So, what did Eric say?" She asked.

"He mostly just listened." Audrey then added, "He did say, next time, I should call him so he can tag along."

"I'm sorry you had to go through that with your mother. Sometimes it doesn't take a lot to set her off." Grandma Josie's eyes searched Audrey's expression. "You do know I'm very proud you, right? You've worked hard, and look at what you've accomplished. Get your medal. I want to see it."

"I left it."

"What? Oh, no!" Grandma Josie's shoulders slumped. "Why?"

"I just had to get out of there before I got really upset." Audrey paused before continuing. "I think she needs to go into AA or something." She opened the refrigerator and soaked in the chilled air, then turned to look directly at her grandmother. "I mean it. There's something wrong with her." She closed the door and sat at the table. Planting her elbows onto the smooth surface, she rested her chin into her open palms and waited for her grandmother's response. It wasn't the first time they'd discussed Claire's coping skills.

"You shouldn't be going into a place like that, but you're right. Your mother needs help." Grandma Josie dried her hands on a dishtowel. "I'll talk to her."

Audrey exhaled heavily. "What're *you* going to say that'll make her pay attention? She doesn't listen to anyone."

"Don't worry about that. You just eat your dinner. It's your favorite."

Josie's chin pointed toward the oven. "Lasagna." She handed Audrey a plate from an overhead cabinet. "All you have to do is take it out of the oven. It's still warm." Since Audrey started swimming, her appetite had doubled.

Grandma Josie picked up her purse from the counter and grabbed her car keys from the pegboard next to the garage door.

"Where're you going?" Audrey asked. She went to the stove and peeked inside the oven. The aroma of melted cheese mixed with pasta and tomato sauce invaded her nose. Her stomach growled, and she realized she was ravenous.

"None of your beeswax. I'll be home in about thirty minutes." Grandma Josie closed the door, then opened it again. "After you finish eating, get started on all that homework you neglected to do earlier."

Audrey scooped a large spatula full of the lasagna into her plate and listened to the garage door rattle closed. She knew her grandmother was on her way to Bernie's Highway Inn.

⌘

After cleaning up, Audrey went upstairs and climbed out her bedroom window onto the balcony. Reclining in a patio chair, she observed the October sky. Usually, this calmed her, but tonight she barely noticed the magnificent display of orange and purple. High temperatures gripped the community during the afternoons, but with fall approaching, the day cooled significantly as the sun set. She rubbed her arms to combat the evening chill.

The sound of a car engine approached, and Audrey leaned forward to watch her grandmother park in the driveway. With homework waiting, she started back inside. Just as her foot touched her bedroom's plush carpet, her ears caught a note clinging to a gentle breeze. She tilted her head to the source. In the waning light, down the street lined with blooming crepe myrtles, a dark figure approached. Strolling casually, he whistled a tune heard on the radio. Audrey went to the railing and leaned over. With arms crossed in front of her, she called out softly.

"Romeo, oh, Romeo. Where art thou, Romeo?"

Eric looked up, overtaken with desire at the sight of her. Even in the fading light, she was striking. Thick dark hair curled around her smooth, delicate face and spilled in front of her.

"She speaks. Oh, speak again, bright angel. You are as glorious as the stars tonight." Eric went to one knee, raising his outstretched arms. Just as Romeo did in the school theatrical play, they attended earlier in the day.

"Where're you headed, my handsome prince?" Audrey covered her mouth and giggled. Her eyes scanned the neighbors' yards for spectators, but the street was quiet. Kids already inside for the night, preparing for baths or bed.

"Why, I'm going to meet a fair maiden." He bowed, then climbed the porch steps and pressed the doorbell. The chime echoed inside. She leaned further to listen to the conversation but only heard faint murmuring. Visits rarely occurred during the week, especially on a school night, but after telling him what happened, he must have decided to make an exception.

"Eric's here." Grandma Josie called from downstairs. Her voice reached Audrey through the open window.

A moment later, he too climbed out and stood at the railing next to her. Without a word, they gazed across the lawn toward the darkening road. Street lights flickered to life one by one.

He turned to face her, but she continued to watch the lights, so he tugged her arm. She straightened and looked into his eyes. Unable to hold his stare, she rested her cheek on his chest. He wrapped his arms around her and cradled her head with his hand. His heart pumped loudly, stirring a recently discovered need within her.

"Are you sure you're okay?" He asked.

Audrey looked into his eyes and put her fingers over his mouth to silence him. He kissed them gently. His lips moved to hers, tenderly at first, then urgently. Audrey responded by wrapping her arms around his neck. Eric's mouth traveled to her throat, then her chest. His hands caressed her back and moved to her hips. Audrey's body tingled, and her breath quickened. With breasts aching to be touched, her legs relaxed and parted slightly. Instinctively, his hardness nudged between them. She pushed back, causing him to shudder. Then, his lips stopped reaching for hers. Audrey drew his head toward her for another hard kiss.

"We can't," Eric breathed into her mouth. He held her shoulders and gently shifted her away.

"Why?" She tugged his hands toward her.

"Because your grandmother is downstairs, and she made me promise to be a gentleman." He sat down on the patio love seat to conceal what was happening in his lap. Audrey frowned but sat next to him and rested her head on his shoulder. They stayed that way until crickets played love songs in the dark. Eric kissed her brow, then leaned his head back to gaze at the starry night.

Audrey nudged him gently. "Do you love me?"

He didn't answer at first, continuing to peruse the heavens. Then he breathed in her hair and pulled her chin up until their eyes met. "You're my whole world. I'm so in love with you." He leaned down and kissed each eyelid and the top of her nose. Then he placed another on her lips.

A loud rapping came from the other side of the bedroom door. Audrey hopped up from the love-seat and yelled through the window. "Coming, Grandma!"

"You have homework to finish before bed, and it's getting late," was Josie's muffled reply.

Eric stood behind Audrey and squeezed her shoulders. He kissed her once more, then passed through.

"We'll talk tomorrow," he said.

⌘

Eric graduated from high school the following June, but he didn't go to college with his friends. He had a choice, either work as a mechanic with his dad or go into the Navy. To Audrey's dismay, Eric chose the latter. She feared he would end up like her dad, but he convinced her it would be a great opportunity. She wanted to be supportive, but it was hard to be rational. The

Navy assigned him to Pensacola Naval Air Station to work as a helicopter mechanic. While there, he studied for his pilot's license.

Mr. Potter delivered for the post office in Grandma Josie's neighborhood for more than thirty years and knew a lot about his customers. He quickly caught on to Audrey's long-distance relationship with Eric and grew accustomed to finding her waiting for him on the porch. She'd flip through, and if she saw nothing from Eric, her anticipation turned to disappointment. Mr. Potter often feigned forgetfulness and miraculously produced the coveted letters. It wasn't long before she grew wise to his charade and quizzed him daily to tease the mail out. Both Eric and Audrey received something almost every day and talked on the phone a couple of times a week. Eric also rushed home whenever he received liberty, so they spent a few days together every month and on most holidays.

Once when Eric was home during Christmas break, Claire disappeared. The sheriff's office refused to put out a search warrant because she'd gone AWOL before and managed to find her way home. After a week, she called Grandma Josie. She was alone and sick in Las Vegas. From what Josie gathered, Claire and some old rich guy drank and gambled until his wife picked him up. Grandma Josie bought tickets for the couple to fly out and get her. Upon her return, Claire pledged sobriety. Although she appeared sincere, Audrey was dubious that her mother would ever out-grow her Peter Pan Syndrome. Contrarily, Audrey became an independent young woman eager to take on the world's challenges.

One day Grandma Josie received a brochure with a coupon for a discounted prediction in Cassadaga, Florida. She thought it would be fun to organize a day trip with some of her girlfriends. They all went for an afternoon of lunch and soothsaying. When she returned home, she couldn't wait to tell Audrey what happened.

"It was the weirdest thing," Josie said to her granddaughter, who had just sifted through the mail, and climbed the porch steps. Audrey timed her arrival home from work to coincide with mail delivery and made a game of appearing on the sidewalk in front of the house just as Mr. Potter's mail truck rounded the turn onto their street.

After graduating from high school, Audrey got a job with the town newspaper, answering phone calls and did most of the filing. She dreamed of becoming a journalist like those who breezed into the office and typed out their news articles daily. Her letters to Eric included stories about things she learned by keeping her ears open and listening to their little town's latest happenings.

Josie took a large swallow of iced tea, then returned the glass to the antique table sitting between the two rocking chairs. Condensation bubbled along the tumbler's outer wall and produced tiny rivers that traveled haltingly to the crocheted doily, doubling as a coaster. The little ice cubes tinkled and dissolved into the sweet, brown liquid.

Josie pushed her heel into the wooden floor to produce a slight sway. She enjoyed sitting outside during the colder months, but the temperature had climbed to an unusually warm and humid afternoon. The other shoe-less foot lay across a crate of oranges. Audrey strolled across the porch to the empty rocking-chair.

Once seated, she looked closer at her grandmother and noticed the gleam in her eyes. She looked like a kid with a secret in desperate need of sharing. Something was up. "You look like you swallowed a canary. What did you do?"

"Who me? Nothing. The ladies and I just went to lunch

today."

"You and your friends haven't been together in a while. Did you hear some juicy gossip? Is that what you can't wait to tell me?" She grinned. "I know how you ladies can talk." The fragrance from the oranges reached Audrey's nose, and her mouth watered.

"Oh, you know—the same old stuff. Sandy's husband ran off with that waitress down at the café. The skinny one?" Her eyes never left Audrey's face. "Oh, and they changed the date for this year's flower show."

"Uh, no. Is that going to be a problem?"

"Well, it might. The date is now in June."

"Why, you planning to be somewhere else in June?" Audrey cocked her head, intent on extracting the secret her grandmother wasn't telling.

Josie leaned forward, and her eyes glowed. "Speaking of canaries." Her voice became bubbly. "A little birdie told me you and Eric would be husband and wife." There it was—the Cheshire Cat grin with a yellow feather between her teeth.

Audrey's mouth fell open. It took her a moment to gather her thoughts. "Where'd you hear that?"

"Well, actually, it was more like an old crow." Her eyes twinkled.

Audrey, ready to change the subject, looked down at the oranges. "What have you been doing? You must have been busy with more than just lunch."

"Don't they look delicious? I bought them from a farmer selling his leftover harvest beside the road on our way home." Grandma grabbed a large bright one and handed it to Audrey. Inhaling the sweet aroma, she pushed her thumb into the naval and peeled the rind away. After separating the pieces, Audrey slipped one into her mouth. The juice ran down the edge of her hand to her wrist, and she grabbed the kitchen towel sitting in Josie's lap.

"Okay, time to spill it." Audrey realized that maybe her phone conversations weren't so private, after all.

"So, it's true." Grandma Josie rocked harder. Her chest puffed out, and she hugged herself. "An old palm reader told me you're marrying this June." Her eyes searched for truth in Audrey's expression. "You never said a word."

"Well, we've been talking about it, but nothing solid."

"She said specifically, a June wedding and a honeymoon in a tropical paradise." Josie clapped her hands giddily. "I knew you two were getting serious!" Josie's mouth flew open, and her eyes widened. She stopped rocking and leaned forward. "If the wedding's in June, we need to start planning!"

Grandma Josie was so excited that she wanted to give them the best wedding gift ever and paid for a honeymoon to The Bahamas. Eric left the Navy at the end of his contract, and then the two got married on June 7th, 1980. They landed in Nassau the following morning.

"Whoa! Wait a minute! I thought you were going to start this story at your wedding, and I get no details about it?" Izzy asked, now sitting up.

Audrey bit her lip and looked out the window.

"Oh, come on! Was it a big wedding? Little wedding? Give me something."

"You know what? You seem to be much better." Audrey's mouth was suddenly dry, and she cleared her throat. "Why don't you tell me a little more about you?"

"I already told you I'm a singer in a band."

"But that can't be all you do. Don't you work anywhere?" Audrey's eyes narrowed, locking onto Izzy's expression.

Breaking into a high-pitched giggle, Izzy looked down the aisle in both directions. "I think that cranberry juice caught up to me. I'm going to hit the loo, and then I'm going to see if I can get another round of drinks." She unbuckled her seatbelt, but before she stood, she leaned toward Audrey. "Let's just say I work in the insurance business." She winked, then moved toward the back of the plane.

What did that mean? Audrey suddenly didn't feel so good. The plane dipped, and her stomach rolled.

When Izzy returned, Audrey was covered from head to toe beneath a blanket. Leaning close, she listened to Audrey's breathing. That's when she noticed the journal poking out of Audrey's carry-on bag.

CHAPTER FIVE

Puzzling Gift

Audrey dragged Eric by the hand through endless rows of collectibles in the Straw Market situated just off Main Street of Freeport in The Bahamas. After having a memorable honeymoon week, the couple decided it was time to find a gift for Grandma Josie to show their appreciation. When they reached the end of the last row, Audrey's shoulders sagged, and she shook her head.

"Nothing but hats, sundresses, and t-shirts. I don't think we're going to find anything." Her smile disappeared.

"How about we look around in some of the shops?" Sweat accumulated on Eric's brow.

"We did that yesterday, and everything was way overpriced, remember?"

"We should take a closer look at those conch shells that guy was diving for on the dock. Maybe he'd make us a deal if we buy two. One for Josie, and one for Claire."

Audrey shrugged. The shells were beautiful, but they didn't look as if they came from the bottom of the ocean, but rather from the expensive shell shop at the end of the pier. Audrey knew her new husband all too well. His purchases typically were thought out, keeping a close eye on the money they saved. Many a night, they snuggled on the porch and whispered promises and dreams for their future.

Eric wanted to buy a helicopter business. His idea was that they'd move to Miami once they had enough money and give sightseeing tours to snowbirds along the coast. He always talked about it. Audrey didn't like the idea as much but tried to be a positive force with his plans. It seemed like a big step, and she wasn't crazy about moving so far from Palm Glade.

When Eric was a kid, his mom and dad both worked full-time jobs to make ends meet. He and his older brother, Michael, were latchkey kids. Michael walked Eric to and from school every day and made him macaroni and cheese from a box for dinner when their parents had to work late. Their dad worked at Harvey's Auto shop and hoped to one day buy it when Harvey finally retired. He put money into a savings account every month to go toward that dream. Their mom worked at the Super Foods grocery store as a meat wrapper. She worked with the butcher, placing cuts of meat into trays, then wrapped each in plastic. It was a good job, and her wages were higher than those of the cashiers.

Unfortunately, the store didn't provide insurance. When Eric's mom received her breast cancer diagnosis, she depended on his dad's coverage for medications. It only covered part of the surgery and chemotherapy. After a few doses, her hair fell out, so she shaved the rest of it off and started wearing a scarf. As her health declined, she missed several days because she was too weak to go in. Her co-workers took up a collection and presented her with almost a thousand dollars. Eric remembered her laughing and crying when she left work that day. After she died, the hospital bills arrived. Their dad worked two jobs to pay the mortgage and withdrew money from his savings to buy groceries.

Michael took their mother's death hard and started failing in school. By the time he got to high school, he had stopped going altogether. Their dad tried to get him some tutoring help, but Michael wasn't interested. He believed he wasn't good at anything and went from job to job, never staying interested in any one thing. Michael didn't enjoy working on cars like his dad and Eric because his mind didn't think that way. Instead, he was very creative and drew disturbingly beautiful pictures of dark dragons and wizards like those in J.R.R. Tolkien's Lord of the Rings.

One day at the garage, a man was short on cash and paid for his auto repairs with an electric guitar. Harvey had no use for it, so their dad brought it home and thought he could sell it. Michael picked it up and liked the way it felt in his hands. He decided to learn how to play and spent all of his free time practicing in his room. After he learned to chord three songs, he joined a band. Without a decent place to play, the group eventually broke up. Undeterred, Michael kept playing and got pretty good. He joined a heavy rock group called The Tongue Twisters, and they started playing in hotel lounges before he was old enough to drink. When he turned eighteen, the guys moved to Miami, where they played in bars every weekend. Audrey and Eric went to see them in Miami a few times, and the band played the music at their wedding, including the march as they walked down the aisle.

⌘

After several hours of trudging through the Straw Market, Audrey shrugged her shoulders. She released a sigh, adding a heaviness to Eric's heart. He wanted nothing more than to make her happy. Friends from home assured them the Straw Market offered unique but inexpensive island gifts, but so far, the couple hadn't found anything worth buying.

"Come here." He wrapped Audrey into his arms and breathed in deeply. She smelled of shampoo mixed with sweat. His mind traveled to the previous day.

While on a snorkeling cruise, they'd slipped inside the lifeboat and made love while the other passengers dove among the reefs. Audrey had the naughty idea, he remembered. They were a little clumsy at first until they figured out how not to rock the boat. Or so they thought. Their initial clamoring must have drawn attention because when they emerged from beneath the tarp, an audience of several passengers applauded them. Audrey hid her crimson face in Eric's shoulder, and he waved with a sheepish grin.

Now Eric rubbed Audrey's arms while his eyes scanned the aisles of tables. "Let's try a little longer, but remember we still have all day tomorrow to find something."

The further they went, the less congested the rows became. A table sat at the far end of the last dirt road, but Eric was sure it wasn't there on their first pass.

"Did we see that one before?" He asked.

The table sat away from the others, hidden beneath large mossy oaks with low overhanging branches. Weeds made their way up and around the wobbly legs, so off-balanced the top leaned to one side.

"Maybe the seller just arrived, but they set up fast. Weren't we by this way a few minutes ago?"

"There's nothing wrong with your television set, "Eric said.

Audrey giggled, "Do not attempt to adjust the picture."

"We are controlling the transmission. You are about to experience The Outer Limits. "Eric tickled her waist, and she jumped.

"You just gave me the heebie-jeebies!" Audrey shuddered.

"Well, it is Friday the 13th."

"Oh my gosh! Is it?"

An older man behind the table beckoned to them to take a closer look. A flat leather cap covered his thin gray hair, and bright red suspenders held up his baggy jeans. Glasses with thick lenses perched on his nose made his blue eyes appear large and wet.

"Step right up! If you're looking for a unique gift to take home to a special person in your life, I have just the thing." He pulled on his suspenders with his thumbs, allowing them to spring back onto his chest to make a crisp snapping sound.

Eric took Audrey's hand and they shared a glance. The thought that this could be just what they've been looking for passed between them.

⌘

Rows of colorful miniature wooden dolls covered the table, each five to ten inches tall. Women clothed in beautiful dresses and head-scarves. Men in professional attire. Some painted in holiday themes, and others were of various animals. Red parrots, yellow giraffes, and green frogs were just a few. Every doll was varnished to a glossy sheen.

Audrey's eyes pored over the display of beautiful artwork. The gentleman picked up a blond-haired female doll in a red sequined coat and placed it in Audrey's palm. Its hair was short and curled around tiny ears. With a bright smile and eyes that looked merry, it seemed almost whimsical. He held the bottom half in place and pulled the top away. Audrey looked on as a smaller doll appeared inside. She was dressed in a painted coat, similar to the one before it, also comprised of the red sequined material. Her blond hair flowed down her back. Audrey lifted the top half of this doll, and inside was a young girl with curly blond hair. Beneath her was a young boy with light-colored hair. Each wore a charming smile. Inside the boy doll sat a tiny baby wrapped in a red blanket. With eyes closed, it appeared to sleep soundly.

"These are called matryoshka, or Russian nesting dolls, and they were used by many to tell traditional Russian stories or fairy tales," the man said.

"They're beautiful, don't you think, Eric?" Audrey held it out and replaced each of the dolls until the largest single matron stood in her palm.

"They're great. What about these?" Eric reached for a man doll.

"Matryoshka dolls often follow a common theme, so what you have there is a group of Soviet Leaders." The man leaned toward Eric and pointed. "You see that one is Brezhnev, inside is Khrushchev, followed by Malenkov, then Stalin, the smallest is Lenin." Eric opened each doll until he came to Lenin. The man smiled. "Amusing, no?" His focus returned to Audrey as Eric replaced the Soviet Leaders inside each other.

"What do you think? You like?" The gentleman asked. He eyed Audrey intently.

"They look so, well." Her feet shuffled. "Old." She shook her head. "Not bad old, but cool. I've never seen anything like them." Audrey set her blue shopping bag on the ground next to the table and picked up a set from the animal collection. The noonday sun shone off the high gloss red and green finish of a spotted frog. She held it up to her hazel eyes. The artistic designs were intricate and precise.

"They are ancient, indeed. Just to give you a bit of history, this set was made in 1890 by a man named Vasily Zvyo, something or other. Anyway, he,"

"Vasily Zvyozdochkin!" A voice croaked from behind him. Eric and Audrey both leaned to the right to see a little old lady sitting in a crooked lawn chair behind the elderly gentleman. Neither noticed her before.

"He was famous doll maker in old country." She sucked in a wheezing breath and continued. "He stole design from Sergey Malyutin, who was folk craft painter at Abramtsevo!" Her voice rose sharply like a door forced to allow entry. One that hadn't opened in a hundred years.

⌘

The man shook his head and rolled his eyes skyward. "Mama knows the history of the matryoshka better than me."

He stepped aside to give Eric and Audrey a better view of his ancient mother. Her bony arms, no more than sticks, poked out of a flowing silk dress with red, blue, and purple colors. A blue cap with gold embroidery sat snugly on her gray head, and a wide leather belt encircled her tiny waist. Her wrinkled face held bright blue eyes that focused on Audrey. Weeds curled around and through the legs of the old aluminum lawn chair. It seemed they would swallow her up if she sat there long enough.

"Please forgive my son, Yuri. He has no manners." She covered her mouth and coughed. Returning her hand to her lap, she grinned with stained, crooked teeth.

Eric raised his eyebrows, and his mouth turned down.

Audrey returned his stare, and her shoulders inched up.

"Yuri, I'm so thirsty. Bring me water, please!" Her gnarled fingers scratched at her throat.

Yuri let out a deep sigh. He shook his head, and his hands dropped to his sides.

"Would you excuse me while I go for water? Mother can entertain you with stories of the Old Country while I'm gone. I should only be a few minutes."

"I don't mind, do you, Eric?" Audrey's eyes pleaded.

A dark cloud moved in front of the sun. After a week in paradise, the couple knew a daily thundershower was imminent. Many of the tourists moved to vacate the Straw Market and find shelter. Eric felt they should do the same, but he hesitated. One of the dolls would be the perfect gift for Audrey's grandmother, and he didn't want to miss his chance of ticking off that box. Shrugging his shoulders, he thought, maybe just a few more minutes.

"I will tell you all the mysteries of the matryoshka." Yuri's mother dragged another old lawn chair closer to hers and patted the seat, peering up at them.

The hairs on the back of Eric's neck stood up, and a shiver ran through him. Something in the way the old lady looked at Audrey gave him the creeps.

"I think we should be getting back to the hotel. It looks like rain." Eric trailed Audrey to the chair. She giggled when she lost her balance and fell into the flimsy seat.

"You know, you look familiar to me. Have you ever been to Florida?" Audrey cocked her head and gave the woman a sideways glance.

"I have been around the world." Her icy blue eyes met Audrey's. "Have you?"

"Me? No. This trip is my first time out of Florida. Why?"

"No matter." The ancient woman took both of Audrey's hands into hers and held them between twisted fingers. They were tinted an icy blue and looked dry as cracked leather. Audrey tried to pull away, but the crone held on tighter until Audrey went still and looked into her eyes. The woman leaned closer until she was inches from Audrey's face. Audrey tried to look away but was captivated. Eric peered up at the darkening sky and caught a glimpse of thick black clouds sparked with jagged strokes of lightning. When he returned his focus to the two in front of him, the flashes reflected brightly in the older woman's eyes.

⌘

"Matryoshka is very beautiful, no?" Her voice sounded as if it was coming from deep inside her, much like a wolf's menacing growl. "They are very mysterious with secrets waiting for the right person to possess them."

Eric leaned down and squeezed his bride's shoulders. Her eyes broke free from the stare to look up at him, but her face was slack without expression. Audrey's eyes held the blank stare of someone sleepwalking.

The old lady squeezed Audrey's hands, and she cried out in pain but was quickly drawn back into the dark blue eyes.

"Some matryoshka are said to have special powers. Some call it black magic. I've been waiting for just the right person to come along. Years, I've been waiting, and here you are. You are the one." The woman giggled, then loomed over Audrey, who slid down in the chair, their eye contact never broken. "Do you accept?"

Eric heard and saw enough. No longer would he allow this ridiculousness. Audrey looked ill.

"That's it. We're out of here!" He reached down and pulled her arm. The woman hung on, but the trance broke when he heaved Audrey from her firm grasp. He wrapped Audrey in his arms and backed right into Yuri, who returned from his search for water. Later, Eric wondered just how long Yuri had been standing there.

"I have your water, Mother, and I'm sorry it took me so long. All of the vendors are closing up because of the storm." Yuri's eyes darted from his mother to Eric and Audrey. "What's going on here?"

Seeing his mother's condition, he rushed to her side and knelt in front of her. Her head was leaning forward, and her cap had fallen over her eyes. Her thin gray hair stuck out at odd angles, and when he pushed her hat back, her eyes remained closed.

Yuri gingerly took her claw-like hand and placed a cup into it. Then he retrieved something from around her neck. Her eyes stayed shut, even as she whispered hoarsely. Yuri leaned his ear next to her lips. After a moment, he nodded and turned his attention to Eric and Audrey. He stood slowly and walked back to the table, shaking his head. "This isn't the way," he mumbled to himself.

Eric looked into Audrey's eyes and held her upper arms tightly. Her eyes weren't focusing, and she appeared to be in a semi-conscious state.

"I am sorry about that. Please don't pay any attention to my mother's rantings." Yuri looked around and rubbed the back of his neck. His eyes softened. "You see, Mother has been diagnosed with Alzheimer's and sometimes has episodes. I didn't think I was gone that long."

He reached into a cardboard box below the table and fumbled around. He placed something into a crumpled brown paper bag and handed it to Eric.

"Here, for the lady. Sorry about the trouble. Now go, before you get caught in the storm." He turned his attention to his mother. "I need to put her to bed." His head nodded to a tiny camper a few feet back within the trees.

Eric put the brown paper sack into Audrey's blue shopping bag and slung it over his shoulder. The skies opened the moment he guided her away from the table.

"My head feels like it's splitting apart." Audrey's hands held her face and allowed Eric to guide her. "I'm so dizzy." They walked quickly as the rain cascaded down.

"Just a little further, you can make it!" Eric shouted, holding her up in his arms. He surveilled their surroundings as they came to the market exit.

A man on a pay telephone turned his back to them as they passed and whispered into the receiver, "It's on the move." Audrey's knees went limp, and Eric used his strength to hold her up, then rushed her through the gate into the street.

⌘

Like many tourists caught in the downpour seeking shelter, they scurried beneath the awning of a gift shop. After a few minutes, Audrey no longer felt wobbly. Her hair hung limp on her shoulders and dripped down her arms. Eric handed her the blue shopping bag, made sure she seemed okay to wait, then went inside for a towel. She stood among other tourists.

As the rain drummed onto the cobbled street, she breathed in the aroma of the fresh summer shower and immediately felt better. With her back to the store and her foggy brain clearing, she wondered, what happened back there? She shook her head to jog her memory.

That's when someone tugged the blue shopping bag. Thinking it was Eric, she looked around only to find other tourists waiting. Hmm, she thought and returned her attention to the street. After a couple of minutes, someone yanked the blue shopping bag once again hard enough to pull it off her shoulder, but she held on.

"Madame, I believe you have my bag," a tall, dark-skinned man said. He pulled the straps again.

"No! You can't have it. It's my bag." She jerked it free from his grasp.

The people around her backed away to watch the scene unfold. The man's eyes darted around the crowd. With so many witnesses, he relented and apologized.

Backing away into the downpour, he turned and ran into the middle of the street, dodging a crowded trolley car at the last second. The driver rang the trolley bell impatiently, never slowing the car's progression. The rain continued to come down hard. Audrey looked for Eric but couldn't see him inside the store. Concerned tourists waiting alongside her asked if she was okay. Eric emerged from the shop drying his hair with a beach towel and noticed everyone looking at him.

"What?" He asked. "Did I miss something?"

CHAPTER SIX

Misgivings

Audrey **slept several hours** before Eric woke her. "How're you feeling?" His gaze focused on her relaxed expression.

She shrugged, then stretched her arms overhead. Eric kissed her cheek, then snorted into her ear like a pig. She playfully pushed his mouth away.

"Better. I guess I needed that nap." She sat up and looked around the room. It was a standard hotel room, but over the week, she had grown fond of it. Is it possible to be so happy and in love, she wondered? Next week they'd figure out how to start their life as husband and wife, but for now, this was perfect.

"Hey, listen." Eric squeezed her hand. "You get a shower, and I'll go down to the lobby to pick up the tickets." He slipped on his flip flops, then strolled to the door. They had waited all week for the dinner cruise, which would be the highlight of their trip.

Audrey got to her knees on the edge of the bed and saluted. "Aye, aye, Captain!"

When the door closed, she stumbled over the comforter and onto the floor. Her foot connected with something.

"Ouch!" She rubbed her toe and reached beneath the bed. Her fingers landed on the cloth handles of her blue shopping bag. What's this? She hauled it up, setting it on top of one of the many pillows the hotel afforded them and pulled out a wrinkled brown paper bag. Hmm, Eric must have bought something for me as a surprise. I wonder if it's a special bottle of wine to celebrate the end of our honeymoon. Sometimes he can be so romantic, she thought and smiled to herself. I shouldn't open it. She dropped it back inside the blue canvas and returned it to where she found it, then proceeded into the bathroom and closed the door. A minute later, she came out and returned to the bed. What the heck, I'll just take a peek.

Inside the crumpled bag was a matryoshka from the Straw Market. When did he get this? Turning it over in her hands, she tried to open it. No luck. There must be a latch or something.

After searching its painted surface, she gave up and tossed it onto the bed. It rolled, came to a stop, and smiled up at her. She bit her lip and put her hands on her hips. Turning on her heel, she made her way back to the bathroom.

Before going in, she stopped and looked at herself in the mirror. The, You be Jammin! T-Shirt she wore that morning, complete with sweat stains, smelled ready for the dirty-clothes bag. Slipping it over her head, she had nothing on beneath except her bikini bottoms. There was a considerable contrast in the color of her skin where her top once covered her breasts. How pale she must have been the day they left Palm Glade. Everyone at the Gazette is going to love my tan, she thought.

She turned to look at her bottom in the mirror from behind

and noticed the doll lying on the bed, still looking at her. Audrey went over again and picked up the nesting doll with hazel eyes and long dark hair like her own. She held it up for a better look. The matryoshka, that's what the older man at the market called it, wore a beautiful emerald-colored gown. She leaned back with her free hand to open the closet door next to the full mirror. Keeping her eyes on the doll, she pulled out the dress she was planning to wear that night—an emerald-colored gown.

⌘

"What are you doing?" Eric whispered in her ear. Audrey jumped and dropped the doll.

"Crap! I told you not to sneak up on me like that!" Audrey tossed the gown onto the bed, then dropped to her knees to search beneath for it.

"I thought you'd be ready by now. The ship sails in thirty minutes." He leaned over and squeezed Audrey's bare shoulders, then slipped past her. He turned and threw his body backward onto the bed, just missing the gown. With hands clasped behind his head, he watched Audrey's toned bottom poke up as she continued to reach for the doll.

"What are you looking for?"

"Uh." Audrey looked up at him. "Did you buy one of those dolls this morning?"

"No, I thought we decided to get the shells from the pier." Eric thought a moment. "Oh, wait a minute. That old guy handed me a bag with something for you. I forgot all about it."

Audrey stuck her head back underneath the bed. The matryoshka was just out of reach. "I can't get it."

"Take your shower, and I'll see if I can reach it before I get ready to go." Eric laughed.

When Audrey stepped out of the bathroom, she was alone. On the bed, Eric left a note. Next to it, the matryoshka. Meet me in the lobby for the most exquisite experience: your Romeo, Eric.

Audrey quickly dressed, applied a bit of mascara and lip gloss, then tossed her hair under the blow dryer for a couple of minutes. She took a quick look at herself in the mirror. Her form-fitting gown with a slit up the side and low-cut neckline showed off her curves in all the right places. She grabbed her room key, matching clutch purse, and sandals, then headed for the door. She took one glance back at the matryoshka who was gazing up at her. "We don't look half bad, do we?" She went down and met Eric in the lobby.

⌘

A cab waited outside the hotel. Along the way, they hit all the green lights to the port, so they made it to the ship, Your Lucky Day, with minutes to spare. The vessel, originally a cruise ship, had carried about 800 passengers around the Greek Islands. Once retired and decommissioned, the company sold it to a business in The Bahamas, who converted it into a party boat. With the right marketing, it became a big draw giving tourists a unique island experience.

Exclusive restaurants served meals on the top deck so passengers could enjoy delicious cuisine while they viewed the beautiful islands. The level below was a bar with a large dance floor and a live band that played during the evening cruises. A cigar bar, daiquiri, and martini bars made up the deck below that. The entry-level where Eric and Audrey came aboard housed poker tables, craps, roulette wheels, and slot machines. Cabins available to rent nightly or for the weekend resided on decks two and three. The bottom of the ship contained mostly crew quarters.

Eric counted them lucky to get a reservation at the trendy Japanese Steakhouse because bookings remained full all week. Once on board, the couple leaned over the railing and amused themselves, watching workers scurry around the dock. Lifeboats hung above them, and Eric wrapped his arm around Audrey's waist.

"What do you think? You want to check them out later?" Eric winked and poked her gently.

"I'll take a rain-check." She squirmed away from his fingers. "I don't think I'd be able to climb up there in this dress." She reached up and kissed his cheek. He leaned over the side to check out the crew working the ropes and preparing to set sail. She gazed at him. I'd love to stay here in this moment forever, she thought and squeezed his arm.

The gambling ship moved slowly away from the dock and out into the Atlantic Ocean. Eric and Audrey left the railing and went up to the restaurant deck. Once inside the Japanese eatery, they sat at one of the many oval counters which featured grill top cooking. Tourists claimed most of the seats. As many as ten regular tables, which sat twelve, filled the center of the large room. The entrees remained on the high end, but the restaurant still packed in patrons to enjoy drinks and fine dining.

"What happened to you today? You had me worried." Eric shouted over the din of conversations held around the restaurant. The chef put on a show of comedy and culinary flair with food on the searing hot surface at their grill top.

"What are you talking about?" Her eyes widened. "I had to dry my hair. Besides, we made it here with minutes to spare."

Audrey turned her eyes to the grill. The chef made a heart out of the rice and used his spatula to give it a beat pointing to Eric and Audrey. The other passengers at the table applauded and congratulated them on their newly wedded status. Eric must have said something when he made the reservation, Audrey mused. Red-faced, she smiled and thanked their dining companions.

"I'm talking about when we were at the Straw Market earlier today. Remember, the old Russian lady? You looked like you were going to pass out."

"I must've gotten too much sun. That old lady was creepy, though." Audrey thought back to their morning experience and took a small bite of chicken.

"Saki!" The chef shouted and picked up a plastic bottle full of a clear liquid. He squirted the Japanese liquor into open mouths around the grill. When the stream reached Eric, he opened his mouth wide and stuck out his tongue to make a bigger target. The Saki hit the back of his throat for a good five seconds until he raised his hands to signal he'd had enough. He swallowed and finished with a grin. Audrey waved the bottle on, shaking her head. Eric leaned over and put his arms around her shoulders and kissed her sensuously. After a few seconds, she gently broke free.

"You're such a cad." She used her napkin to wipe his cheek, and he leaned in for another kiss. She grabbed his chin and popped a shrimp into his mouth. He washed it down with beer and gazed at her.

"Did I tell you how beautiful you are? That dress makes me hot." Eric took the napkin from Audrey and kissed her palm.

"Only every time I wear it," she whispered in his ear. She took Eric's beer and set it on the table. "If you want the full package tonight, you better slow down, or you'll be snoring before we get back to the room."

Eric and Audrey talked several times about starting a family right away and wanted to take every opportunity to make that happen. While in the Navy, he was sent overseas to a base in the Middle East and maintained helicopters for six months.

In his letters, he always wrote about how much he wanted to have kids. Once, he sent Audrey a picture of himself in full gear with five children of various ages wearing giant smiles. One held two fingers behind Eric's head while the youngest boy's arms clung tightly to his neck. Another sat in his lap. A rifle lay against his opposite knee, reminding Audrey of where he was. Even though he wasn't in Vietnam, it still made her worry and think of her dad.

Eric gauged his alcohol consumption level and agreed to slow down on the beer. He tugged her neck toward him to kiss her forehead, then waved a nearby waiter over and asked for a tall glass of water. When the waiter reappeared with the drink, Eric peered up at him. The waiter returned his stare.

"Hey, you look familiar. Do I know you from somewhere?" Eric tried to clear his head to remember.

⌘

"He works in this restaurant. You probably saw him when we boarded."

"Will there be anything else, sir?" The waiter asked.

"Nope." Eric shook his head. "That's not it, Audrey." Then to the waiter, "You're a local from here, aren't you?" Eric cocked his head and continued to stare at the man. "Hey, weren't you in the Straw Market today?" Pause. "Wait a minute, I remember now. You were following us!" Eric rose slowly, still holding his napkin. "Audrey, is this the guy who tried to rob you today?" He looked down at her. Audrey's mouth dropped open.

"You are mistaken, sir." The waiter backed away. Eric moved to follow.

"Eric, what are you doing?" Audrey reached for his arm.

The waiter turned and collided with another staff member carrying a tray full of drinks. They both crashed into a table of diners. He scrambled to his feet and ran for the exit. Eric dropped the napkin and hurried after him.

"Eric!" Audrey screamed. Diners sat frozen, and cruise staff stood looking on.

"I'm so sorry about this!" Audrey said, looking around the quiet room. She backed into the door, then pushed it open to follow her husband onto the outer top deck and into the night. The ship rocked as it cut through the dark ocean. They were at least twenty miles from the closest island.

Audrey did her best to catch up, but Eric stayed several yards ahead, pursuing the waiter to the stern. The dress made it difficult for her to maneuver, and she felt a few stitches in the back come apart when a chair snagged the hem. Her ankles wobbled in her sandals, never built for running, especially on a moving vessel.

She called out to him several times while negotiating around unaware passengers who attempted to dodge her approach. Avoiding deck furniture became her focus. The ship rolled through the rough surf at a brisk clip with a crew unaware of the drama playing out on the top level. She reached the back only to see Eric leaning over the railing.

She ran to his side. "Eric! What's going on?" Audrey grabbed his arm and pulled him away. The horror in his eyes was unmistakable.

"He jumped!" Eric bellowed and leaned over the rail once again. His head turned in all directions, searching the ocean below.

"What? No, he didn't."

He grabbed Audrey's upper arms and looked into her eyes.

"Yes, he did."

"But that can't be." Audrey's mouth was agape. Her eyes searched Eric's face for a hint of humor. He had to be joking. "Please don't tell me that!" Her bottom lip began to tremble.

"We've got to stop the ship and turn around!" Eric's voice cracked several octaves higher than usual. They both leaned over as far as they could and searched the dark sea. All the while, the wind blew, and the deck dipped.

⌘

The ship's captain contacted the local police and returned the vessel to the island of origin to investigate what Eric and Audrey witnessed. The restaurant manager dispatched a lineup, presenting all members of his crew to the authorities. When asked, Audrey couldn't say whether the waiter in question was also the man who accosted her on the island. After several hours of questioning, the authorities determined the waiter wasn't an employee of the ship. Many of the guests remembered the scene in the restaurant, just as the couple described. Eventually, all hands returned to their duties to prepare for the next cruise.

After a long and tiring night, the couple returned to their hotel. It was well after 2:00 A.M. Eric slipped his key into the lock and opened the door. A single bedside lamp burned dimly. Before they stepped into the room, their housekeeper appeared behind them. She was tiny, maybe four feet, nine inches, with short dark hair. In her early fifties and originally from Indonesia, she spoke in quick, clipped sentences. Eric and Audrey only knew her as Sammy. She kept their room spotless throughout their stay and added subtle touches like leaving cute animals made with a towel. Nightly mints on their pillows made their stay extra special. Her round face, typically graced with a perpetual smile, appeared flushed. Her mouth, anxiously drawn into a frown.

She quickly ushered them in, but not before stealing a glimpse down the hall in both directions. She stood with her back to the door and stared at the couple for a moment before closing it. Eric and Audrey gazed at her suspiciously. She pointed to a towel that covered something on the bed.

"Where did you get that?" Sammy asked.

"What?" Eric pulled the towel away and found the matryoshka smiling up at them. "This doll?" Eric picked it up and showed it to Sammy. Audrey looked from Sammy to the matryoshka, then glanced at Eric. Sammy's eyes darted away, not wanting to look at it.

"Islanders are superstitious and say matryoshka is not good for The Bahamas." It was apparent Sammy was desperate to leave the room, but her eyes softened. She knew all too well what dangers being young and in a foreign country meant and only wanted good fortunes to befall the couple.

"What do you mean?" Audrey asked, walking over and reaching for Sammy's hand. Sammy turned away and wrapped her arms around herself. Audrey immediately put her arm around Sammy's shoulders and squeezed gently.

"Your whole body is shaking." Sammy relented and let Audrey hold her.

"We picked it up at the Straw Market earlier," Eric said. "Actually, it was yesterday since it's after midnight." He dropped the hand that held the doll to his side and used the other to run his fingers through his hair.

"Come, sit down and tell us what you know." Audrey coaxed Sammy to the bed while Eric stuffed the matryoshka back into the brown paper bag and returned it to the blue shopping bag. He tossed it onto the bed, then as an afterthought, placed it out of sight underneath.

"Return it where you bought."

"Okay, but what makes it so bad?" Eric said. He knew there were a lot of superstitions among the Islanders.

"Islanders say Russian doll bring bad luck to any who possess. Some say it holds black magic."

"But I don't understand, an old man and his mother were selling a table full of them in the Straw Market yesterday," Eric said. "Why would they sell something like that? Especially if it's?" Eric shook his head. "Evil?" He barely contained a smile.

Sammy looked directly at him. "Tourists buy them, but locals stay away."

"Alright, how's this? We'll return it first thing this morning after we get a couple of hours sleep." Eric said.

"But I was thinking about giving it to Claire," Audrey said.

"Don't take home!" Sammy's eyes widened. "Return it."

Audrey glanced at Eric, then helped Sammy to her feet and walked her to the door. "Thank you for telling us." She squeezed Sammy's hand affectionately and said goodbye.

"Maybe we can grab a couple of those shells on the pier before we go home," Eric said after Audrey closed the door.

"It doesn't make any sense. It's just a doll."

⌘

Not able to sleep, Audrey rose and dressed just as the sun peeked over the horizon. The last full day of their honeymoon in the Islands looked to be another beautiful day in paradise. Eric wanted a few more hours of shut-eye, but Audrey rustled him out of bed, then pulled him through the Straw Market by the hand with the blue shopping bag banging against her side.

"Slow down! Why are you in such a hurry?" The market once again came alive with tourists from all over the world. Audrey continued pulling his hand through the colorful hats, bags, and t-shirts.

"Come on! I want to get rid of this thing," she said. "Then, I need to find a phone to call Grandma Josie."

"Do you believe a doll can be bad luck? I'm starting to believe you're as superstitious as Sammy." He shook his head and laughed.

"I'm not superstitious, but that doll gives me the creeps, and I don't want to bring it home with us." Audrey stopped pulling Eric and turned to look at him. "There's something wrong with it." She eyed the shoppers milling about and lowered her voice. "I had a dream last night that it slipped out from under the bed and tried to kill you. You couldn't breathe, and with my whole body paralyzed. I couldn't help you."

"Wow! How'd I get away?"

Audrey looked at him. "You didn't."

"What?! It's a doll." He couldn't help but laugh again. "It's old. Your grandmother's old too, but you don't think she's creepy. Although it would make the perfect gift for Claire." Eric winked at Audrey.

She glared at him, "Last night, you were all for returning it and getting them both a shell." Her forehead creased, and her jaw felt tight. She turned and continued walking past the booths. Eric shrugged his shoulders and followed grudgingly. They walked by a young girl of about twelve with a comb and an empty chair.

"Braid your hair?" She called out to Audrey. "Cheap! Only five dollars?"

"No, thank you," Audrey said without breaking her stride.

"Hey, I thought you planned to get your hair braided today." She kept walking. "Wait, Audrey, come back. I was kidding!" Eric grabbed her hand and turned her around. Tears were in her eyes. "What's wrong?! Oh, I'm sorry, Babe. You know I was kidding, right?" He wrapped his arms around her and pulled her to his chest. Audrey released a sob. Her body shook as the tears fell. "It's okay." Eric breathed in deeply and held her. Tourists ignored them, continuing to shop.

"Why did that waiter jump overboard!" Audrey cried openly. "What happened to him?"

"Shh. It's okay. Maybe there was a boat waiting to pick the guy up. Who knows?" Eric kissed the top of her head and squeezed tighter. After a few minutes, her shoulders sagged beneath him, and she wrapped her arms around his waist.

"But that doesn't answer the question of why." She looked around the busy market as she waited for Eric's answer.

"You know what I think?" Eric guided her chin to look up at him. "I think he was the thief who tried to steal your bag, so he was afraid I was going to get him arrested. The guy's a local. He probably does that sort of thing all the time. I bet he knows every inch of the waters around here, and if a boat wasn't waiting for him, he probably just swam back to shore."

"I don't know. That's a long way to swim." Audrey's brow furrowed.

"They're great swimmers here. Remember the guy on the pier bringing up shells? Like a fish."

Audrey shrugged her shoulders and looked down at the ground. Her sobs subsided. "I still think the sooner we get rid of it, the better." She was feeling more composed. "Do you think it kind of looks like me?"

"Uh? Where did you get that idea? Have you noticed what a fat round body she has?" He winked.

"But that dress. It looks like mine."

"Honey, no doll can hold a candle to you, especially in that dress." He smiled. "Come on, let's go back to that old man and return his voodoo doll. Then we can find a phone." Eric put his arm around Audrey's shoulder, and they continued their return trip to the matryoshka table.

The table stood in the same place, but this time, devoid of merchandise. The two lawn chairs where Audrey and the woman had their conversation sat as they did the day before.

"Hmm. I wonder if the old man packed up the nesting dolls and left for good?" Eric walked around the table, put his hands on his hips, and looked at the flattened space the small camper occupied the previous day.

"They cleared out right after you left here yesterday." A man with dark skin made tough by long sunny days sat cross-legged in the shade of a giant oak. He had white dreadlocks that fell to his shoulders and a short gray beard. Mirrored aviator sunglasses covered his eyes, and a cane lay balanced across his lap. His left hand was petting a sizable yellow dog seated next to him.

⌘

Eric shaded his eyes to block out the sun and get a better look at the man beneath the oak. He returned to stand beside Audrey. The temperature already on the rise caused his shirt to dampen.

"So, you saw them leave?" Eric asked. He looked from Audrey to the man.

"Eric, he can't see," she whispered and touched his arm.

"I'm not totally blind. Just mostly. But you'd be surprised at what I can see, although not always with my eyes. It's more of what I know."

"So, what do you know?" Eric said.

"I know you're the tourists who came here yesterday and were given a matryoshka doll by the old Russian lady."

Audrey walked over and sat down in front of the older

gentleman, even as Eric tried to stop her. Her reflection was visible in his sunglasses.

"Is it okay if I pet your dog? Audrey asked.

"He's not mine, but he would probably be okay with it."

Audrey reached out and let the yellow dog smell her hand. He laid down and allowed himself a good head rub. He was clean with a collar, complete with tags.

"He's beautiful, but he must belong to someone." Audrey scratched behind his ears.

"He answers to Buddy, but he belongs to the streets. He knows every inch of this city and never has to worry about his next meal. Neither do I when we're together. Sometimes we work as a team. You see, we're performers. My name is David Sanders, but around here they call me Davie."

"Nice to meet you." She held out her hand. Davie didn't respond, so she returned it to her lap.

"You're from the United States. Someplace in the southern region?" Davie asked.

"Yes! We're from Florida," Audrey said. "It's my first time out of the country."

"The Bahamas is a great travel destination, especially for a first trip. I took a vacation here one day and never left."

Eric looked at him skeptically. "How does one do that? Didn't you have a job and family to return to?"

"How does one manage such a drastic move?" Davie used his thumb and forefinger to tug on his beard. "Not as easy as it sounds."

Eric glanced at some tourists heading in their direction, who stopped to shop at a nearby table. Audrey looked down at Buddy. The couple waited to hear more.

"I worked for a large oil company when an accident occurred, taking most of my sight. The company settled out of court for a couple of million dollars. When I came to the islands on a weekend getaway, I liked it so much I decided to stay. I found a cottage on the outskirts of town and lived there alone until I found a puppy going through my trash. I took him to the local vet to get the required shots and started calling him Buddy. The name stuck."

Eric and Audrey shared a glance.

"Buddy was a quick learner, so I taught him several tricks, and before long, we were doing routines in the park on Sundays. Tourists love it and drop tips into a hat." He picked up a worn straw fedora lying next to him and put it on his head. "All the locals know Buddy and treat him like a king whenever we stop by."

"What a wonderful way to live your life." Audrey's voice was cheery. "I'm Audrey, and this is Eric." She looked up at her husband and reached for his hand. "We're here on our honeymoon."

"Well, this is a great place to enjoy your honeymoon. Congratulations on your marriage." Davie held out his hand. Audrey smiled, and with her free hand, accepted Davie's.

"You're a pretty smart dog, aren't you, Buddy." Audrey rubbed behind his ears. He turned over onto his back so she could start on his belly. "Buddy, you're spoiled!" She giggled but complied eagerly.

"Can you tell us anything more about the old lady and her son? Are they from around here?" Eric said as he sat down next to Audrey. While still on his back, Buddy laid his head in Eric's lap. When Eric relaxed enough to rub his neck, Buddy closed his eyes.

"Not a lot, but I overheard them talking. They seemed determined to pass off that doll. The locals say it has special powers, and they're afraid. They say there's a curse attached to it."

"Yeah, we heard that. You don't believe it's cursed, do you?" Eric asked.

"It's not important what I believe. It's what certain others believe that's important."

"See Eric. Something isn't right with it."

"Do you have any ideas about where they may have gone?" Eric asked. "I think the old lady was sick."

"Can't say, but I know they aren't from here." He stopped and thought a moment. "We have several shops in town run by local merchants that might be more helpful. Most of the islanders know things. Oh, and I think there's even a gift shop on High St. next to the Pirate Museum. I don't believe the owner is local, but I heard he's Russian. He may at least know of them, or perhaps, give you some direction."

"Great! We need to return this thing before we head back home." Eric got up and wiped the back of his jeans. "We'll check it out, thanks." Buddy sat up. Eric extended his hand to help Audrey to her feet, and she gave Buddy one more ear rub before accepting it.

"If the Russian shop doesn't know how to help, maybe the college can. I believe they offer a few Russian courses, so perhaps they'll know about any Russian folk on the island.

"Maybe we'll learn something while we're there." Audrey winked at Eric.

"I'd be careful about who you show that doll. Some may have less than ethical plans for it." Davie used his cane to stand as well. He was tall and thin with baggy beige pants and a matching shirt. Buddy stayed next to him.

"Is that what you meant by 'certain others'?" Eric asked.

"The Bahamas are beautiful islands, but we get our share of shady characters. Not locals; they're all good people. But organized crime does frequent the islands from time to time. That's what happens when you have something beautiful. There's always someone who wants to take it from you."

Audrey gave Buddy one last rub. "Thanks for your help, Mr. Sanders. It was nice meeting you."

"Please, call me Davie. You be careful walking around this town with that thing, you hear."

"We'll, do." Eric gave a salute.

"Eric, don't be silly," Audrey whispered. "It was nice to meet you too, Buddy. Mr. Sanders is lucky to have such a good friend." They started back down the dirt-packed lane and merged into a group of tourists. Davie waved at them while he stared straight ahead.

"Just Davie," he said again to himself. "I see a lot more than you think." He reached down, found Buddy, and caressed the top of his head.

⌘

The couple walked along High Street, looking in store windows. They almost missed the Russian shop before noticing a handwritten sign that said, I Love the USSR, and entered through a glass door smudged with old fingerprints. The couple breathed in stale air even though a ceiling fan turned. The stink reminded Audrey of Bernie's Highway Inn back home minus the scent of beer. She bit her lip, and her brow wrinkled. Eric returned her nervous stare, then tickled her in the ribs. She giggled, brushing his hand away.

Shelves mostly bare supported cobwebs hanging in one corner. Audrey's eyes followed one web upward to ceiling tiles with orange spots the size of frisbees where rain seeped in. Fluorescent lights dangled in a row the length of the store. Two were lifeless while another burst on and off intermittently. A

Chill ran up her arms, and she hooked one through Eric's at the elbow.

Single sets of pale blue and yellow porcelain mugs sat along a shelf to their right on the row, leading to the shop's rear. They waited for someone to emerge from that direction. When no one appeared, Audrey took a step back to get a better view and collided with a wire jewelry rack perched in the corner next to the front window. She turned too late with her arms out to catch it, not wanting it to clatter to the floor. Earring sets and necklaces hung from the mostly empty stand. It wobbled precariously before settling back into its stance, and she blew out a heavy sigh.

An antique rotary-style telephone with intricate golden leaf patterns sat above several stacks of dinnerware shelved to their left against the wall. Inside a glass case below the phone lay two ornate Faberge Eggs nestled in satin fabric and lit by the soft glow of an interior bulb.

"Hello? Is there anyone here?" Eric called out toward the back of the store.

Audrey tip-toed to the egg cabinet and noticed a pile of what looked like several broken matryoshka dolls lying upon one of the empty shelves directly behind it. She waved Eric over to see.

"They look like the same dolls," she whispered and leaned closer to get a better look. Eric being taller and having a reach advantage, bent over the case and picked one up.

"They do." He turned the high glossed piece of a female doll over. On the back, what looked like a hinge had been smashed. "That's weird." He showed Audrey.

"Can I help you?" A voice from behind them broke the stillness. Eric dropped the doll piece back onto the pile, and Audrey froze. They turned to see a man dressed entirely in black. His thinning hair combed over the top of his head appeared to be coated with some sort of gel. His thin mustache sat above a smirk, and his dark eyes pierced them with a hard stare.

"Oops! Sorry, but somebody already broke it," Eric said. He grabbed Audrey's hand and squeezed gently.

"That's right. We found it that way." Her tone purposely sounded nonchalant. "Do you have any that aren't?"

The shop owner frowned. He slid past the couple and moved behind the case. He picked up a plastic trash can full of empty soda bottles and candy wrappers, then scooped all of the dolls' remains into it with a loud clanking sound. He set it on the floor behind him and returned his attention to the couple. Slowly, he folded his long fingers together onto the counter as if in prayer.

"We do not. Now, is there something else that you would like to see? How about an authentic Fabergé Egg?" His lips peeled back into a grin while waving a hand, palm up across the display case.

Eric examined the eggs as if interested. "You want to look at one?" He asked Audrey. The shop owner pulled a set of keys from his pants pocket and bent down to unlock the case. When he reached in, Eric leaned over the counter to get a better look at the trash can. The man noticed and moved to block Eric's view. The two men straightened and stared into each other's eyes. The man in black drummed his long fingernails on the glass.

Audrey looked at the two. "Does this mean you don't have any matryoshka dolls for sale?" She asked and pulled Eric's arm so he'd back off. The two men continued to stare. Eric broke first and smiled at Audrey while the shop owner maintained his focus.

Finally, he said, "That is correct. We have no matryoshka. Is there something else you need?" He crossed his arms over his chest, and his eyes broke away.

"But what was that? They looked like a bunch of those nesting matryoshka dolls from Russia." She pointed behind the case.

"Very bad fakes. Complete forgeries, but I can spot them a mile away. We only deal with authenticity here."

"Do you ever have any dealings with the Russian man and his mother in the Straw Market?" Eric said.

"I know of no Russians selling in the Straw Market."

"None?" Audrey lifted a single eyebrow. "We hoped you could help us find them. They were old, and we think they accidentally gave us someone else's purchase. We'd like to return it since it isn't ours."

"Perhaps, if you give it to me, I can pass it on to them."

"But didn't you just say?" Audrey shook her head, choosing not to complete her question.

The shop owner stared at her, then asked, "Do you have something to sell? A matryoshka, perhaps?" The shop owner asked.

"Uh, not really." Audrey grabbed Eric's hand and coaxed him toward the door with the straps of the blue shopping bag tightly draped over her shoulder.

"We're interested in the matryoshkas, though," Eric said, glancing at Audrey. "Hold on. It's okay," he said to her and brushed her hand away. Then to the shop owner, "Can you share any information about them? Someone told us you might be knowledgeable since you sell Russian stuff."

"Most matryoshkas are nothing more than cheap painted wood, but some are worth a few dollars. For obvious reasons, nesting dolls with locking pieces or puzzle entries are worth more. Are you sure you don't have one? I can tell you if it's 'The Real McCoy' as they say in America." He glided around the counter and stood close to Audrey, towering over her. "You know, some are said to be cursed." Her mouth dropped open as she stared up at him.

"We've heard, but we don't believe in curses." Eric ignored Audrey's attempt to catch his eye. "Why are the puzzle dolls worth more?"

"Some have treasures hidden within them." The shop owner's eyes gleamed. "A toy or maybe something more. You could be in danger if you have one. People from the islands are very superstitious and sometimes irrational."

"Let's go, Eric."

"I take it you aren't from here?" Eric asked. He mouthed to Audrey, "Wait a minute," and held up his hand.

The shop owner snickered while shaking his head. "No, I am from Russia. I only come here to sell Russian goods. And buy."

"Well then, can you direct us to the college?" Eric allowed Audrey to pull him to the door.

"The college?"

"We thought we might check it out before we return home."

The shop owner thought a moment. His long fingers held flat together under his chin pointed skyward. "You know, maybe the college can help you. I hear they have an extensive research library and probably have books on the matryoshka."

"That sounds great. Thanks. Can you turn us in the right direction?" Eric asked. Audrey opened the door.

"We'll find it." Audrey yanked Eric out onto the narrow sidewalk.

"What are you doing? I was trying to get some directions." He shook his head, but she pulled him further away from the Russian shop.

The shop owner called to them from the door. "Thompson Boulevard. Just ask anyone, and they will tell you how to get there."

"Thanks for your help," Eric called back. Then to Audrey, "Will you stop pulling me?"

"Not until we are far enough away that my skin stops crawling." They crossed the street to the next block. "Besides, what was that stare down about?"

"He started it." Eric laughed. "He's hiding something, and I'd like to know what it is."

The couple dissolved into many tourists who moved in every direction along the sidewalk and narrow street.

After witnessing their assimilation into the crowd, the Russian glanced across the street. A constable propped against a light post stared directly at him. The shop owner went back inside and took the old phone off the shelf. Its cord, just long enough, allowed him to set it on the glass case. He picked up the headset, dialed, and waited for an answer.

"I think it was here. Yes. A young couple, but they are just tourists. No, but I think they are curious. They babbled on about returning some merchandise to a couple of old Russians in the Straw Market. The woman is carrying a large bag." He waited then said, "I didn't get the opportunity. Too many people are hanging around outside. Oh, and that nosy Constable is out there again." He listened for a few more seconds. "Of course." A smile spread across his thin lips, and he hung up.

After returning the phone to the shelf, he walked to the back and entered a tiny office. He opened a desk drawer, took out a Beretta, and made sure he had it loaded. After sticking it into the back waistline of his jeans, he covered it with his shirt. With a black Bahama hat in hand, he returned to the front of the store and peeked out the window. The constable was no longer there, so he locked up and headed in the same direction as the couple. When he reached the end of the block, Buddy stepped out from behind a trash can across the street and began to follow with Davie attached to the end of a leash. His cane tip-tapped along the gray sidewalk.

⌘

The college campus was like the rest of the Island, lush and beautiful. Red hibiscus and yellow elder adorned the walkway while mighty banyan and royal poinciana trees afforded lots of shade for students congregating between classes. A summer shower added a glittery sheen to the lush grass and evaporated within minutes.

Audrey wondered what it would be like to take classes at such a beautiful university. Before they decided to get married, she dreamed of taking journalism classes at Palm Glade Community College. Would it be so bad if we missed our plane, she thought? What if we stayed in The Bahamas forever? I could take classes, and Eric could fly tourists around the islands. Mr. Sanders certainly has the right idea. I could finally get that puppy Dad promised me.

She breathed in the fragrance of sweet purple and yellow bougainvillea growing beneath the red brick buildings' high row of windows. In front of the administration building was a bank of pay telephones, and Audrey's thoughts returned to reality. She used one to call Grandma Josie while Eric went inside to get information and possibly use their library to learn more about the matryoshka.

"Good morning Audrey. Are you enjoying your honeymoon?" Grandma Josie asked when she answered the phone.

"Are you kidding? It's so beautiful here. How can I not?" She twisted the phone cord between her fingers. "I just had a wild idea! What if we missed our plane and had to stay here a while longer?"

"That sounds like a lovely idea, but how will you explain it to the Gazette? I saw Molly at the grocery store, and she says the temp they hired isn't working out. She's never worked in the newspaper business and is having a hard time."

"Oh, no!" Audrey sighed. "They don't have to worry; we'll be home tomorrow."

"I think your mother is missing you too. She keeps stopping by the house, asking when you're going to be home."

So, how's Claire doing? Please tell me she's sober." Audrey's eyes scanned the transparent wall dividing the phones from each other, offering a bit of privacy. Scratched into the Plexiglas with a sharp object was: Dial 242-8213 for Tarzan and a swinging good time. Some things don't change no matter how far from home you travel, she thought.

"As far as I know. How's Eric?"

"He's good. But what do you mean? Do you think she's been drinking?" Audrey asked.

"I don't think so. You shouldn't worry so much about your mother."

"You're right, but I can't help myself. If Claire starts drinking again while we're here enjoying The Bahamas,"

Josie interrupted. "News flash, Audrey. If she falls off the wagon, it won't be your fault. She's a grown woman and makes decisions for herself."

"I know, but."

"But nothing. You go and have fun with that wonderful husband of yours. That's who you should be thinking about."

"You're right, of course. I just wanted to thank you again for all you've done for us. This trip is fabulous. And guess what? You won't recognize me when we get home. My skin is so dark."

"That's what I want to hear. What time is your flight back?"

"I'm not sure." Audrey exhaled onto the plexiglass to create condensation and drew imaginary hearts on the booth's wall with her finger. "I'll ask Eric and give you a call again when we get back to the hotel."

"Great, I'll be there to pick you up at the airport. Remember to take lots of pictures for your wedding album. I already sent off the photos from the ceremony and reception to be developed. They should be here next week."

"I will. I love you, Grandma."

"I love you too, Darlin', and try not to worry unless there's a real reason to do so. If anything happens with your mother, I'll take care of it. Okay?"

"Okay. Bye, Grandma."

"Bye, Baby."

Audrey sat down on the bench next to the phones to wait for Eric. She opened the blue shopping tote and extracted the brown bag. After a glance around and finding herself alone, she took out the matryoshka. The natural sunlight helped her see it in a whole new way.

⌘

Upon closer inspection, she realized the doll was a young mother-to-be. Its belly was round and protruding as if the baby would come soon. She turned it over and found an inscription on the back. It said, от матери к ребенку. She looked at the bottom and noticed more writing. Знание - сила/мощность из влияние was spelled out. Was that Russian? What did it mean? Now she was curious. She tried twisting the head, but the doll stayed locked.

A pair of voices increased in volume along the wide

sidewalk behind her, so she tucked the doll back into the crumpled sack and returned it to the shopping bag. Hooking the straps over her shoulder, she laid her arm across the top. Her foot bounced to a song playing in her mind. It was a song covered by Eric Clapton and now quite popular around the islands. The couple danced to 'I Shot the Sheriff' in many of the bars they visited during their honeymoon. The feeling of doing something a little criminal, like in the song, made her feel somewhat daring. Although what she and Eric were doing was nowhere near killing a sheriff. But the doll wasn't a typical Russian nesting doll either. She peeked behind herself once again.

A girl not much younger than Audrey, wearing a crisp skirt suit, walked briskly with what appeared to be her mother chasing behind, trying to keep up. The girl stopped in front of payphones while looking at a map. Both mother and daughter wore their hair up in neat French braids. They spoke with the same island lilt Audrey became accustomed to during their time in The Bahamas. The mother wore a dress with large red flowers.

"Good morning." The mother said. "Do you know where we can find Bradley Hall?"

Audrey looked around, hoping someone who worked at the college was within range. Not finding anyone, she answered. "Sorry, I don't go here. I'm just visiting."

"Oh? You look like a student." The woman smiled with dazzling white teeth. "We are here to see if this beautiful college is good for my Rosi. She's so smart."

"Mama, don't embarrass me," Rosi said.

"What? You don't think you're smart?" The lady said to her daughter. To Audrey, "She's going to be a doctor."

"Wow, that's great." Audrey smiled.

"Thanks," Rosi said. "We're supposed to meet a tour group in front of the administration building in about ten minutes." She looked around.

"I think that's the administration building, so you're in luck." Audrey's head tilted toward the tall building in front of them. A small number of people assembled at the corner. "Maybe that's your group over there?" Audrey's shoulders inched up.

"Oh yes, maybe that's where we're supposed to be." The mother said. "Are you going to become a student here?"

"Me? No, I'm just waiting for my boyfriend. Oops, sorry. I mean, my husband. We just got married last Saturday. We're from Florida."

"I have an uncle who lives in Miami. Maybe you know him? Oscar Knowles? He's in real estate." The mother said.

Audrey shook her head. "No, we don't go to Miami much."

"So, you're on your honeymoon! That's so romantic, and this is such a great place for a honeymoon. If you decide to come here to college, my Rosi is a great friend."

"Ma!" Rosi rolled her eyes but smiled as she did. She folded the map. "Let's go see if that's the group we need to be in." She waved to Audrey, and they headed for the gathering. "It was nice meeting you and happy honeymooning," Rosi said.

"Thank you. Good luck with your classes." Audrey watched them scurry toward the small crowd. Rosi's mom put her arm around her daughter's shoulders and squeezed.

Audrey recalled some of her friends having similar mother/daughter relationships and how much fun it was to spend the night with them. She didn't dare invite her friends to spend the night with her for fear of Claire's drinking habit. Would things have turned out differently if Daddy didn't go back to Vietnam? Maybe Claire would've been more like Rosi's mother? She giggled to herself. Probably not.

The main doors opened, and Eric strolled out toward her.

"What's up? You look like you lost your best friend." He sat next to her.

"Just thinking about what a beautiful place this is." She shook her head. "What'd you find out?"

"We're in luck. This college has a Russian history class."

"That's a good thing?"

"Maybe we can find out about your doll. It can't hurt to ask." Eric grabbed Audrey's hand, and they walked across the campus to the social science building. They took in the college along the way, and both appeared to enjoy the new adventure they were on. It's almost like a scavenger hunt, Audrey thought.

⌘

Professor Rodin lectured from the podium, clicking through the slides displayed on the giant screen in front of the auditorium. Eric and Audrey slipped into seats behind the class at the top.

"Nicholas II was deeply conservative and maintained a strict authoritarian rule. He expected good Russians to show self-restraint, devotion to community, deference to the social hierarchy, and a sense of duty to country." Click. "Many turned to their religious faith as a source of comfort and reassurance. Who can tell us how this was a problem for the people of Russia?

Professor Rodin peered up into the darkened auditorium while the sleepy students glanced at one another. One student sat forward awkwardly and raised his hand.

"Okay, Felix." The professor clasped his hands behind his back and strolled away from the class toward the screen. He looked at the floor and waited patiently for the answer.

"Uh, Nicholas II used this as a way of getting political authority?

"Okay, and how did he do this? Anyone?"

"He bribed the priests." Someone shouted. The students giggled.

"Yes, that's one way of interpreting it. He exercised his will through the clergy." Click. "More than any other modern monarch, Nicholas II attached his fate and the future of Russia to the notion of the ruler as a saintly and infallible father to his people. This idealized vision blinded him to the actual state of the country." Click. "With a firm belief that Divine Right granted his power to rule, Nicholas assumed that the Russian people were devoted to him with unquestioning loyalty. How did Russian citizens react to this oppression?" Click, click. He looked around at his class. Only one student had her hand raised. A blond wearing a red bathing suit top beneath a pair of faded blue coveralls cut off high on her thighs. He smiled and nodded for her to answer.

"So, the people wanted to participate in making decisions in the government. You know. So that it would be more democratic for everyone."

"That's right! I see some of you have been reading." He winked at her, and her blue eyes looked down coyly. "So, Russian intellectuals promoted Enlightenment ideals such as the dignity of the individual and the integrity of democratic representation." Click. "Russia's liberals, Marxists, and anarchists supported these democratic reforms and a growing opposition movement began to challenge the Romanov monarchy openly well before World War I." Click. Click. "Lights, please." Ding, ding, ding.

It was the end of the class period. The pupils closed their notebooks and filled their backpacks. "We'll continue the events leading up to the revolution on Thursday. Remember to read Sections 18 through 20 and be ready for a quiz."

The pupils moved toward the exits. Only the blond-haired girl lingered at the podium. She and the professor discussed something that made them laugh before her friends called her to catch up. She backed away toward the door, then turned to join them. Their giggling echoed as they retreated down the hall.

The professor gathered notebooks and slid them into his backpack. He threw one loop over the shoulder of his faded island shirt and started for the side exit. His attire included leather flip flops and jean cutoffs. His hair was sandy blond, bleached from the island sun, and his skin was tanned.

"Excuse me, Professor Rodin?" Eric said. He and Audrey descended from the top to join him.

The professor turned around, and his face showed him to be about fifty. He smiled. Round wire-framed glasses were perched on his slender nose with irises a lighter hazel than Audrey's.

"That's me. You aren't in this class." He watched them approach, lowering his brow. He cocked his head.

"No, no, we aren't. We went to the main office, and they sent us here. Would it be possible to ask you a few questions?" Eric said.

"I have another class in about 45 minutes." His eyes slid toward the exit. "What's this about?"

Audrey reached into the blue shopping tote, extracted the brown paper bag, and handed it to him. He looked inside a moment, then closed it and returned it to Audrey.

"We were hoping you might be able to tell us a little about it," she said, putting the crumpled bag back into its hiding place. Another bell echoed throughout the auditorium.

"I'm headed to my office if you'd like to join me." He turned and walked out the side door with the couple following close behind.

⌘

When they reached his office, two young ladies with beautiful skin, the color of rich cocoa, sat in the hall on an old wicker sofa. Music heard through a set of headphones connected to a cassette player sat between them. One of the girls stood as they approached.

"I'll be with you in a few minutes, Kalie. You don't mind waiting, do you?"

"Grammy says I must see you today." Kalie sat back down. Her friend put the headphones over her ears and continued writing in a notebook. They were both dressed in tank tops and shorts. Kalie leaned back against the sofa cushion, crossed her long legs, and bounced one golden-sandaled foot.

"Okay, get your notes together while you wait." Professor Rodin unlocked the door. He showed Eric and Audrey to a couple of wicker chairs matching the sofa in the hall.

The tiny office waited in darkness, lit only by a lamp set next to a large computer monitor. When the professor flipped the wall switch, an overhead fluorescent bulb illuminated the room. The desk, covered with files, papers, and books, took up most of the room. Professor Rodin sidestepped to reach his chair. He removed a stack of textbooks balanced on it, set them on the floor, and then sat across from them. Large books, some opened while others stacked four high on the desk, sat precariously on mountains of paper and files. Much of it appeared to be notes, correspondence, and graded essays. A cabinet standing against one wall held more stacks. The middle drawer stood open with a load of files balanced on top.

The couple glanced at each other. I have a terrible feeling that maybe we're wasting our time here, Audrey thought. This guy's either scatter-brained or, at the very least, unorganized.

"The Nutty Professor," Eric whispered. Audrey giggled.

Professor Rodin attempted to fold his hands on one of the paper mountains but quickly abandoned it with a sigh. He let his hands fall to his lap.

"Term papers. Need I say more? So?" He waited for a beat. "You want to show me what you have?"

Audrey set her shopping bag upon a stack of folders on the floor, then handed the paper sack to the professor.

"Would you lock that door for me, Mr.?" The professor asked, pointing behind them.

"Reynolds. Eric Reynolds, and this is my wife, Audrey. He reached over the desk, and they shook hands. Audrey did the same.

Eric locked the door. Then Professor Rodin took out the matryoshka. He held it up to the lamp. His face changed from mildly curious to complete wonder.

"Where did you get this?" He tried to open it without luck.

The couple explained how they came upon the doll in the Straw Market and how their hotel maid said was cursed. They went on to tell him about some of the strange things that had happened since they came into possession of it. Professor Rodin listened without speaking. When they finished, he smiled and shook his head.

"It sounds like you've had a taste of how superstitious the locals are here on the islands. I wouldn't worry about the guy who went overboard either. Believe it or not, that's not that unusual.

Audrey's eyes narrowed. "That just seems dangerous."

"The locals are great swimmers, and the laws are a little different here than they are in the United States."

"See? That's what I said!" Eric agreed.

The professor stood and searched for a book from the bookcase behind his chair. Overflowing with volumes on

Russia, especially Russian history, the professor found the one he was seeking.

"Here we go. Secrets Uncovered: The Soviet Union of Yesterday. We might find something here." He laid the massive book on top of a stack of files and opened it to the Contents Table. Eric and Audrey tried to look, but he quickly flipped to a page somewhere in the middle.

Voices heard outside the office filtered through the thin walls. Then, someone jiggled the doorknob and knocked loudly. Professor Rodin shook his head but continued his search through the vast edition of Russian history.

"Is he in today? I need to see him before I fail his class," A muffled male voice said.

"Wait your turn, I'm next," they heard Kalie say.

"I'll be late for class; I promise I'll only take a minute. You love me, don't you?" The male voice said.

"Get off me, Tony!" Laughter burst out from several more students waiting for the history instructor.

Rodin stopped a moment and closed his eyes. He appeared to say a little prayer then continued to flip through the ancient book. Eric squeezed Audrey's hand, and his eyes brows arched up.

"Here it is." The professor turned the volume around for the couple to see. Both stood to get a better look. The page showed an antique male doll painted beautifully wearing a robe with a bright blue sheen. He flipped through before they could read much. He stopped at one particular page, then opened the lid to a small copy machine next to the bookcase and began duplicating.

"Hopefully, this should give you some basic information on the matryoshka." He searched around under some files and pulled out a stapler, then stapled five pages in all before handing it over. "Why don't you leave it here with me, and I'll do some research? You can pick it up tomorrow." Another loud knock on the door.

"Would you give me a minute, please?" The professor said to the door. Then to Eric and Audrey, "Right now I'm just pressed, it being the end of the semester and all. When do you go back to America?"

"We're on a flight to Miami tomorrow," Eric said. "But we appreciate you taking the time to talk with us. Once we're home, we should be able to find out more about it."

"Oh, so soon? If you give me your address, I can send you what I find. As you can see, I have plenty of books on Russian history."

"That's a very kind offer. We may take you up on that," Eric said.

"Well, here. Take my office phone number, at least." He scribbled on a notepad and tore off the sheet. Audrey dropped it into her shopping bag.

"Thanks, if we don't find out what we need to know, we'll give you a call," Eric said.

"Excellent. Now I guess I better see what's going on out in the hall." Professor Rodin stood and made his way toward the door. Audrey stood as well, but Eric stayed seated. He looked at Professor Rodin and waited. "Oh, here you go," Professor Rodin handed the doll over, and Eric slipped into Audrey's shopping bag.

"Oh, wait," Audrey took the doll out again and showed it to the professor. "Can you translate Russian?"

Professor Rodin held it under the desk lamp to get a better look. "I see, yes, there is some writing here on the back."

"There's some on the bottom too," Audrey pointed out. Eric looked at her and cocked his head, his mouth a thin line.

"I found it while waiting for you after I called Grandma Josie," Audrey explained.

Professor Rodin turned the bottom up and saw the inscription. "Ah, here it is." He slid his glasses to the top of his head get a clearer image. "If I'm not mistaken, I believe it says something about power and knowledge. Hmm." He searched his mind. "And maybe influence?" He looked at the other inscription on the back. "This one says, mother to child." He turned it over again. "Yes, I see she is, with child. How odd." He used his finger to rub the doll's protruding belly. He returned his glasses to his nose.

"Huh, I thought maybe it must have some sort of meaning." Audrey opened the brown bag and held it out to Professor Rodin, and he carefully placed it inside.

CHAPTER SEVEN

The Detour

The **Kuban Korner** sat across the street from the campus. The clatter of plates and conversation heard through a large open window assured Eric and Audrey the place was crowd-pleasing. Once inside, the aroma of spicy chicken and pork mixed with onions and peppers overwhelmed them, and their stomachs came alive with hunger. The owner had painted the walls lime green with murals of colorful parrots perched on branches of tropical trees. Servers rushed about delivering food and drinks to tables of mostly students and faculty members on lunch break.

The couple found a booth in the back, hoping to gain a little privacy. Eric stood in line and placed their order while Audrey stayed at the table and flipped through the pages Professor Rodin copied. Confusion set in when she found most of it written in Russian. She did tease out a few critical points: The matryoshkas they observed in the Straw Market the day before resembled ninety-nine percent of the matryoshkas found worldwide. Many contained smaller dolls hidden within, increasingly more petite in size. Antiquities specialists considered only a tiny sample to be rare collector's items. Even fewer had an obscure form of entry, such as a latch or puzzle.

I wonder, she thought. Audrey took out the nesting doll and hid it with her body by turning to face the wall, then scanned the restaurant for anyone watching. A bright yellow parrot mural with red wing feathers peered down at her as if she were a tasty insect. Eric moved up another space in line.

She turned the doll over in her hands and rubbed the smooth surface along the head and body. Continuing to feel her way down the back and bottom, she felt the engraved inscriptions. Her fingers moved around to the front, feeling for anything out of place but found nothing. She began again, her touch lighter and slower this time. Then, the soft pad of her thumb snagged on something. She peered at the doll between her thighs, but nothing stood out. Still, she did feel something. Her index finger slid over it once again, and there it was—a small catch at the bottom of the rounded belly. Eric bent down to read the menu on the counter and placed their order.

Audrey continued with light pressure all around the edges, then gently squeezed the sides of the protruding stomach, and heard the whisper of a click. The belly popped open. Her breath caught in her throat. Covering the doll with the blue shopping bag, she looked around once again. Everyone was eating, not paying any attention to what she was up to in the back booth.

Within the protruding stomach, she found red satin material. While gently tugging until it separated from the doll, an object the size of a large walnut fell into her hand. Flipping it over to get a better look, she found a tiny doll painted to depict a baby, wrapped in a metallic emerald blanket. Only the face was visible. Eric finished ordering and sat down across from her.

"That took forever, but they seem to be pretty fast once they get your order." He looked across at her. "You hungry?"

Audrey cupped her hands and reached across the table. "Take a look." She eyed him mischievously, then opened her palms just enough for him to take a peek. She returned them quickly to her lap. "Did you see?"

"What was that?"

"A baby, I think. It came right out of her stomach."

"What?! Let me see it again."

Audrey showed him, then explained how she found it. She returned it to the satin material and placed both mother and baby into the blue bag. The waitress brought their food, and while eating, they attempted to decipher more of the copied pages. After the server collected the dishes and refilled their drinks, Audrey brought the infant out again. This time, she had a feel for how the matryoshka worked and opened it with ease. Rubbing her finger along the smooth edges of the baby's emerald blanket, she found another clasp. Audrey pressed it with her thumb, and the baby popped open.

"Whoa!" A blue oval stone about a nickel's size, attached to an antique gold chain, was inside. She cupped it in her hands beneath the table and took a closer look.

⌘

"What'd you find?" Eric's eyes also scanned the diner. Many patrons had left, taking the noise with them. He kept the volume of his voice low so as not to be overheard.

Audrey held the necklace under the table toward him in her cupped hands. "Take it."

He held it close and took a peek, then returned it to her. Audrey reassembled the matryoshka.

"I'll be back in a few minutes." She left the table for the restroom with the blue bag. The room was small, with a single sink and counter area. She took the necklace out once again and held it up to her chest in front of the mirror. Slipping the chain over her head smoothly, she admired how the stone looked on her.

It made her feel pretty and warm inside. Everything felt right with the world. Like she had no worries about the future or problems at home. She felt relaxed, like after drinking a glass of wine, but without the side effects. More importantly, she felt like she could do anything.

The door opened, and in walked a woman of about fifty in a colorful flowing blouse with matching pants—an American tourist. Audrey tossed the opened matryoshka back inside the bag and tried to appear casual. She adjusted her tank top and shorts while looking at herself in the mirror. She eyed the woman.

"Oh, excuse me. I didn't see an occupied sign." The tourist moved to back out.

"I'm just using the mirror." Audrey tried to sound calm, but her heart was pounding. The matryoshka's head stuck out of the bag, so she turned to face the lady to block her view.

"Oh, what a beautiful necklace." The lady came in and closed the door behind her. "Did you get it here on the Island?"

"Ah, actually." Audrey frowned. "Umm, sure." She fumbled with the doll and bag behind her.

"How unique, it has brown swirls in it. They appear to be moving around in a circle." She leaned in for a better look. That's when her eyes froze, and her face became slack. Motionless, she stared at Audrey's chest. Audrey's temples began to throb. It felt like someone was beating on her skull from the inside, trying to get out.

"Are you alright?" Audrey asked. The woman didn't respond but kept staring at the necklace. Taking hold of the lady's shoulders, Audrey gave her a quick shake. Slowly, the tourist looked into Audrey's eyes. Waving her hand in front of the woman's face, she got no response. The woman continued to stare into Audrey's eyes as if in a trance. It was like her body was there, but her mind had checked out.

"Hey, don't you need to use the restroom? Why don't you go into that stall? Maybe you'll feel better."

The woman turned and went into the stall. Audrey took off the necklace and quickly placed it back inside the matryoshka. The pounding in her head subsided a bit, but her face looked pale in the mirror. With the matryoshka back inside the shopping bag slung over her shoulder, she waited. A toilet flushed. The woman came out and looked at Audrey as if seeing her for the first time.

"Oh, sorry, I didn't hear anyone come in."

"Are you okay?" Audrey asked and stood next to the door. The woman made her way to the sink.

"I'm fine. Thank you. You? We heard this was a good restaurant, but I think the fish may have been bad." She washed her hands and looked for a towel. "My stomach is feeling a little queasy, and I feel a headache coming on." The woman shook the water from her hands into the sink and looked at herself in the mirror. Her face appeared drained of color. "So, what brings you to The Bahamas?"

"We're on our honeymoon." Audrey's brow wrinkled as she stared at the woman.

"That's so romantic. Get your new hubby to buy you something nice. The jewelry here is inexpensive and yet unique." The woman stepped to the door, and Audrey moved aside to make way.

"Are you sure you're feeling okay?"

"I'm fine. Enjoy your honeymoon." She smiled wanly before the door closed behind her.

Audrey looked at herself in the mirror one more time and found color returning to her cheeks. That was strange, she thought. She left the restroom as well.

⌘

"Where have you been?" Eric now sat in the booth with his back against the wall. "I was ready to send someone in to look for you."

Audrey sat across from him. "Something bizarre just happened." She gave him the short version.

Eric finished his tea and appeared lost in thought. He dropped an ice cube into his mouth and crunched. "I bet we could sell it for a bunch of money."

Audrey stared at him, incredulously. "How could you even think of selling it?" She waved the copied pages at him. "Remember what Professor Rodin said about the inscription? It could mean something important."

"I agree, it's a little unusual, but it's still just a doll with a secret compartment. Probably some kid's toy." His eyes lit up. "Hey, a Cracker Jack nesting doll!"

"Well, that's some toy." Audrey narrowed her eyes. "I know what I saw. Something happened to that lady. She kept looking at the necklace like, like, I don't know, like she was hypnotized or something." She rubbed her temple. "All I know for sure is what I felt. It gave me a terrible headache, but at the same time, it made me feel good. Exceptionally good. I can't explain it."

"Take it out. Try it on me."

"What? Wait a minute. I thought we were trying to keep it a secret." Audrey glanced around the empty cafe. A teen stacked dirty dishes from a used table into a large plastic tub.

"There's nobody here."

"We can't risk someone seeing it." She looked across to the large window at the front. A constable stopped by the door and peered in, then moved on. "Remember, we aren't in the United States. If someone wants to take it, they can, and I don't think the police will do anything about it."

"That's probably true. Alright, let's go back to the hotel, and you can try it on me there."

They left the diner and walked along the sidewalk, not remembering how they got there.

"Where are we?"

Audrey reached inside the blue shopping bag and produced a street map.

"We're right here." She pointed to a cross street showing the front of the college.

Eric stood next to her and tried to decipher which direction they should go and how long it would take to get back to the hotel. A black Cadillac cruised up beside them and stopped. The passenger side window eased down, and the Russian shop owner leaned over from the driver's seat and smiled. His dark sunglasses didn't reveal his eyes, but Audrey felt them all over her.

"Where are you headed?" The heavy lunch hour traffic still congested the street. An orange Mercury Cougar with loud mufflers attempted to inch around the Cadillac, and the impatient driver honked his horn. The shop owner laid on his own horn in response then looked out at the couple again. "Get in. I'll take you back to your hotel."

⌘

Eric looked at Audrey and said, "You want to ride?" She

shook her head and started down the sidewalk. The last thing she wanted to do was get into a car with the creepy Russian. As she walked, she noticed a couple of local women looking at her and whispering to each other. Then she remembered what the Russian shop owner said about some of the local islanders being irrational about their beliefs. When she looked behind her for Eric, she saw Davie and Buddy on the street's opposite side.

"That's odd. Either this town is tiny, or Mr. Sanders and his sidekick are following us."

"Come on, Audrey. We need to get back to our room so we can start packing, and he can get us there in a few minutes." He stopped, and his eyes followed her line of vision. "I don't think we should be walking around with that thing anymore. At least not until we find out what it may be worth." He reached out to her. She looked back at the ladies as they hurried down the street.

She stared at Eric for a moment, her mouth a tight line, then relented. "Okay, since we seem to be lost."

They climbed into the back seat, and the Cadillac eased into traffic. Audrey looked out the rear window to see Davie and Buddy running into the street toward them. She nudged Eric, and he looked also.

"Thanks for the ride. We never got your name," Eric said as he turned his attention to their driver.

"My name is not important. I am glad to help out when tourists get lost in our city. But," He braked at the red light and lifted his hat off his head. "I am C.A. Bortnik." He looked back at them and nodded. When he faced the front again, they could see he needed a trim. His oily hair curled at his shirt-collar and around his ears.

"How long have you lived here in Freeport?" Eric asked.

"Oh, on and off for about five years." He glanced at the

rearview mirror. "I travel to Moscow many times a year to bring goods to sell in my shop."

"What does C.A. in your name stand for?" Audrey asked.

"I was in Russian infantry. It stands for my rank." His fingers appeared elegant, gliding across the steering wheel like playing the piano. After riding for a few minutes, an empty parking lot came into view on the left, and he maneuvered the Cadillac into a parking space. He slid the gear shift into park, then turned the key to kill the engine.

"Why are we stopping here?" Eric asked.

"This is my warehouse. I just need to pick up a few things for the store. Come. See what I have. You will like it. Maybe even find something to take home with you."

Eric and Audrey gave each other nervous glances as Mr. Bortnik climbed out of the driver's side and closed the door. He bent down and looked at them through the backseat window. Dark clouds were gathering behind him.

"Come. We will only be a minute, and then I'll take you to the Blue Dolphin."

"Let's go in before we get caught in the rain." Audrey swung the bag straps over her shoulder and waited for him to open the door. "Maybe we'll find something in there for Grandma Josie and Claire. Remember, we still need to do that."

"I think we should just go on to the hotel and pick up something in the gift shop."

"Well, he's not going to take us right now, and I don't want to walk in the rain. Do you?" Audrey said. The sky looked angry, almost black.

⌘

With a flat roof and corrugated walls, the warehouse was

pale aquamarine—possibly an old fishery in the past. Several large sliding doors evenly spaced along the front with tall weeds growing within the asphalt cracks exuded neglect. Bortnik went to one on the far left and keyed the padlock. It opened noisily with the scaping of metal. Once inside, he slammed it shut, then flipped on the lights. The room expanded into a cavern full of shelves laden with cardboard boxes stacked high. The dim lighting gave the interior a yellow hue, and the odor, dank as a wet dog, hung stagnant in the gloom. Beads of sweat accumulated across Eric's upper lip and his shirt instantly dampened.

"It should be right down this way." Bortnik didn't appear to be bothered by the heat and coolly strolled down a narrow aisle of boxes. His strides were long, so the couple upped their pace for fear of getting lost. Stopping at every intersection, he cocked his head as if in thought, then moved on. Sometimes he switched directions and made several turns. "Wait till you see what we have. You'll love it."

"It's like a maze in here." Audrey peered at the walls of boxes all around and wondered what he had packed inside. Dead bodies? She thought. A shiver ran down her spine.

"Yes, it is a maze. We have collected valuable merchandise from all over the world into this one warehouse."

"We? Do you work with someone else in your shop?" Audrey asked.

Bortnik stopped. "No, just me." He stared at her for a moment, then continued in his search. "Me and Russia." Audrey and Eric locked eyes.

"Mafia stuff," Eric whispered and smiled at her. She didn't think it was funny.

"What makes you so confident that isn't true?" She whispered back.

"You sure have a lot of stuff. Is it all for your shop?" Eric asked. He didn't want to worry Audrey, but he wondered why the store shelves were so empty.

"Most is for the shop, but some are returning to Russia."

Audrey slowed down. "I have a bad feeling about this," she whispered. Should we be following him further into this place like a couple of sheep? She thought. Eric dragged her along behind him.

Bortnik mumbled something.

"Say what? I didn't get that last thing you said." Then Eric said to Audrey. "Come on. He'll leave us here if we don't keep up."

Bortnik turned a corner, but when the couple reached it, he had vanished. They stopped and stood close together, waiting for him to reappear.

"Which way did he go?" Audrey whispered. She moved to the aisle she thought he went down, but Eric put his hand in front of her.

"Wait. Hear that?"

On the other side of the box wall, they heard scratching.

"Rats! Oh, yuck!" Audrey grabbed Eric's hand and called out, "Mr. Bortnik! We've lost you."

No response.

"Okay, time to get out of here." Eric led Audrey back down the row, but they quickly found themselves lost. Unsure which way to go, they waited. Audrey paced in a circle.

"Did you tell him the name of the hotel?" She asked after completing a full round. She scanned the boxes for anything familiar.

"I don't think so. Why?"

"Because he said he would take us back to the Blue Dolphin, remember?" Audrey stopped, and her eyes widened. "Just before he convinced us to come into this hell hole." Her voice rose an octave.

The barometric pressure dropped, and lightning thundered overhead. A few pings pattered on the tin roof. Then the rain came cascading down hard as marbles. The lights flickered and went out. Audrey jumped into Eric's embrace. Their eyes slowly adjusted to the darkness, but the boxes remained deep in shadow.

⌘

"Great! Let's go this way." Eric pulled Audrey into the aisle on their left, and just when they thought they would find their way out, Bortnik reappeared. He came toward them carrying a cardboard box with the flaps opened.

"Hee Hee! I found it!" Bortnik walked past them. They quickly fell in behind him.

"Why did you leave us back there?" Audrey felt the sting of tears.

"Sorry about the lights." He stopped and faced them. "They go out all the time when we have a storm, but they'll come back on once they reconnect the power line."

"And that will happen, when?" Eric asked.

"Oh, maybe by tomorrow. Or next week." Bortnik snickered.

"But I can hardly see!" The boxes felt as if they would consume her. Then, something ran over her sandaled foot. She squealed and hopped behind Eric.

"Follow me." Bortnik rolled his eyes to the ceiling. "I will show you the way." After a few quick turns, he took them to a clearing in front of the doors and set the box onto the dusty floor. He stood up straight with palms turned up.

"What?" Eric asked curtly.

"It's a whole box of matryoshka!" Bortnik bent down, reached in, and pulled something out. They saw he was holding a monkey from the dim light that came from the high dirt-streaked windows. He put it back and took out another—a zebra. "See! All kinds. What you want, yes?"

Audrey kneeled and reached in. She brought out a seagull. Then a rabbit. "These are animals. We were more interested in the dolls of people. Specifically, women."

Bortnik began extracting the dolls, twenty-four in all, looking for people. No luck. Then he tossed them back into the box. "You take these. I can trade you for your doll."

Eric and Audrey looked at each other.

"What makes you think we even have a doll?" Eric said.

Bortnik laughed. "Everyone knows you have matryoshka." He shook his head. "I can trade you. An excellent deal for you."

"Wait a minute, who knows we have a doll?" Eric asked. He took Audrey's arm and helped her to stand.

"Everyone on the island. You should trade. Not safe for you to have it."

"Why isn't it safe?" Audrey asked.

"Let's go, Audrey. We can find our way back to the hotel." He ushered her toward the door.

"Wait!" The couple stopped and turned in time to see Bortnik lunge at Audrey. He grabbed the blue shopping bag and pushed her into the wall, but she held on tight. Eric grabbed him firmly by the arm and threw him to the floor on his back. Bortnik sat up and reached behind him into his waistband, but his smirk turned into a frown. Eric glared at him as if daring him to attack. Audrey held her breath. Bortnik sat still and waited with his knees bent, wiping his hands on his black jeans. He scowled at the couple but didn't attempt to move.

"You okay?" Eric looked Audrey over. He brushed her clothes down, then hugged her. The rain had subsided into a light sprinkle, so they left by the same door they entered earlier.

⌘

When they reached the Blue Dolphin, they found Davie and Buddy standing outside the main entrance. While Davie conversed with the valet, Buddy noticed the couple duck around the side of the hotel. His tail wagged.

"Maybe we should ask them why they are following us," Audrey said.

"I'd rather not. I have a feeling Mr. Sanders has shared our little secret around town." He couldn't shake their encounter with Mr. Bortnik.

A back door was open, so they passed through the kitchen where chefs and wait staff were busy preparing the hotel's dinner entrees.

Eric checked Audrey from head to toe once they were safe inside their room.

"I'm fine."

Eric wanted to go to the police, but Audrey convinced him not to. The law would confiscate the matryoshka as evidence.

"We should get rid of it anyway," Eric said.

Audrey sat on the bed and peered up at him. "If only we could give it back to the old man and his mother. Do you think something happened to them?"

"They dumped the thing on us and skipped town is what I think. If we take it home, we'll need to protect it. Maybe get a safety deposit box for it until we have it appraised. I bet someone in the U.S. will buy it."

"Maybe we shouldn't be so hasty."

"This morning, you couldn't get rid of it fast enough," Eric said. "Now you don't want to be hasty?"

"I just think now that we know a little more about it, we need to consider all of our options." Audrey wasn't ready to part with it. At least not until they understood more about it. She took it out and turned it over in her hands. Eric watched her. She couldn't get over how good the necklace made her feel and longed to try it on again.

"I guess I can agree with that, but that Bortnik fellow wasn't fooling around."

"It must be worth a lot, or he wouldn't have tried to trade a whole box of matryoshkas for it." She found the catch beneath the belly much more quickly now that she knew where it was. Once opened, she pulled out the necklace and set both mother and child to the side.

She handed the chain to Eric. He held it up to the light so they both could get a good look at it. The stone glistened with the color of robin's eggs, but instead of speckles, it contained the brown swirls the lady in the bathroom noticed. The chain was thin and delicate, appearing antique.

"I don't see anything special about it." He handed it back to her.

"Well, I think it's beautiful." She put it on and went to the mirror to admire how it looked. Again, she had a feeling of warmth, and it made her feel calm. Almost invincible. Like nothing could hurt her.

She turned to face Eric and grabbed his hands. He immediately felt pain shoot up through his arms and into his head. He let go, and his eyes glistened with anger.

"What the hell?" He stepped away. "Damn, Audrey, you shocked me." He sat down in the chair.

She knelt in front of him. "See, I told you there's something odd going on with this thing." He held his head in his hands with his elbows on his knees. She tried pulling his hands from his face.

"Don't touch me."

Audrey fell back with eyes wide and leaned on her elbows. Eric's face was red. His eyes closed tight, and his mouth an unseemly grimace.

"I'm so sorry," she whispered and flung the necklace onto the bed. Eric had never spoken to her like that. Tears welled up in her eyes, and she laid her head on his lap.

He eventually wrapped his arms around her, and they sat together without moving. Then he breathed in deeply and gently lifted her. They stood with arms wrapped around each other.

"Do we have any aspirin? I believe this day has caught up with me. Maybe you can try to use that necklace on me after I take a nap, but I bet it won't have any effect on me." He smiled wanly and gently tugged her hair. "Sorry, hon, I'm drained right now." He moved toward the bed. "I hope I'm not getting sick."

Audrey watched him lie down. "Yeah, sure. I'll get you a couple out of my travel bag. You okay?"

"I'm fine. I just want all this crazy doll stuff to be over."

Audrey returned with aspirin and water from the bathroom. "Do you think Mr. Bortnik was telling the truth about the whole Island knowing we have the doll?"

"It's possible, being a small town and all. Don't worry. We're taking it home with us." Eric took the aspirin, then pulled off his shoes. He leaned back on the headboard and pushed pillows behind his head.

"I'm not so sure we should sell it right away," she said. "We don't even know what it's worth. Maybe it's worth millions." She sat down and leaned against his chest.

"Or, maybe it's not worth a cent. Have you thought at all

about why the Russians gave it to you in the first place?"

"Because she was getting too old to keep it?" She waited a moment, then continued. "You said I looked like I was in a trance yesterday. What if she was wearing the necklace when I sat next to her?" Audrey was sure something just happened with Eric even though he didn't remember, so it made sense that maybe she wouldn't remember if the lady used it on her.

"But why wouldn't the son want to keep it for himself?" Eric said.

"Maybe it's too dangerous for such an old guy?"

"That's an interesting thought. Maybe it's too dangerous to keep, and those gypsies saw us as a couple of suckers." He yawned. "You know. The Russian Mafia and all?" He nudged her gently. "Whatever's going on with it, I think maybe it's too hot to handle, so we just need to lie low until we get home." His eyelids felt heavy, and his head still throbbed.

"It's as if it takes control of peoples' minds somehow." She sat up and looked at him. "People get crazy when they think they can control others."

"And power-hungry. That Russian lady and her son were probably running from someone. Maybe the Mafia *is* involved somehow or even the police."

"That waiter who jumped off the ship was the same guy who tried to steal my blue shopping bag. I know that now. I bet he knew I had the doll. That's what he was after."

"Yeah, and remember, the blind guy knew we had it. The same goes for Bortnik, the Russian shop owner." He massaged his temples. "It looks like all the wrong people know we have it. I'm starting to think they'll do anything to get their hands on it."

"Anything?" Audrey asked. Eric shrugged.

"We're probably over-analyzing it, but we'll keep it hidden until we leave tomorrow. And, when we get home, we'll have it appraised. Maybe then we could afford two helicopters." Eric tickled Audrey's side, and she squirmed away.

"What time is our flight?" She asked.

He yawned again. "Two o'clock. Check out from the hotel is at noon so we can catch a cab straight to the airport."

"I should call Grandma Josie to let her know what time to pick us up. I'm still worried about Claire, but she wouldn't tell me anything. She just kept telling me to enjoy my honeymoon."

"She's right, you know. Your mother's a grown woman and needs to start taking care of herself."

"But she's been doing good, and I just don't want to mess that up."

"Audrey, you have nothing to do with it." Eric closed his eyes a moment, then opened them. "Claire is going to do what she wants when she wants to, and you're not going to change that. No matter how much time you spend with her."

"She's just had it so hard since daddy died."

"I seem to remember hearing about some things she'd done even before your dad died."

"Don't start, Eric."

"I'm just saying. You do so much for your mother. What has she done for you? Really, done for you? Your grandmother is the one that's always been there for you since way before I met you."

Audrey sat up and faced him. She crossed her arms and let out a sigh because they'd had these conversations before.

"But she's my mother. Don't you get it?" Anger flashed in her eyes, as well as regret and something else that looked a little like wishful thinking.

"I do get it. I once had a mother too."

"Yeah, then you should understand." Audrey wasn't ready to up.

"Okay. Hypothetical." He peered at her. "Let's say we're on a boat in the middle of the ocean: you, me, and Claire. A terrible storm comes up, and both Claire and I fall into the water. You only have one life preserver. Which of us would you throw it to?"

"That's easy. You're a great swimmer," Audrey giggled.

Eric looked hurt. "Yeah, that's what I thought."

"I was only kidding, but that's unfair."

"Can't you see? You're obsessed with your mother. Don't you realize she only cares about Claire?"

Audrey's eyes started to water. She hated it when they fought. They rarely disagreed on anything except when it came to Claire. The matryoshka smiled up at her from where it laid on the bed. A knock at the door shattered their discussion.

⌘

"Put that away." Eric got up and looked out the peephole. He shook his head and returned to the bed to lay back down. "Speak of the devil. What timing."

Audrey grabbed the matryoshka pieces and the necklace, then tossed them into a drawer. "Who's at the door?"

"See for yourself."

Audrey peered out, then looked back at Eric. He covered his face with a pillow.

"Oh no!" She whispered.

"Now, I definitely have a headache."

Claire was in the hall, sitting on a suitcase with her chin in her hands. She wore a sheer blouse with a bikini top beneath and a pair of tiny white shorts. Her large hoop earrings peeked out of her thin blond hair, styled just below the jawline. She looked like she used to when she was getting ready to go out. Audrey hadn't seen her mother look like that in a long time. She breathed in deeply, then opened the door.

"Claire? What are you doing here?"

"Oh, baby! I couldn't stand you being away from me any longer. I just had to see you." She stood.

Audrey looked down the hall in both directions, then grabbed her mother's hand and her suitcase. She pulled them both inside.

"How did you get here?"

"How do you think? I took a plane. Like you." Claire walked over to the single chair at the end of the bed and plopped down. Audrey set the suitcase next to the door.

"But you can't be here. We're on our honeymoon."

"Hey, Eric." Claire hung her sandaled foot over the arm of the chair and swung it back and forth. She leaned her head over the chair's high back.

Eric raised his hand in a half-hearted wave without emerging from beneath the pillow. Audrey came over and sat on the edge of the bed to face Claire.

"Does Grandma Josie know you're here?"

Claire laughed. "Well, of course not." She sat forward, returning both feet to the floor. "Your grandmother tried to keep the name of your hotel a secret, but I saw it written on a pad by her phone." She grabbed Audrey's hand and squeezed. "Aren't you happy to see me?"

"Well, of course. But we're flying back tomorrow."

"Not a problem. Maurice and I plan to gamble and hang out in the sun for a few days. Maybe I'll get me one of those drinks they put in the coconut shells with the fruit on top." She winked.

Maurice was one of Audrey's dad's buddies from the Marines. For whatever reason, he felt he needed to take care of Claire, but, of the two, he was a bigger alcoholic. On many nights, Audrey found them hanging out in the bars spending his pension checks.

"Have you been drinking?" Audrey asked.

"Not really." Claire looked away from her daughter. "Okay, maybe just a couple of those little bottles they sell on the plane." She exhaled deeply. "Don't worry. I'm not drunk if that's what you think."

"Yet." Audrey went to the door and grabbed the knob. "You have to go home."

"You're not my mother. You need to stop telling me what to do."

"Would you ladies take your fight outside," Eric said through the pillow. "I'm trying to take a nap."

Audrey glowered at the pillow, then returned her attention to Claire. "I'm going to call Grandma to let her know what time we're landing in Miami tomorrow. I bet she won't be happy to hear where you are."

"Suit yourself. I just missed you." Claire inspected her nails. "This was Maurice's idea, by the way. I never would've thought of it on my own."

"You sure about that?" Audrey knew her mother well. "Okay, we'll figure this out so that everyone's happy. You hang out here and try to be quiet, okay?" Audrey turned on the television and lowered the volume. "Where's Maurice now?"

"The last time I saw him was at Calico Jack's. You know that place. Great music? Live band?" Audrey did know the place. She and Eric spent several nights over the week celebrating their marriage there. They rode in pedicabs to and from the bar because it wasn't within walking distance.

"You left him?" Audrey asked incredulously.

"He's a big boy. He'll show up sooner or later."

"What? Wait, he's coming here?"

"Well, of course. The guy needs a place to crash too."

"Oh, my God!"

"Audrey." Eric breathed.

Audrey whispered to Claire. "Okay, I'm going downstairs to make the call. Can you sit here quietly until I get back?

Claire saluted, then put her index finger to her lips. Audrey grabbed her key and left the room.

⌘

Grandma Josie wasn't happy to hear about Claire crashing their honeymoon, but Audrey assured her that she would take care of it. Claire will be on a plane home tomorrow at the latest, Audrey told her. Then thought to herself, I just have to keep her out of the bars. I'll give Maurice's ex-wife a call, and she can take care of him.

Afterward, she sat beneath an umbrella by the pool and gathered her thoughts. She needed a plan. The sun was sinking toward the evening hours, and the temperature was a few degrees cooler. A mother played in the water with her toddler. The baby girl squealed and giggled until her face sunk below the surface, and water went into her nose. She came up coughing and crying, but the mother soon got her laughing again. At first, it seemed cruel, but Audrey realized the mother was teaching her daughter to swim. That's the kind of mom I'll be, she thought, and a smile spread across her lips.

Eric was right. Now that they were married, it was time Claire took care of herself. How can she think it's okay to crash our honeymoon? Eric's not going to be happy if my mother stayed with us our last night, and neither am I. Maybe she can get a room in the hotel.

Audrey took a detour by the check-in counter in the main lobby before going upstairs. A young woman wearing a crisp red jacket was on the phone, but she noticed Audrey approaching and hung up.

"Can I help you?"

"We have a room, but I was wondering if you have any vacancies. My mother flew in and is looking for one tonight."

"I think we are pretty booked up, but let's see." She scanned through a massive black ledger. "Oh, yes. We have a room on the sixth floor still available and one on the ninth." We're getting calls about a wedding party coming in this weekend, so we're filling up fast. Should I reserve one for you?"

"I'll send my mother down, and she can book the room. Thank you for checking." Audrey headed for the elevator. All I have to do now is see how much cash Claire has on her. If she doesn't have enough, maybe we can use some of our wedding gift money. I'm sure Eric would say it's going to a good cause. She smiled.

When Audrey unlocked the door, the television played softly, sounding like a game show: Hollywood Squares or something. The next thing she noticed was how dark it was. The heavy drapes that hung open earlier were closed tight. Her eyes adjusted to the darkness and looked for Claire. The chair was empty. Maybe she left. Problem solved. Audrey mentally slapped herself on the cheek for thinking such a thing.

The bathroom door was closed, and no light emanated from beneath. Audrey stepped over to the bed to check on Eric. He wasn't feeling well when she left, so she hoped he got some rest. With his eyes closed, his face appeared contorted into a grimace. She felt his forehead thinking he had a fever, but it was cool. He must have been hot enough to take his shirt off because he was bare-chested, and the comforter lay loosely around his waist.

"Eric, are you okay? You're worrying me." The blankets moved on the other side of the bed, and a dark figure flopped onto the floor.

"Oops!" Claire stood. Her hair was a jumbled mess, and she wore nothing but her skin. It appeared ghost pale in the darkness. Almost translucent.

⌘

Audrey's brain wouldn't accept what her eyes told her. She stared at Claire with her mouth open. Not looking up, Claire rushed to the chair where Audrey had left her only an hour before and began putting on clothes. In shock, Audrey could only watch her. She willed herself to turn on the bedside lamp.

"Now, girl, I don't want you to be upset." Claire pulled her blouse over her head, then put on her sandals. "I hope you don't think anything was going on." She laughed, then looked at the floor. "I was just helping him get undressed. You know so that he could rest?" She looked into the mirror and pushed her fingers through her hair.

"Why were you naked here in our room?" Audrey's voice was a whisper.

Claire stopped and looked at Audrey but didn't respond. Instead, she looked at herself again in the mirror and rummaged through her purse. She took out a lipstick tube and applied a deep red color, then smacked her lips together.

"You took your sweet time, and I got tired of waiting. I decided to lay down and take a nap. You know I always sleep in the nude." She walked over to Audrey and put her hand on her arm. Startled by the touch, Audrey jerked out of her thoughts.

"Don't touch me." She pushed her mother's hand away, then noticed the necklace around Claire's neck. She scooped the stone into her hand. "Where did you get this?"

"It was in the drawer." Her shoulders inched up. "So, I tried it on." Audrey let go, and Claire took it from around her neck and held it out.

Audrey grabbed it and stared at it in her hands. Her mind raced. What have I done? This thing has just destroyed my marriage. She breathed a heavy sigh, and tears started to down her cheeks. Her body shook.

"I bet Eric bought it for you. It looks like something he'd buy." Claire went back to the chair, grabbed her purse, and slung the strap over her shoulder. "It's kind of plain, but like it. It made me feel weird. I don't know, wonderful. Like everything is right with the world, I guess." She strolled to the door. "Now, see what you did? I'm getting a headache." Her hand went to her forehead. "You're always stressing me out. But I know what I can do to take care of a headache. Don't you worry about me." She winked at her daughter.

Audrey felt like throwing up, her stomach became full of acid. Her face paled.

Claire snickered. "I'm sorry, Audrey. It looks to me, you've picked a real winner for a husband. As I said, we didn't have sex if that's what you think, but you have to ask yourself, can he be trusted? He let me take his clothes off without a single complaint. He just kept staring at that silly necklace."

"Please leave, mother."

"I'm going." She picked up her suitcase and left the room, letting the door bang closed behind her.

Audrey turned to Eric, grabbed him by the shoulders, and shook him. Nothing. She slapped his face hard and shook him again. "Wake up! Wake up!"

His lids fluttered open without focusing. After what seemed like forever, his eyes settled on Audrey's face. When she saw he was awake, she went into the bathroom and slammed the door so hard it vibrated on its hinges.

"Audrey?" Eric sat up and grabbed his throbbing head in both his hands.

CHAPTER EIGHT

Exposed

On the way to the airport, the couple didn't talk. They said all there was to say the night before. Audrey sat as far to the right as was possible in the back seat of the cab. Eric reached over, grabbed her hand, and squeezed gently. She sucked in her breath but allowed it for a moment, then returned it to her lap. She couldn't get the thought of him and Claire together out of her head. During their argument, Eric proclaimed no memory of what happened. His only defense was he must have slept through the whole thing, but he apologized anyway, which irritated her more. The thought of Claire sexually touching Eric made her skin crawl. But what Claire said about trust just before she walked out still echoed in her head.

The cab drove through town, and both looked out of their respective rain-streaked windows. The buildings with the vibrant colors they witnessed when they arrived now looked pale and drab. The poverty in the area was evident and depressing.

Many of the homes were not much more than corrugated steel boxes, and some didn't have front doors, but instead, an opening covered by a curtain. Indoor plumbing in this area was a luxury most couldn't afford.

Someone should do something for these people, Audrey thought. If I ever come back, I'm going to help out somehow. Maybe I could start a collection at our church. She looked over at Eric. He looked defeated. Will we still be married this time next year, or was Claire right all along? The taxi pulled up to the airport drop-off area. My mother is the one I can't trust. She sighed. God, I know I shouldn't blame him, but how could he do such a thing if he loved me? Tears stung her eyes, and she swallowed a sob.

They got out of the cab at twelve-fifteen and went inside. Tourists in island shirts crowded the lobby and dragged suitcases into ticket lines. After about an hour of line surfing, Eric and Audrey reached the counter and received their boarding passes. They tagged and checked their luggage, but Audrey kept the blue shopping bag tucked safely under her arm.

By the time they arrived at the gate, it was one-thirty, and the passengers were already boarding. I wonder how Claire is going to get home, she thought. No longer my problem. She'll just have to figure it out on her own.

Audrey turned to look down the long row of gates behind them after waiting in the boarding line for about ten minutes. Many tourists were heading for places in Central America, Canada, and Europe, but most were returning to the United States. Before she returned her eyes to the person in front of her, out popped Buddy from the crowd. He was followed by Davie holding the end of a leash and tapping with his cane. Audrey turned back around quickly and squeezed Eric's arm.

"That blind guy and his dog are coming this way," she

whispered.

Eric turned to look and nodded to acknowledge he saw them. "Don't turn around again, and maybe they won't see us."

"Why do they keep following us? They seemed so nice yesterday."

"Why else? I'm sure they want the doll." Eric stole another peek behind them. They stopped at a counter a couple of gates down where passengers were waiting to board a plane to Orlando, Florida. They spoke with the flight attendant for a few minutes. Now, acutely aware of his surroundings, Eric noticed Mr. Bortnik with the gambling ship's waiter also walking in their direction.

"They'll have to get in line," he said, facing forward again.

"Who?"

Eric put his index finger to his mouth and grabbed Audrey's arm. He led her out of line to hide amongst a crowd waiting at a gate further down. Some of the passengers looked at them with interest but returned to their conversations when the couple ignored them and avoided eye contact.

"What's happening?" Audrey whispered.

"They're coming."

"Davie and Buddy?"

"No. Bortnik and that waiter." He tugged Audrey out of their line of sight and was sure they hadn't seen them. Not yet, at least.

"You're kidding, right?"

He shook his head. "I wish I was."

The couple hid around a corner next to a bank of pay telephones. C.A. Bortnik and the waiter walked past them, looking in all directions, and headed toward the couple's flight gate. They went to the counter and spoke with the attendant, then strolled up to a security officer. The officer looked around, searching the crowd. The three continued to carry on a conversation.

Davie and Buddy also walked over to that counter. When they did, Eric and Audrey backtracked around the corner and hid among groups of passengers. They eventually slunk past all the gates before theirs and ducked inside a newspaper shop. They slipped behind a row of books out of sight from the door.

"What're we going to do? We'll miss our flight." Audrey said.

"Can I help you?" Asked the store clerk.

"We're just looking, thanks," Audrey said in a clipped tone.

The clerk regarded them suspiciously but returned to the counter to help another customer. Eric went to the door and looked back toward their gate. Passengers were still boarding, but the waiter stood close to the entry door and propped himself against the wall. He scrutinized passengers as they proceeded past him to board the plane. Across the lobby, Mr. Bortnik talked on a payphone where the couple had hidden minutes before. Eric scanned the rest of the gates in both directions, but Davie and Buddy weren't visible. He watched Mr. Bortnik hang up the receiver, then wave to the waiter to follow him. They both headed back past the gates toward the newspaper shop.

Eric crept back behind the rack where Audrey stood waiting. They watched the two stroll past their hiding place. Eric reached for Audrey to pull her into a hug as he always did since high school. She saw it coming and stepped away, then looked at the floor.

"You know, maybe we should just give it to them. I seriously don't think it's worth dying over. Do you?" He gazed at her. "I don't know how many more times I can tell you I'm sorry." She crossed her arms over her chest, held her elbows tightly, and stared off into the distance.

⌘

"Let's go. We'll just go straight to our gate and get on the plane." He grabbed Audrey's hand, and they went back to their boarding gate. The door was closed when they arrived.

"We're supposed to be on that flight to Miami," Eric said to the flight attendant at the counter. She wore the same island shirt as the other flight attendants and a red hibiscus flower behind her ear.

"I'm sorry, but they're already backing out and heading to the runway."

Eric and Audrey walked over to the large glass window to watch their airplane, directed by two men with orange vests signal information to the pilots. The loading ramp had already retracted, and the plane pulled away from the building. The couple returned to the counter.

"Now, what're we supposed to do?" Audrey asked.

"Well, you can go back to ticketing and see if they can get you another flight."

"How much will that cost?" Eric asked.

"I'm not sure. The airline may charge you the whole amount or pro-rate your fare, depending on why you missed the flight. Do you know how to get back to the ticket counter?"

"We'll find our way, thanks," Eric said.

Davie and Buddy sauntered through a crowd out of the airport's main entrance. Once Eric was sure they were gone, he led Audrey back to the ticket counter. With the evening flight booked, they chose to wait until the next morning. Luckily, their tickets were pro-rated.

"It makes more sense now. Those two thugs are working together," Eric said. "This whole thing is starting to smell like the Black Market." He handed the tickets to Audrey, and she stuffed them into the shopping bag. "But that still doesn't explain Mr. David Sanders and his dog."

"They want the doll." Audrey noticed a bank of pay telephones and headed in that direction. Eric followed. "I need to call Grandma to let her know we aren't going to make it home until tomorrow."

Eric dug in his pocket and pulled out some change. "You think this will be enough?" He handed her all his silver.

"I only plan to be on the phone for a minute, so that should do."

"Then we can grab a cab back to the hotel to see if we can get our room back," he said.

They claimed some chairs in front of the phones. Audrey went to make the call, and Eric scanned the lobby for Mr. Bortnik and the waiter, but there was no sign of them. He quickly took note of all of the possible exits, just in case.

Audrey was vague on the phone, choosing not to say anything about the men following them. I'll explain the whole story when we get home. She also decided not to mention what happened with Claire. Instead, she said Claire left without saying where she was going.

After she hung up, she rejoined Eric and noticed Professor Rodin coming in the main doors with Kalie, her suitcase in tow. The two walked to the ticket counter, and Kalie left her luggage with them to load onto a plane. On their way to the gates, the professor saw the couple sitting in the chairs and told Kalie he would be just a minute.

"So, you're heading back to the states?" Professor Rodin asked. Kalie stood to the side, waiting.

"Our luggage is already on the way," Eric said. "We, however, can't leave until tomorrow morning."

"Oh? Why's that?"

Eric and Audrey glanced at each other, not sure what to

divulge.

"We missed our flight," Audrey said.

Professor Rodin looked perplexed. "But, your luggage didn't?"

"It's a long story," Eric said. He leaned forward and put his forearms on his knees. "They told us they would hold our luggage at the ticket office in Miami. We have another flight scheduled for 9:00 in the morning."

"Ah, so you have another night in paradise."

"Is it okay if I go to my gate, Professor?" Kalie asked. She sighed heavily, and her shoulders slumped while playing with her bracelets.

"Sure, here's your boarding pass. I think you can handle it from here." Kalie took it and headed toward the gates. She was tall and thin with long legs and creamy dark skin. She wore large bracelets on both wrists that jingled when she moved, and hoops dangled from her ears. Her white flowing sundress reminded Audrey of something an Egyptian princess may have worn.

"See you in a couple of months, Kalie," Professor Rodin called.

Kalie waved without looking back and hurried to her gate.

"She's a good kid, but like most, a little immature. Her grandmother asked that I watch out for her while she takes classes here. Both her parents died a couple of years ago. She's been living with her grandmother ever since."

"I kind of know the feeling," Audrey mumbled.

"Pardon?"

"Oh, nothing." Audrey shook her head.

"So, what are your plans now that you have an extra night?"

"First, we need to see if we can get our room back at the hotel," Eric said, raising his hands in explanation. His eyes narrowed at anyone who appeared to be walking in their direction. Audrey stretched out her foot and touched his leg lightly, and his eyes focused on her.

"Why don't you give them a call before we take another cab?"

"Yeah, okay, that's a good idea. We're kind of running low on cash. If we call and all the rooms are full, we can skip the taxi ride back and look for another hotel closer to the airport."

Audrey gave him the change left from her call and a brochure with the hotel phone number on it. He looked around the lobby once again, then walked to one of the payphones.

"So, do you like living here on the island?" Audrey asked Professor Rodin. He sat down beside her.

"Love it. The people are friendly, and there's always a party going on somewhere." He grinned sheepishly.

"But you're here full time, right?" She asked.

"I go home sometimes in between semesters to see my family, but yes, I live here."

"You seem more American to me. Your accent sounds like you're from someplace out west. Maybe California?"

"Wow! Good ear."

He appeared almost adolescent with his hair falling under his glasses and into his eyes. He shook his head, and his eyes sparkled beneath the florescent lighting. The John Lennon style glasses made him endearing. If I were older and not married, I'd be interested in this guy. She thought. He's an educated, worldly professor, even if he is a bit disorganized. She glanced over at Eric on the telephone, and a wave of sadness washed over her.

"So, have you been?" He asked.

"To California? No, never, but I've met a few people stationed at the naval base in San Diego."

"I spent many years in L.A. doing stuff like going to college, surfing, and partying."

"Yeah? What made you move from that paradise to this one?"

"I guess the same reason as everyone else who lives here but was born elsewhere. I came here on vacation and fell in love with the slower pace of the island life. And of course, the sunsets." He winked at her.

Eric hung up and strolled back to sit on the other side of Audrey.

"Well?"

"They already rented our room." He frowned. "And they booked all the rest for a wedding. They won't have anything open until Monday."

"We'll be back home by then," Audrey said. "I guess we should check the other hotels to see if we can find something."

"It is June, you know." Professor Rodin said. "The Bahamas are hosts to thousands of weddings during the summer months, especially in June."

"We can relate." Eric took Audrey's hand and squeezed. "We didn't get married here, but we're on our honeymoon." Audrey's eyes glazed over.

"Well, congratulations! I thought there was something special about you two."

He put his hand to his chin and thought. "I tell you what. I have a boat that I like to putter around in sometimes. I plan to sail out tonight to some of the other islands to celebrate the summer solstice.

"But that's not for another week, right?" Audrey said.

"Sure, but the locals on the islands like to celebrate the whole month. There's always music and fireworks. And lots of food and drink."

"Hmm. Sounds like fun," Eric said.

"Why don't you be my guests? There's plenty of sleeping

room below deck so you can spend the night, and I can bring you back tomorrow in time to catch your plane."

"That's a generous offer, but we can't impose on you and your weekend," Audrey said.

"Nonsense! I'd love to show you some of the other islands, and you can tell me what it's like to live with the alligators."

"Are you sure? We can find a room somewhere on the island and just hang out in town tonight." Eric said.

"Hey, you're on your honeymoon. This week should be the best week of your life. One, you'll never forget." He stood. "It's settled. You're my guests. Come! Your chariot awaits."

The newlyweds followed him to the parking lot across the street to a black convertible Mercedes.

"Man, I guess college professors make pretty good money here," Eric whispered to Audrey.

"Not really." Professor Rodin overheard him. "I received a large settlement recently from back home." He jumped into the driver's seat. "Hop in. Oh, and call me Tom."

Eric climbed into the back and left the front for Audrey. She set her blue shopping bag between her feet and put on her seatbelt. She had a pretty good idea they might be in for a wild ride. On the way to the marina, the professor showed them all the beautiful places they somehow missed during their stay.

The boat turned out to be a fifty-foot twin mast schooner named Anastasia after his grandmother, who recently passed away. Ah, the large settlement from back home, Audrey thought. It makes sense that he has wealthy relatives. They received a quick tour of the top deck, and then he took them below to their sleeping quarters.

He opened the closet. There were a couple of swimsuits, shorts, blouses, and about five dresses. It was the property of his last girlfriend, who left him the month before. Audrey was about the same size, and he told her to help herself. Most of the stuff still had tags. Rubbing elbows with the rich and famous made the couple feel uncomfortable and out of place. They glanced at each other, then without a word, decided to enjoy it because it would be a once in a lifetime event. After all, they were on their honeymoon.

Thomas looked at Eric's six-foot, two-inch frame and apologized for not having anything in his size. Eric was okay with what he was wearing anyway. Professor Thomas Rodin left them alone to settle in and went up to start the schooner's engine.

⌘

When they closed the cabin door, Audrey looked for a place to hide the blue bag and ended up squeezing it between the wall and the double-sized bed. She pushed the mattress over the top. Eric laid down and watched her change into a pair of culottes and a peasant blouse. I wonder why the professor's last girlfriend didn't take her clothes with her, he thought. The relationship must have ended badly. People with money don't think about it like us regular folks. Anyway, the clothes fit Audrey, and she looks happy to have something to wear.

Audrey took her hair out of the ponytail and let it fall around her shoulders. Her arms and legs appeared tanned from their week in the sun. To Eric, she looked like a princess. When she looked in the mirror, she saw him watching her but pretended not to notice.

"Audrey," His eyes locked onto hers. "You must know how much I love you."

She looked down at her hands, and although she tried to fight it, tears welled up in her eyes. She sat down on a chair and put on her sandals. If she feels she can't trust me, I don't think I can stand it, Eric thought. She closed her eyes and mouthed a few silent words as if praying. I know she feels betrayed, so I need to find a way to make it up to her. We have to get past these hurt feelings. Maybe we can at least enjoy this moment. We are preparing to sail around the islands on a sailboat. Something neither of us had ever done before.

"Audrey, please." Eric sat up and faced her.

"It's going to take some time. Give me some space right now." She put her sunglasses on the top of her head, stood, and walked out of the room. It felt to him like she just stepped out of his life. He hung his head and sat forward with his forearms on his thighs.

Thomas was behind the wheel when she climbed the steps to the upper deck. "Come, have a seat here and watch while I raise the sails."

He cut the engine, and the boat slowed its movement through the clear blue water. Audrey gripped the handrails when their forward progression changed. They were moving out of the mouth of the marina with the bow pointed into the vast Atlantic. Other sailboats passed them on their way back to shore, and many of their passengers waved. Audrey waved in return then tilted her face toward the sun. The breeze felt amazing. She put her sunglasses on as Eric came up to the top. He made his way toward them with his hands in his pockets.

"There you are, have a seat. We're about to go for a boat ride, my boy!" Thomas laughed, which made Audrey smile. He's just a big kid with his toys, she thought.

"You enjoy this," Audrey said.

"I do! My grandparents taught me to sail when I was old enough to walk, so it's in my blood."

"Do you need any help with anything?" Eric asked.

"Have either of you sailed before?"

Eric and Audrey both shook their heads no.

"Then sit back and relax. I do this at least once a week." The professor pointed to the two long poles running parallel to the boat. "Just keep your eye on the booms." He climbed to the top deck and untied the sails, then returned to the wheel. He advanced a crank next to him, pulling the sails up to the top of the mast. "This is one of the best reasons to move to The Bahamas. I promise you're going to love it."

Once again, Audrey wondered what it would be like to live on the islands, but her heart sank when she looked at her husband. Working at the Gazette allowed her time to become familiar with statistical reports. The stats for newly married couples staying married after the first year weren't in their favor.

Thomas poured them each a glass of red wine, then finished cranking. He hopped up and tied the sails off again. They immediately billowed out, and the boat moved into the open waters. The bow cut into the waves splashing along the sides, and the vessel rocked in time like a rocking horse. Both Eric and Audrey held on at first but quickly adjusted to the cadence and relaxed. The wind blew through their hair, and Audrey returned hers to a ponytail. The boat hugged some of the smaller islands, venturing close to shore. The professor turned out to be an excellent sailor. The sun continued its trek to the west, and by the time they neared Castaway Cay in the Abaco Islands, it had dipped into the horizon.

⌘

Thomas lowered the sails and dropped the anchor just offshore. They rode a water taxi to the beach where party sponsors encouraged laughter, dancing, and all-around fun. A Calypso band beat out island melodies complete with steel drums, bongos, ukuleles, and flutes. Most everyone got into the atmosphere, and Audrey felt her body move to the music when she stepped off into the sand.

Men in island shirts went around taking mixed drink orders. Several long tables stood covered with food and alcohol. Claire would love one of those drinks in the coconuts, Audrey thought. She crossed her arms and muttered under her breath. "I should order one just to spite her."

"What was that?" Eric asked.

"Nothing. Just thinking out loud."

They sat at a picnic-style table and watched the festivities while the professor talked with some locals. He seemed to know a lot of them and appeared quite comfortable. Eric left Audrey at a picnic table to see what was at the food bar, then returned with barbecued pork, beans, coleslaw, and two large cups of beer.

The sky gradually darkened, and the island breezes settled. They ate silently at their table beneath a Banyan tree. One of the waiters lit their torch, and the breeze caused the flame's shadow to dance as if in time to the music.

Thomas strolled over to their table and said it was about time to go if they wanted to watch the fireworks from the water. Eric returned their empty plates to the employees behind the food table and thanked them. Audrey said she needed a minute to go to the lady's room.

"Are you going to be alright? I can go with you," Eric said.

"I'm fine. I'll just be a few minutes."

She started down the restroom path located a bit into the forest, away from the party area. She carried her sandals in her hand and carefully placed each foot on the hard-packed earth. She wobbled just a little and giggled at herself. The beer and the wine from earlier made her feel a bit off-balanced. After going about twenty-five feet from the festivities, she heard someone behind her.

"I said I was fine, Eric." She turned around, but nobody was there. She looked through the trees to see Eric sitting at their table, talking to Professor Rodin.

Hmm, that's odd, she thought. The bathroom area was about thirty feet in front of her, so she continued in that direction. Next, she heard a rustling and turned again to look. There was Buddy. His head was down and turned to the side, his tail wagging. He walked gingerly toward her.

"Buddy? What are you doing here?" She bent down to rub behind his ears, and he licked her face. Hearing footsteps, she looked up and saw Davie walking up the path toward her. She stood straight.

"Buddy, here boy," Davie said. Buddy ran back and greeted his master with both paws to the chest, which Davie deflected with ease. He rubbed Buddy's head and floppy ears. "Is that you, Miss Audrey?"

Audrey had just enough beer to speak her mind, and she did. "You know it's me. I'm not falling for that blind con anymore. Why are you following us?"

"I'm sorry?" Davie stopped in front of Audrey and looked directly into her eyes. Without his sunglasses, she could see his eyes were the color of dark honey, and they smiled at the creases. There were dark scars around both and along the bridge of his nose. "I had no idea you were here on Castaway Cay. I come here every year to take part in the Solstice Celebration."

"Yeah? I know you've been following us. We saw you outside the college yesterday and at the airport this morning."

"New Providence is a tiny island. You're bound to see the same people from time to time."

"Oh?" She said with sarcasm. "Well, we even saw you talking to the valet outside our hotel." Audrey put her hands on her hips. "That's too many coincidences, even for me."

Buddy sat, and Davie rubbed his head. "Truth is, I saw you with your husband and another gentleman back there at the table. When you started up this path alone, I decided to follow you."

"To steal the matryoshka, right?"

"To what? No! I don't want to steal it. I just wanted to warn you about it." Davie said.

"You've already done that." She turned to continue her trip to the restroom.

"You don't understand." He grabbed her arm.

"Let go!" She turned and pulled away from him.

"Listen, I've been hearing about you showing it all over Nassau, and I just want to you be careful." He held his palms up to her. "There are some very shady characters around, and if they know you have it, they will do anything to take it from you."

"Yeah? And one is standing right in front of me."

"What you plan to do with it is your business." He pressed his lips together in a slight grimace. "You shouldn't keep it, though. It's too dangerous. If it falls into the wrong hands," He shook his head. "Well, let's just say it could be a bad thing."

Audrey's eyebrows scrunched together, and she stared at him for a beat. "How bad?"

Davie took a step a little closer and listened for anyone within earshot. When he was satisfied, they were alone, he continued. "By now, you must know it isn't a regular nesting doll." He waited for her response, but she kept silent, so he said, "Have you opened it yet?"

"Why?"

"If you haven't, don't. But if you have, then you'll understand why I'm telling you this. Because what's hidden inside is what everyone is after."

"And what's that?"

He cocked his head. "Control." His voice lowered. "And in the wrong hands, pure evil. From everything I've heard on the islands, that Russian woman you met in the Straw Market was its Keeper, and she didn't just pick you at random. She chose you. You're now it's, Keeper."

"You're crazy!" She backed away from him, then turned to run.

"Keep it safe," Davie said to her back. "And hidden!"

She hurried into the bathroom, slammed the door, and engaged the lock. Her mind raced. After a long minute, she heard a knock on the door.

"Go away! Or I'll scream," she shouted.

"I'm sorry?" A woman's voice came from outside. "My girls need to use the bathroom, but no rush."

"Just a minute."

The mother and her girls waited patiently just outside the door for their turn.

"Sorry, I thought you were someone else." Audrey held the door open. As they passed through, she scanned the outside area and found no sign of Davie and Buddy.

⌘

She hurried back to the table while looking for the golden lab and his partner. They are partners in crime or whatever you'd call it, she thought. He said I'm now the Keeper. What did he mean by that?

The group of people drinking and celebrating was getting larger and louder. Some sang along to the music while others danced. She thought about how her parents made her go to the ship's parties and how intoxicated people got. Her mother's laugh was always the loudest.

As she strolled by, she noticed several people clumped

together, swaying to the music. Then she heard a familiar giggle and froze. She turned to see Claire right in the middle of the group dancing to the rhythm. In her hand, she held a pineapple with a straw poking out the top. I can't handle this right now, Audrey thought. She's a big girl, and she did manage to find her way out here so she can find her way home.

Audrey continued trudging through the sand toward the picnic table where Eric and the professor waited. Then she thought more about it. I bet she's drunk and probably alone out here. Audrey turned and walked back toward her mother. Claire swayed with closed eyes, unaware that Audrey was coming to her rescue like she always had.

"Hey, you ready?" Eric asked and squeezed her shoulders gently from behind. She looked up at him. Claire would make a scene anyway, Audrey thought. Now is not the best time for Eric and Claire to be in the same hemisphere.

"Let's go," she quipped. Eric dropped his hands to his sides and took a step back. He waved his palm toward the water and bowed to usher her to the taxi. The professor's head cocked to one side, and he frowned.

Audrey decided to keep her siting of Claire and her meeting with Davie to herself for the time being. There was no sense in upsetting Eric. She could tell him later or maybe even after they got home. On their trip to the boat, he asked her what took her so long in the restroom. She told him her first lie.

"There was a long line." She avoided his stare.

After climbing back on board, the professor handed them both a jacket and set sail again. The islands looked like tiny dark masses off in the distance in three directions. The Abaco was on their left, New Providence behind them, and the Eleuthera Island on their right. In front of them, the open sea.

Thomas dropped the sails, then the anchor. He poured more

wine all around. They sat comfortably out in the middle of the ocean, waiting for the fireworks to start.

"We'll have a great view anchored here," Thomas said. "We can sit back, enjoy this beautiful island night and drink all the wine we want. We don't even have to worry about getting a ticket for drinking and driving." His eyes appeared glassy, and his voice contained the slightest slur.

"Sounds like a great plan to me," Eric said. He was feeling pretty relaxed himself by this time.

"To the sea!" Thomas said, raising his glass. "I can't think of a better place to be right now." Eric clicked glasses with Thomas, then held his glass out to Audrey.

She tapped the rim of her glass to his, then took a small sip. The temperature dropped several degrees since the sun disappeared into the ocean, and she thanked the professor for the jacket. Wrapping it tightly around herself, she stared out into the Atlantic. The waters were calm and quiet, except for tiny waves lapping against the boat's hull.

Eric drank his wine in one swallow and looked over at his wife, who was now gazing up at the sky. The moon was waxing, but the stars were bright, and they lit up the cosmos. She had taken her hair down once again, and it fell around her face.

She could easily be one of the great goddesses of the universe, just like one of those stars up in the sky, he thought. It broke his heart to think she didn't know how he felt. He looked away and wiped his eyes with the back of his hand, pretending to have almost fallen asleep.

"Stay awake young man!" The professor joked.

"It's just so perfect out here." He sat up and breathed in the salty air.

"I love it!" Thomas said. "If I had my choice, I'd be out here every day."

"The guy who recommended that we go to the college for information is from Russia. Do you know him?" Eric asked. "You seem to know a lot of people."

"Most of the people I know work at the college, and we all help out the less fortunate in the community. The English department hosted the party we went to on Castaway Cay. All the proceeds go to charity."

"That's great! Right, Eric?" Audrey said, not sure where he was going with his questions.

"Yeah, that's great," he said to Audrey. To Thomas, "I'm talking about the guy who runs the Russian gift shop. I thought there might be a chance you knew him since you teach Russian history, and he's from Russia."

"No, I don't think I've met him. Maybe I should look him up."

"Don't. The guy is kind of a creep." Audrey's lip curled, and her nose wrinkled. She shook her head at the memory of their encounters with him.

"Well then, I'm glad I haven't had the pleasure of meeting him." He laughed heartily.

"We should tell the professor what we learned about the doll," Eric said.

Professor Rodin poured Eric another glass of wine and reached over to fill Audrey's, but she declined. "I hope the information I copied for you was of some help."

Audrey glared at Eric while the professor perused the sky for lights.

"It was helpful, right, Audrey?" Eric said.

She raised her eyebrows and pursed her lips. You need to drop the subject, she thought.

The professor's attention returned to the conversation. "Did it help?"

"A little," Audrey said. "We did figure out how to open it."

"Is that so? Well, at least that's a step in the right direction."

"We plan to have it appraised when we get home," Eric said. "It could be worth a fortune."

"Or it could be worth nothing, right Eric?" Audrey said. "I wonder when the fireworks are going to start."

"Why don't you go get it? You can show the good professor how to open it and even what's inside. Wink, wink!" He accentuated the winking gesture.

"I think you've had too much to drink," she said.

"Nah, I'm good as gold. Get it. I want to see if Tom here can appraise it for us." Eric smiled. "If it sells for enough, we can buy that business we've been talking about."

Audrey sighed, then stood. She shot Eric an angry stare before climbing the stairs. He noticed but ignored her.

"Oh? What kind of business?" The professor watched Audrey go. He suspected before but now knew the newlyweds were having a tiff.

"I learned to fly helicopters in the Navy, so I want to buy one and start a scenic tour business flying tourists up and down the beach. Audrey will take care of the office work, and I'll do the flying and the mechanics, of course."

"That sounds like a great idea. I know the beaches in Florida are beautiful, and the tourists will love it. Very exciting."

Audrey returned, carrying the matryoshka in her hand without bothering with the blue shopping bag. She sat between Eric and Thomas, holding it lovingly in her hands between her knees. She looked up at the Professor.

"You ready to see this?"

"Sure." He twisted toward her for a closer look. Eric looked away. He decided he hated that doll and didn't want anything to do with it.

Audrey used her thumb as she had before, running it along the belly's bottom edge. The door sprung open with an audible click, and the red satin blanket spilled out. Audrey tugged it the rest of the way into her hand, then unwrapped it. She held the baby up to the professor for a closer look.

"May I?" He asked and held his cupped hands out. She looked at him for a moment, then relented. Once she placed the baby into his hands, he brought it carefully to his chest and peered at it. He gently rocked his hands from side-to-side to see it from all angles.

"Impressive!"

"Let me show you something." Audrey reached for it.

"There's more?" He handed the baby back.

"Are you sure you should open it, Audrey?" Eric asked.

"Hey, showing him was your idea, but maybe he can tell us what it means."

She took the baby back into her hands and used her thumb, running it around the edge, and just like the mother, it clicked when it popped open. Audrey reached in, pulled out the necklace, and held it up for the professor to see.

"Ahoy there!" A man's voice yelled from the bow of the boat. All three stopped talking and looked in the direction of the shout they heard.

⌘

Audrey quickly returned the necklace to the baby, the baby back into the mother, then hid it inside her jacket's interior pocket. She glanced at Eric, who was now alert. The professor stood and looked at them questioningly.

"Someone, you know?" He asked. They both shook their heads negatively.

"Permission to come aboard?" The same male voice asked.

"It could be someone with engine trouble. We get that sometimes out here. I'll go up and see who it is." Thomas said. "If it's for anything else, like drugs, or booze, I'll send them on their way. We get that too from time to time." He went to the front of the boat, and they heard him lower the ladder. After a few minutes, some people came aboard. With their view obscured and too dark to see, the couple waited without speaking.

"Sorry to interrupt, but we've been out fishing all day, and when it was time to head back in, our motor was dead. We were rowing to shore when we saw you anchored, so we decided to row to you instead." The man continuously chattered. "We said to ourselves, now there's a beautiful boat. Maybe we could beg a ride from you when you head ashore. Is it alright if we tie up behind your boat?" He had an island accent. "I hope we aren't interrupting too much. We promise to be no trouble."

"Oh, no problem at all." They heard the professor say. "We're just waiting to watch the fireworks, and then we're planning to hit the sack. Got an early day tomorrow." He led the way for the three to follow him back to the stern. Audrey leaned over to get a better view but could only see Thomas coming down the starboard side.

"As I said, we'd be no trouble. If you can just drop us off when you head in, we'd certainly be obliged."

"Of course. We'll be heading over to New Providence when the sun comes up. My two guests have an early plane back to the States tomorrow."

"We don't mind sleeping up top here, then a ride to New Providence would be perfect."

"It's no trouble," Thomas said again. "Come have a seat. I'm sure we can all get cozy. I'd like you to meet my guests. Oh, and by-the-way, I didn't get your names." Thomas said, turning around to look at them.

Just as she saw his face, Audrey remembered where she'd heard that voice before. It was the waiter from the dinner cruise. He was holding Claire by the arm, and she looked like she'd been crying. When the professor turned to introduce the couple, the waiter pushed him down into his seat at the wheel.

"What the?" The Professor's eyes were as big as saucers. Claire whimpered when she saw Audrey.

"Why are you holding my mother?" Audrey said, glaring at the waiter. Eric sat up straight with clenched fists.

Claire pulled free of the man's grip and ran to Audrey. They hugged each other while Audrey looked her over.

"Are you okay? Did he hurt you?"

"Oh, Audrey, I'm so sorry. I was just trying to have a fun vacation. You know?" Claire said.

"What happened?" Audrey asked.

"I don't know what happened. Those guys said they knew about a much better party, and they said it was on another island. When I changed my mind, they got crazy and threw me into a boat. I just liked the people at my first party. You know?" She smelled of rum and pineapple, and her eyelids drooped. A signal Audrey recognized when her mother had too much to drink.

"What's going on?" Eric asked.

"I know who you are. You're the guy who tried to steal my bag. You jumped off the gambling ship when Eric recognized you!" Audrey started to stand, but Claire pulled her back.

"No, Audrey, don't!" Claire held on to her.

"And you! I knew we should have called the police after you attacked me, Mr. Bortnik!"

"Please, Audrey!" Claire cried. "Tell me what's happening?"

"Jesus, I know why they've come," Eric said. He shook his head.

"All we want is the matryoshka," Bortnik said. He took his Berretta from the back of his waistband and pointed it at Audrey. "I didn't leave it in the car this time." He smiled.

The waiter pulled out his gun and pointed it at the professor. Thomas tried to stand, but the waiter pushed him down hard and used the back of his hand to slap him across the temple. The professor's head bounced off the steering wheel, causing a cut over his eye. When his trembling fingers found the blood, his eyes grew large.

"Now see here, what's this all about?" Thomas raised his hands to defend his face and drew back as far as his chair would allow. "Take what you want. Just leave us unharmed." His voice shook.

"Give it to them, Audrey," Eric said. "Maybe then they'll leave us alone, and we can walk away from this nightmare."

Audrey looked at him but said nothing.

"Audrey?" Eric said. "They are going to kill us."

The sky burst into bright light as the fireworks show began. Eric reacted by standing up to block Audrey from the gun, but the waiter turned and fired in response. The bullet hit Eric in the chest, and he collapsed onto the deck. Audrey's scream echoed across the water, and she dropped down to him. Claire wept and joined Audrey, trying to hold on to her. She hugged Audrey's back and rocked back and forth.

"It's okay, baby," Claire cried. Audrey pushed her away and returned to Eric.

⌘

"Damn it! How could you possibly fuck that up?" Professor Rodin stood and grabbed the gun from the waiter. "All you two knuckleheads had to do was steal the damn doll from the room while we were on Castaway." He shook his head and held a palm up. "What happened?"

"You told us not to tear up the room," the waiter said.

"Sorry, Commander, we couldn't find it," Bortnik said.

Audrey shook Eric and cried while fireworks continued to explode overhead. She pulled him into a sitting position and felt all along his chest. When she looked at her hands, they dripped with his blood. His head rolled forward to his chest.

"So, instead, you come on board and shoot the guy?" Professor Rodin said incredulously. "Whatever happened to stealth? Get in and out without anyone knowing?" He swung the gun at the waiter connecting it with his cheek. The waiter grabbed his face and went to his knees. "That's for hitting me, you stupid ass."

He sat down and pointed the gun at Audrey.

"Please don't kill us." Claire cried. She pulled her knees up to her chest, covered her ears with her hands, and whimpered.

"I'm so sorry about all this, Audrey," Thomas said. He leaned over toward her with his forearms on his knees and pointed the gun to the deck. "These two stooges were supposed to get the matryoshka even before the old lady dropped it into your hands." He shook his head and clicked his tongue. "And your honeymoon, too. I'm so sorry to spoil it for you. But now, think about what's happening here. It's time to cut your losses and get out with your life." He motioned to the two men.

Bortnik pushed Audrey back, and the two grabbed Eric by each arm and leg, then hoisted him overboard. His body made a tremendous splash, and Audrey scrambled to her feet, leaned over the side, and watched him sink.

"No!" She screamed, and her body shook. She laid her forehead on the edge of the boat and cried deep heavy sobs.

Fireworks continued to explode, lighting up the dark ocean. A few swirls remained on the surface where Eric sank.

"If you don't want to be next, hand over the doll. Carefully. I'd hate for it to get wet," Professor Rodin said.

Audrey slowly turned to look at the three men. They watched her intently, and she released a heavy sigh.

The waiter grabbed Claire and held her elbows behind her back. "Audrey, I'm so sorry. I didn't know," she cried.

Audrey, still sobbing, climbed up on the edge of the stern, turned to face them, and stood. With her right hand, she grabbed the rope tied to the mast and adjusted her balance. She pulled the matryoshka out from her right inside jacket pocket and held it up in her left.

"She'll be next." Professor Rodin pointed the gun at Claire, but Audrey didn't move from her perch. She appeared to be in shock. With eyes searching the sky behind her, she watched the fireworks fly.

"Ah, hell." Professor Rodin shook his head, gave the gun to Bortnik, and then slowly made his way toward her. He beckoned her to come down with an agreeable come-here indication with his right hand and reached for her with his left. "You don't want to do this." Her eyes were unreadable when she stared down at him. She backed further to the edge and rocked from her toes to her heels.

"Audrey, please give them what they want!" Claire cried out.

Fireworks continued to pop and light up the sky. Audrey looked down at the dark ocean, then to the four below her.

"Remember when I got the Most Improved medal?" She said to Claire. "You remember that, right, Mom?"

"Audrey, please, don't do this. You'll drown." Claire tried to break free but then stopped struggling and looked up at her daughter. "I kept your medal," Claire said. "After you left? I know you thought I didn't care. But I kept it. Doesn't that count for anything?"

The wind picked up slightly and blew across Audrey's long dark hair. Her face was bright with the fireworks' grand finale. She looked directly into Claire's eyes, smiled, and shrugged her shoulders. "Sure, Mom." She cradled the matryoshka to her chest, turned, and fell into the ocean.

They all clambered to the stern and looked over. The four waited for Audrey to resurface, but she didn't. There was no sign of her.

"Why are you waiting? Go in and get her!" Professor Rodin said to the other two. "I don't care if she drowns. Just bring me that doll."

"My baby! Audrey, please come back. Don't leave me." Claire cried out. Her body seemed to melt as she slid to the deck.

The two men dove down, but they came up without Audrey or the matryoshka time after time. They complained it was too dark to see anything. After several dives, they climbed back into the sailboat. The waiter went in and tied their craft to the back. Then Thomas Rodin pulled the anchor, and the Anastasia trolled the waters in the area using just the motor and a searchlight. He steered to the closest island, and their eyes scanned the dark silhouettes of docks and houses onshore.

Claire hung over the side and cried out for her daughter's return. After about thirty minutes of trolling, Professor Rodin could no longer take it.

"Would you shut that bitch up?!" The two men grabbed Claire by the arms and tossed her into the water. She came up, coughing and splashing.

"I can't swim," She cried. But the Anastasia continued its slow progression through the murky waters, leaving her behind.

The professor steered the boat from island to island and searched without luck. Audrey was at the bottom of the ocean, or she had somehow slipped past them. The dark waters refused to give up its secrets.

Professor Rodin turned the Anastasia toward Castaway Cay, thinking if Audrey survived the ocean, she might make her way there for help. The two henchmen disembarked and approached the few locals cleaning up after the Solstice party. They let everyone working know a young American woman fell into the ocean and handed out a phone number to call if anyone laid eyes on her. Then, they moved silently into the woods to search the rest of the island. The morning sun started to rise in the east, and with that, fishermen headed out for their morning catch as they did every morning.

Izzy threw the journal onto the seat between her and its author. What is all this? She thought. It has to be a work of fiction. Audrey stirred beneath the blanket and mumbled something in her sleep, but Izzy couldn't make out the words. She must be dreaming. If any of this story is true, it's a miracle the woman's still alive. She must have made it out of the ocean somehow, though. Izzy unfolded a blanket onto herself and ducked underneath. After a moment, a hand slipped out, grabbed the journal, and pulled it beneath.

⌘

In 1974, Commander Vasin, aka Professor Thomas Rodin, was relieved of his commission as Commander of an Infantry Squadron by the KGB Chairman Yuri Andropov. Never given a reason for his firing, he assumed it had something to do with an incident where his commanding officer caught him with a high-ranking general's daughter. He was young and reckless at the time, but his father and grandfather both courageously served in the Russian army, and the family expected him to do the same. Given a choice to either be sent home in disgrace or go undercover as a spy, he chose the latter and went to the United States. He waited for his assignment in California, where he stayed under the radar of the C.I.A. by taking college classes, surfing, and traveling back and forth to Russia on a work/study program. He earned his degree in Social Science, majoring in Russian History and taught part-time at the local junior college. The little-known office within the Kremlin gave Commander Vasin a new identity and paid him well.

Ten years passed in California before he received his first secret communication. His assignment was to confiscate a rare artifact, stolen over two-hundred years prior. Details about the relic were scarce except that a Russian aristocrat smuggled it out of the country in the early 1900s. If Vasin could find this matryoshka or nesting doll and return it to the Motherland, he would become a hero with full military honors.

When he was a small boy, his grandmother told him stories about a nesting doll with unique abilities. The stories included young heroines who used the powers to free the falsely imprisoned and feed the poor. He assumed it was folklore the older people told to keep Russian stories alive. Now he wondered why the Kremlin was so interested in a matryoshka.

Intelligence revealed a couple of sightings of the current Keeper, an old gypsy woman in The Bahamas and Florida around 1975 and then again in 1978. Commander Vasin, now Thomas Rodin, left his comfortable life of part-time teaching and surfing in Santa Monica to become a full-time history professor in Nassau on New Providence Island. The intelligence said he would intercept the doll before the gypsy passed it off to the next Keeper. At least eighty years of age and in failing health, the woman desperately sought the next guardian before she died.

C.A. Bortnik worked as an aide for a high-ranking officer while in the military. Recognized as someone who got the job done no matter what it entailed, made him the perfect choice to assist Vasin. Knowing nothing except the military, Bortnik dedicated his life to the Russian KGB. If answering to a womanizing arrogant beach bum was his assignment, then he would do that. His cover in The Bahamas was to open a Russian shop dealing in exquisite artifacts and antiquities. This experience made him an authority on anything Russian bought in or around the islands, but he focused on finding the special matryoshka. His shop proved to be a great cover to lure unsuspecting tourists with questions or information. He kept the Kremlin advised of sightings and traveled from The Bahamas to Moscow often. From time to time, he paid some of the unemployed locals to follow tourists who acquired nesting dolls to take home as souvenirs.

⌘

Heartbroken, Audrey had fallen from the sailboat and wanted nothing more than to be swallowed up. As her body sank deeper, it instinctively struggled to return to the surface, but the jacket kept pulling her downward. She fought to take it off without success.

Now that Eric was gone, she decided life wasn't worth living and stopped fighting. Into the darkened deep, she went—the same feeling of calm when she sank in the pool many years before came over her, but this time there was nobody to pull her out.

She released a sob, and her mind drifted beyond her fears and took her back into the past. Vividly, she remembered her father's laugh and the safety of his arms. He soothed her tears and made everything wrong seem right, even in their last conversation together. His only concern was to make her feel safe and loved.

"I miss you, Daddy," she cried. She remembered the fair and how she had her fortune told. Her mind skipped forward to the old lady in the Straw Market.

"Oh, my God!" She cried. "Mystic Vamonda?"

When the Golitsyn family arrived in San Francisco from Russia, a world of opportunities awaited them. Once fearful, Vera became independent and set out on her own eager to explore her new home. With a sizable endowment from the Golitsyn family to keep her financially afloat, she made her way to the east coast. From there, she traveled around the world.

Soon after they arrived, Mr. Golitsyn wisely invested their wealth into stocks, such as steel and the movie industry. Members of the Russian government showed a keen interest in those finances but realized the money was untouchable in America. More importantly, they tried unsuccessfully to question Mr. Golitsyn about the whereabouts of a missing antique. A special matryoshka of unknown worth had disappeared from Moscow at the time of their hasty departure. Remembering the dire urgings of Alex's grandmother, Vera never shared her secret with the family, but all the questions about a nesting doll made Mr. Golitsyn suspicious. He knew his aging mother had many secrets, and he wondered if she smuggled something into their luggage. When he questioned Vera about it, she pretended to know nothing.

Vera fell in love with a businessman who made his fortune

in the stock market. Alan Hammond doted on her every whim. They soon had a son whom they named Yuri, after Vera's father. When the stock market crashed, Alan lost most of their money, so Vera used the doll's secrets to find ways to keep them solvent but never told her husband about it. She wanted to but couldn't bring herself to disclose her secret to anyone. When Vera wore the necklace, it made her feel powerful, invincible even. She believed Alex's grandmother picked her to keep the artifact hid for safety's sake, and the only way to do that was to tell no one. She reasoned nobody would believe her anyway.

Tales of odd occurrences in America reached Moscow, and soon the Hammond family began receiving visits from Russian agents. Vera managed to not be at home when they came to visit, and Alan thought their questions had something to do with his dealings with the failed Stock Exchange. The harassment made him nervous, so he moved his family to New York City and found a small apartment without leaving a forwarding address. He accepted a job at a bank.

Now that Alan had a decent paying job, the young family was doing much better, and the baby grew fast. It seemed Alan had a few secrets of his own, and Vera was okay with that. She knew he had to do whatever he could financially to keep them from ending up out in the street.

After about six months, as Alan walked home, someone attacked him and left him to die. A night watchman found him stabbed and bleeding and took him to the hospital where he died three days later.

Vera, now alone with a baby, knew it must have had something to do with the Russians, and they would come for her next. She used the necklace to slip out of the country where she hid with her child. She raised him in Poland but dreamed of getting back to the United States, the place she considered home.

They returned in 1970, again using the power within the matryoshka. She and her son could live somewhat comfortably while traveling around the country, telling fortunes and reading palms with carnival caravans. It was what she knew best. Never needing an address, they stayed hidden from the Kremlin's long arm, but the secretive corner office never stopped searching. They eventually tracked down the mother and son team and quickly deployed an operative to retrieve the matryoshka.

When Audrey and her father stopped in at Mystic Vomanda's fortune-telling tent, they overheard the Russian agent threatening Vera. She felt vulnerable once again and knew she needed to act. What happened to that agent became lore gore in Palm Glade, a story told around many campfires late at night.

When Vera read Audrey's fortune, she recognized the young girl as the one she had seen in her dreams. The next Keeper of the matryoshka. Vera and Yuri kept a close eye on Audrey over the years without interfering in her life. When the girl was old enough and ready to take on the responsibility, they'd reach out to her. The old gypsy wanted to give Audrey a choice to accept or decline the duty to safeguard the matryoshka. Vera felt strongly about this because she wasn't allowed a choice when she took over guardianship.

After a severe illness, Vera became frail and often forgetful. Yuri realized the exchange needed to happen sooner than planned. She had a license in Hypnotherapy, and on her better days, Vera achieved excellent results in the powers of suggestion, even without the help of the necklace. So, Yuri lured Grandma Josie to Cassadaga, where Vera inserted an idea into Josie's subconscious. They needed a way to get Audrey to The Bahamas, where they could pass on the matryoshka safely with time to explain the power within.

They watched and waited for her to arrive, but by the time

the couple married and made it to the islands, Vera's health had progressively deteriorated. Sometimes her mind was sharp, but there were more and more days she didn't know Yuri from a stranger. Also, the Russian agents were closing in once again. The mother and son became desperate to pass it off.

CHAPTER NINE

Reckoning

Audrey **found the courage** to fight her way back to the ocean's surface. A light beam cut through the water, searching in all directions, but Audrey stayed submerged, resisting the urge to surface for air. When the Anastasia passed, she appeared behind it.

"Audrey, where are you?" Professor Rodin leaned over the side and called. "You need to stop this silliness and get back onboard. I promise not to hurt you or your mother."

A sob escaped her as she scanned the ocean for her husband. Maybe he swam to one of the islands, she told herself. The fireworks show no longer exploded overhead, and she looked up into the dark sky to see a multitude of stars shining brightly.

The sailboat's propeller chopped through the water, retracing its initial path several times. With each pass, Audrey submerged herself back into the depths. When they went by a second time, she noticed the motorboat attached to the back and grabbed a handhold giving herself a break from the currents tugging her out to sea. Whenever the searchlight angled back to her position, she held her breath and hid underneath the boat. At one point, Audrey heard her mother's screams, then watched her dog-paddle to shore.

Through the night, she held on and kept out of sight. After long hours, the sun peeked over the horizon. She recognized the island of Castaway Cay and swam to it. Nearing one of the smaller shores, she slunk out of the water. Surrounded by a steep incline where trees and shrubbery grew thick, her little beach appeared hidden from the rest of the island.

She made her way through the trees in search of a road. At the top of the hill, she stopped and leaned on a large tree to catch her bearings. Heavy footsteps behind signaled she wasn't alone. Before she could turn toward the sound, she was grabbed from behind and yanked back. Her head bounced off a broad chest, and the smell of sweat and alcohol filled her nose before a hand clamped over her mouth.

"I have you now," a gravelly voice breathed wetly into her ear. With the man's leg wrapped around her thighs, he extracted a large bowie knife from his belt. "Now, I am going to skin you alive before I kill you."

It was the waiter from the gambling ship—the one who shot Eric. Without thinking, Audrey bit down hard on his knuckle. When he jerked his hand away, she ducked, unwrapped herself from him, and clamored to run. He grabbed her by the hair and snapped her head back. She cried out, then twisted around and kicked him in the groin. He let go, grabbed his crotch, and moaned vehemently. She gathered her wits and darted away from him again but tripped over some tree roots exposed above the sandy soil. She scrambled to her feet, but he dove and tackled her. Audrey let out a garbled cry. Now intertwined, the two rolled the rest of the way down the hill, where he bumped his head on a tree trunk. She freed herself from his arms and crawled to the shore. Her last hope she knew was to out-swim him.

He regained his wits, barreled after her, then tackled her once more, this time in the water. He flipped her over even as she screamed and fought. He plopped hard onto her stomach, knocking the air from her lungs. Now straddling her, he squeezed her ribs tightly with his knees. She gulped for air only to have water pour down her throat. Holding her head under the surface with one hand, he took the matryoshka out of her pocket with the other. Audrey kicked her legs and swung her arms wildly. It wasn't long before she found it difficult to fight. Her limbs became sluggish, heavy as lead weights, and she started to lose consciousness. Her fingers clawed at the sand and landed on a solid object. She grasped it into her fist and swung it wide out of the water, and felt it connect. He let go of her head, and she came up choking. She sensed him fall next to her, but she turned onto her hands and knees, coughed, then threw-up. When she caught her breath, she looked to see him lying on his side. His knife handle pointed at the sky with the blade deep in his neck. With his head submerged, his blood spilled into the water and washed away. The matryoshka lay next to him. She grabbed it and crawled to the water's edge, then collapsed.

⌘

Audrey felt a wet tongue licking her face and heard barking in her ear. She opened her eyes and used his sturdy body to pull herself to a kneeling position, then leaned on him. Davie appeared and assisted her across the beach and back into the forest. He helped her out of her jacket and wrapped her in a towel retrieved from his backpack. Her whole body shook while he dried along her arms and back.

"We need to go now," Davie said gently. His senses scanned the trees. "That guy's friends are searching this whole island for you."

Audrey's bottom lip trembled. "He killed, Eric." She tried to draw in a breath and found she couldn't. The ground spun. She was hyperventilating but couldn't stop herself.

"Okay, calm down. I think you're in shock."

"I can't breathe."

He took her face into his hands. "Look at me." She jerked back, but he didn't release her. "You need to focus on me." The spinning slowed, and her breathing evened out. "There'll be time to explain after we get someplace safe," he said.

"Okay." She nodded, and he let go. Then he helped her stand.

They hiked through the dense canopy until they reached a dirt road. After walking about a mile, the two slipped back into the trees with Buddy staying close to give direction, never more than a few feet away. The trees eventually thinned to reveal another obscured tiny cove. At the water's edge, Davie helped Audrey into a small motorboat. She sat in the middle on some flotation cushions on the floor. Davie instructed her to lie down. Exhausted, she complied, and he covered her with a blanket. Buddy lightly stepped over her to his place at the front, and Davie launched the boat into the water then hopped into the back. The small motor came to life with one crank, and they set out across the open seas.

Audrey woke when the engine quieted. The boat continued to glide silently through the water, and she sat up. The sun had set, but the stars were brilliant. A light breeze blew, and Audrey felt a chill run through her. Her clothes, still damp, clung to her wet skin. A boat ramp cloaked in deep shadow came into view.

"Where are we?" She whispered. Buddy came to her and put

his head under her hand. She rubbed behind his ears, and he sat next to her.

"Just coming back into Nassau. We took the long way to make sure we didn't run into anyone." His voice slightly above a whisper. The boat came to a sandy stop, and Buddy jumped out. "You'll wait in the boat until I tell you to come?"

"Yes." Then it occurred to her she was no longer in possession of the matryoshka. She scanned the boat, then felt around beneath the blanket. Davie waited in silence. She became frantic, "Oh no! I must have dropped it."

Davie reached under his seat and pulled out the rolled-up jacket, and handed it to her. "Are you looking for this?" Audrey looked up at him for a moment before she grabbed it. Upon inspection, she found the matryoshka tucked securely in the interior pocket.

A smile broke across Davie's lips as his eyes stared into the distance. "As I told you before, I'm not one you need to worry about."

She put the damp jacket back on and stuck her fists into the outside pockets. Davie climbed out of the boat and dragged it the rest of the way up the beach. He trudged up the ramp holding onto Buddy's leash to scout the area. It appeared deserted. He returned to the boat and reached in to extend his hand to her.

"Thank you. For everything." Audrey said. His sight seems to be better at night, she thought.

"No need. I hope someone would do the same for me if there ever came a time." He leaned in further to reach her. "You're still in danger. That sailboat you were on has been searching the waters and islands for you."

Audrey accepted his hand, and gingerly climbed out. She pulled the blanket over her head, so just her face showed, and he put his arm around her waist. Buddy led them through back alleys until they came to a small turquoise-colored bungalow with a gray, metal roof.

⌘

Once inside, Audrey found the two-bedroom home neat, with overstuffed wicker furniture and ample pillows. A fishnet with shells hung from the ceiling in one corner of the living room as if just pulled in from the surf. Hanging potted plants adorned every window.

Davie led Audrey to one of the bedrooms. Tastefully decorated, it housed a double bed covered in a thick white comforter. Tropical paintings of large flowers in bloom hung on the walls. A teak dresser, nightstand, and headboard all matched, and a highly polished wooden bench with inlaid designs of more flowers on the lid sat at the end of the bed.

"My daughter comes to visit from time-to-time." He stepped back to allow Audrey in. "There are clothes in the closet, and she's probably about your size, so help yourself."

"Oh, I couldn't."

"Well, of course, you can. The shower is down the hall on your right." He turned to leave but stopped and faced her again. He looked in her direction for a moment. His jaw moved like he wanted to say something but instead said, "You get cleaned up. Then we'll talk."

Audrey stepped into the hot shower when steam began to roll over the top of the curtain. The patter of droplets stung her skin, and chill bumps popped out across her body. The spray penetrated her scalp, and her shoulders slumped. She closed her eyes.

Her mind immediately flowed over the last twenty-four hours and focused on how Eric was thrown overboard like a sack of garbage. The tears returned, and she collapsed into the tub.

Water continued to rain down while Audrey sobbed uncontrollably. Her whole world had fallen apart, and she wanted to give up.

⌘

Regaining her composure, she quickly washed and stepped out of the bath. Wrapping a towel around her wet body, she used another to wipe away the steam that accumulated on the mirror. The image of the red-faced girl with dark hair dripping into the sink seemed unfamiliar. She bent forward and peered at herself. Who are you? She thought. You're not the same person who went on her honeymoon a week ago.

She'd killed a man. It didn't matter that he tried to murder her. Her mind couldn't stop running through it like a movie. When he sat on top of her, she was drowning, and her instincts took over. She killed him to save herself. Nothing could have prepared her for that feeling of desperation and survival. It was brutal. Although she felt guilty and even a little sad for what she did to him, she knew she would do it the same way if it happened again. That doll caused all of this, she thought. She knew from the start, it was dangerous to keep it, but she kept it anyway. It never occurred to her that she or Eric could die because of it.

She found shorts and a t-shirt with a picture of Bob Marley printed on the front and put them on. She entered the kitchen with a towel wrapped around her head and found Buddy eating from a bowl in the corner. Davie made tuna sandwiches, so Audrey took the seat at the round wooden table next to him. All of her energy dissipated into the air, and she hung her head. Missing Eric terribly, tears seeped from her eyes. She caught a glimpse of Davie, waiting for her to speak. Instead, she pulled the towel from her head and rubbed it briskly across her hair.

A Nassau news program ran a story about an American plucked from the ocean by a fisherman. When he pulled in his net, he found a body among his morning catch. After wrapping it in an old tarp, he transported it to a local hospital. The attending physician took one look at the body and prepared for the worst, but grew excited when he detected a faint pulse. He also found a bullet, inches from the heart. Kept sedated during and between several surgeries, they finally removed it, and the victim's chances of survival improved daily.

"I've been listening to the radio, and I think they found your husband." Audrey stopped drying her hair and looked at him. Her sigh so full of sorrow made his chest tighten. He swallowed and continued. "If it's him, he's alive and in the hospital."

Audrey dropped her face into her hands and cried until she couldn't catch her breath.

Davie reached over and pulled them away gently. "He's going to be okay." Her tears subsided. Then, she sharply sucked in her breath.

"I've got to get to the hospital." Standing abruptly, she tipped the chair, but it settled back to all fours.

"Wait a minute. You can't go out. If I'm not mistaken, that man with the knife in his neck is probably dead."

"He tried to kill me!" Audrey sat back down.

"Those men are still looking for you. It's better if they think you've drowned."

"But Eric doesn't know I'm okay. It'll make him crazy."

"Better crazy than dead. Don't you think?" His amber eyes attempted to focus on her. "Those men chasing you aren't playing around. They will kill you both."

"What about my grandmother? She'll worry."

"She can't know either, at least not now." Buddy finished

his dinner and sat on the floor between the two. He watched them, looking at each as they spoke.

"I'm sorry, Audrey. I know this is hard, but it seems you have a bigger responsibility." His stare made her uncomfortable. "For whatever reason, the old woman picked you. I overheard her and her son talking in the market before you and Eric showed up. I didn't realize what it all meant at the time, but I have come to understand it a bit more. Whether you like it or not, you're now the Keeper of the doll." He tugged on his beard and thought, then continued. "As you have already learned, your job will not be easy. Do you understand what that means?" He reached for her to make sure she was listening. "It's very dangerous, so if you want to keep it out of the wrong hands, you must hide."

"Why me? I'm nothing. A nobody." She glanced at Buddy, then looked up. "What if I take it to the police?"

"Taking it to the police will be the fastest way to drop it into the wrong hands. You know what its contents can do. Remember, the police are looking for you as a missing person. Once they find the dead man on Castaway and connect the dots, they'll be looking at you like a murder suspect. You can't trust the police or anyone." He rubbed Buddy's head. "You know you are welcome to stay here as long as you like, but it's not safe for you anywhere in The Bahamas. Is there someplace you can go to in the states? Not home. That's the first place they'll look."

A loud knock on the front door caught them unaware. Audrey's eyes filled with terror and cut over to the living room. Buddy ran to the door and barked aggressively.

⌘

"You need to hide. Now!" He made his way into the living room and listened at the door. Audrey ran back to his daughter's bedroom. He waited until he heard the bedroom lock click into place before releasing the deadbolt on the front entrance. Buddy continued barking, so Davie told him to sit. He quieted and sat next to Davie but maintained a low growl. Davie opened the door and peered out, his scars wrinkling around his eyes.

"Good evening." Right away, Audrey recognized the voice of C.A. Bortnik. "I was driving by, and I thought I saw someone lurking around the back of your lovely home." Audrey sat with her back to the wall and listened. Every time he spoke, it made her skin crawl.

"Oh? That's disturbing." Davie rubbed Buddy's head, then grabbed his collar. Buddy's body was tight and ready to pounce.

Bortnik eyed the dog nervously. "Have you seen or heard anything suspicious tonight?" His eyes peered inside the living room.

Davie closed the door to within a few inches and stood in that space to block the view. "Nope. I haven't heard a thing tonight. My dog hasn't alerted me, and he's pretty good about doing that. As you can see, he's suspicious of strangers."

"Maybe it was just some kids looking for something to vandalize. I'd be happy to take a look around for you." Bortnik leaned forward and tried again to look inside.

"And why would you do that?"

"You know, since you are blind and all. I'm just doing my civic duty. I would hate for someone to commit a crime on a blind man."

"I wouldn't bother myself with worry about that if I were you. My dog is capable of protecting me. As I said, things have been pretty quiet around here."

Bortnik's dark mustache twitched. "Didn't I see you at the Solstice party out on Castaway yesterday?"

"You may have. I went to several parties last night, and actually, I'm tired right now, so if you would excuse me, I need to get to bed."

Davie attempted to close the door, but Bortnik put his foot in the way. Buddy barked and lunged. Bortnik instinctively pulled his foot back, and Davie slammed the door and turned the lock.

Bortnik wasn't ready to give up. "Some islanders told me you were speaking to a woman with long dark hair at the party. Very pretty. An American tourist, I think," he called through the door.

"I'm friends with everyone, but because I'm blind, I can't say how the ladies look. They all sound beautiful to me."

"They are saying this woman is very dangerous. I hear she killed a man while on Castaway Cay, and she stole some artifact that belongs to the Russian Government."

"I'm sorry I can't help you. Have a good evening."

Davie stepped away and moved over to the bookshelf, where he took out a pistol. Checking to make sure he had loaded it, he pulled the slide back to chamber a bullet with an audible click. Davie waited for the sound of footsteps echoing on the sidewalk. When he peeked out the window, he saw the silhouette of Bortnik's dark figure getting into his Cadillac and driving away. Davie breathed out a sigh and tucked the revolver into his waistband. He knew the Russian would be back, probably sooner than later.

⌘

Audrey sat on the bed with her knees drawn to her chest and stared out the predawn darkened bedroom window. A songbird tweeted as the first rays of sunlight peeked throughout the quiet neighborhood. She dropped her forehead to her knees. Tormenting thoughts during the night hounded her still, and her mind continued replaying what happened on the Anastasia, how they shot and threw Eric overboard like his life was worth nothing.

A happier script ran parallel to that—one of her going to the hospital and running into Eric's arms. So relieved to see her, he'd kiss all her tears away. He'd know just what to do and how to make everything better. Together, they'd put an end to this craziness and go home to Florida as Mr. and Mrs. Reynolds. How could I even think he had sex with Claire? She laughed to herself. After everything that happened, she realized her priorities no longer included her mother. She would find a way to get back to Eric so they could spend the rest of their life together.

Reality set in once more, and tears from her tired, puffy eyes burned. The price was too high. People had murdered just to get their hands on the matryoshka. She couldn't put Eric into danger again. He almost died because of all this.

She fell onto the pillow and cried. Why me? She thought. They picked the wrong person. I'm not strong, or dedicated or anything. I'm just a regular, average person, afraid of my own shadow. She looked over at the matryoshka lying next to her. Its eyes stared into hers and seemed to say, 'Now that you know my secret, how can you not protect me?' Audrey looked away. Even after everything that happened, she longed to feel the power of the necklace and realized she could never allow it to fall into the wrong hands. I may be too afraid to put it on again, but I'll make sure the Russians don't take it from me, she swore to herself.

Davie listened through the bedroom door for a moment before knocking. He looked down at Buddy, who stood beside him. "Audrey, are you awake?" He hesitated, then said, "I have a plan."

⌘

The small harbor bustled with activity. Boats, water taxis, and ships of various sizes crowded the docks. Buddy grew excited with the smell of fish all around. Audrey wore a long dress adorned with large tropical flowers designed to hide any figure. She stayed close to Davie locking her elbow around his. They passed rows of tables laden with the morning specials - star fruit, bananas, mangoes, and of course, all kinds of fish. Everything was sold fresh directly from the boats docked there.

Dark sunglasses covered most of her face, and a large floppy hat with a wide brim completed her ensemble. On her shoulder hung a sizeable striped beach bag full of Spam, bread, and fruit. Tucked into the bottom was the jacket with the matryoshka. The locals went about their business without a second glance her way. Some called out to Davie to say hello and to pet Buddy. Audrey glanced about searching for anyone who might show more than a passing interest in her.

"How much further? I'm afraid someone's going to recognize me." Audrey found it difficult to believe she was blending in. Back home, her get-up would attract all kinds of looks.

"Calm down, or you'll draw attention to yourself. There are excellent deals down here, but visitors miss out since only a few venture this far from downtown." He touched her arm, and she gazed up at him. "Take me to the last row. Don't worry. Nobody down here cares much."

They were getting close to the end when Buddy ran ahead to a forty-foot boat. It had a pale blue paint chipped cabin perched squarely in the middle of its topside. He jumped across the water and onto the deck, then ran to a large woman who sat on a kitchen chair spray-painted white. She rewarded him with a hug and lots of petting. Once he finished his greeting, he ran up and down the length of the boat. His eyes stayed focused on the water below, and he barked at fish swimming near the surface.

"It looks like Buddy found who we're looking for." Davie ushered Audrey toward the pier's edge. The dark water swirled several feet below. "I have someone I want you to meet."

The woman stood and watched them approach with her hands attached to her fleshy waist. Her canary yellow tank top stretched tightly, not entirely covering her round belly. Her cut-off shorts hung low on her hips. Buddy jumped up and put his front paws on the railing, while the woman walked over and dropped the gangway.

"Good morning, Janey!" Davie shouted as Audrey assisted his cross over. Once onboard, he hugged the large woman. Audrey followed behind, then stood beside him. Janey pulled out a couple more chairs from inside the cabin and invited them to sit.

"So, Davie, how you hangin'?" Janey's voice boomed.

"Oh, so-so. Same ole, same ole." His drawl became slower, and his accent thicker. "How about yourself?" His sunglasses flashed, reflecting sunlight. "You selling anything special today?"

Janey reached behind her inside the cabin. She brought out a bottle of brown liquid with a foreign label and held it out for Davie to touch. Rum. "Best stuff yet. Picked it up in Cuba." She said in that familiar island lilt.

Davie smiled and shook his head. "Woman, if they catch you, they'll put you under the jail."

"They won't catch me." She giggled. "Don't you know the Governor General's my biggest client?" Her laugh filled the boat and pier nearby. A man in the next vessel waved, and Janey waved back. He pulled large wahoo and dolphin from an iced cooler and hung them from hooks for customers to buy.

"So, how much are your special elixirs going for?" Davie asked.

"$200.00 a bottle. I could get more, but I decided to give a good deal since I got so much. My brother, Bruce, is dropping them all off now. This here bottle's all I kept."

"What? You aren't drinking now, are you?"

"Oh, Lordy! You know I can't stand the stuff." Her head tilted back. "Dis for my brother. He like a snort sometimes."

"Ah. I see." Davie sat quiet a moment. His face turned toward all the boats in the harbor, waiting for their place at the docks. He leaned toward Janey with his elbows on his thighs, "So, where are you heading out to next?"

"Leaving for Tampa this morning as soon as Bruce gets back." She leaned inside the cabin again and pulled out a box of cigars. "What do you think of these?" She opened it and handed one to Davie, then offered the open box to Audrey. Audrey shook her head, so Janey took one out for herself and lit it. She sucked on it until her jowls worked out a fair amount of smoke to dispel into the air. "Dis here's my weakness." She leaned back and blew a smoke ring. "The real deal and worth a lot more than rum."

"Gran Habano?"

"Yes, siree, nothing better."

"I have to agree. Nothing has as sweet an aroma, lit or not."

"Hey, wait a minute. Hold the phone." Janey sat up straight. Her attention switched to the young woman hidden behind the giant sunglasses and floppy hat. "You haven't introduced me to your friend."

"This is Audrey." Davie grabbed Audrey's hand. She looked to him for reassurance. He nodded to her and smiled as if to say everything is going to be alright.

"Hello." Audrey felt like Janey could see right through her silly disguise.

Janey peered at her but waited to hear more.

"I got huge favor to ask." He took his sunglasses off, and his scarred eyes attempted to focus on Janey. "Normally, I wouldn't ask for a favor such as this, but it's vital."

"Okay." Janey looked around to make sure there wasn't anyone within earshot. The man selling fish was haggling prices for his catch with a restaurant owner. Janey then leaned in. "I'm listening."

"She needs to get to the United States, but she can't go the typical way that most tourists go if you know what I mean."

"That's so?" Janey leaned back and looked sideways at Audrey, then tilted her face to the sky and blew smoke. "You don't look dangerous."

"It's very nice to meet you, Miss Janey." Audrey stuck out her hand.

Janey scratched her head and looked at Davie, who had returned his sunglasses to his sun-sensitive eyes and waited.

"Well, hell. It would be a pleasure having you aboard." Janey accepted Audrey's hand and squeezed. "I don't need to know no details. We got plenty of room." She leaned in. "There are bunks below and even a head when nature calls."

"Thank you!" Audrey said. "I can't pay you now, but I'll send money when I get to where I'm going."

"No need. We're already sailing in that direction. We'll head for Florida today. Dock offshore overnight in Miami, then putter around to Tampa tomorrow. That work for you?"

"Yes, thank you."

Davie stood up and pulled out a wad of cash for Audrey. "This should be enough to get you to where you can hide for a while. At least until you can find a more permanent place to stay."

"Oh, no. You've done too much already. I can't accept it."

"Yes, you can, and you will. Besides, I have more money than I can spend in ten lifetimes."

Audrey felt her eyes welling up. "I'll never be able to repay you for all you've done for me."

"Just stay safe." He took her hand to help her to her feet, then placed the cash into her palm. After slipping it into her beach-bag, she wrapped her arms around Davie's neck.

"Don't cry. It will work out, and you'll be fine," Davie whispered into her ear. Buddy nudged Audrey's hip with his nose. She released her embrace.

"I'm going to miss you so much, Buddy." Audrey knelt and hugged him too, then rubbed behind his ears.

"Let's get you set up down below. My bro should be here any minute, and we'll be pushing off." Janey led Audrey through the cabin to the deck below.

When Janey returned, she sat down once again across from Davie. She picked up her cigar from where she left it prized between an iron loop on the boat-rail used to tie rope.

"Some people are looking for her. If you encounter anyone on the trip, she would be safer if she stayed below."

"How much trouble is she in?"

"Enough." He pulled out another wad of cash and held it out to Janey.

"Nada, you know I'm a sucker for lost causes. Keep your money. I'll make sure the girl gets to Florida in one piece."

"Thanks, Janey. She's been through a lot." He patted her shoulder.

"I've known you to help sad sacks in trouble before, but this one seems important to you."

"She's special." Davie rubbed his eyes beneath his

sunglasses. "I'll see you next week?" He stood and returned the cash to his pocket. Buddy ran to his side, and Davie clipped him to the leash.

"For sure. We'll be here."

"Oh, and one more thing. I didn't want to say it in front of Audrey. She's nervous enough. The police are looking for her." Davie and Buddy stepped over to the edge of the boat.

"Hey, you know me. Folks don't call me, 'The Smuggler,' for nothing." Janey watched them cross over and walk back along the dock. Her brother Bruce appeared out of the crowd and hopped on the boat just before his sister retracted the gangway. Davie heard the boat's engines come to life. He stopped and bent down to rub Buddy behind the ears and to voice his thoughts. Buddy sat. "I hope the girl gets to where she can be safe. What do you think, Buddy? Will she make it?" Buddy wagged his tail and stood, and they continued back toward the pier's beginning and the shoreline.

⌘

When Claire went overboard, she splashed her way to shore on one of the smaller islands. She laid down on a picnic table until someone finally called the police to say a woman was sleeping in the park. She asked everyone who would listen to help her find her baby. The law thought they were searching for a lost child until they tracked down Josie in Florida.

Josie received the phone call from the constable in The Bahamas, boarded the next flight out, and then went straight to the police station. Claire lay on a bench, wrapped in a blanket, and sleeping in an interrogation room. Josie took her to the hospital, where they admitted her for dehydration and shock.

Eric awoke to Grandma Josie's concerned face looking down at him. His mind was confused and struggled to remember. When his head cleared, his memory returned, leaving him with many questions. Most importantly, "Where's Audrey?" He tried to pull himself up in bed but immediately felt intense pain and fell back, agony written across his face.

"You need to take it slow. Someone shot you, and you almost died." Grandma Josie poured some water into a cup and held it out to him. "Have a sip; it might make you feel better." Worry lined her forehead.

"I just need to know if Audrey's okay." He noticed Josie had been crying. "Tell me." He looked into her eyes. "Where is she?"

A sob hitched in her chest, and she turned away. After a few deep breaths, she said, "We don't know." Her shoulders sagged, and she turned to him once again. "The police called me three days ago because they found Claire at a park on one of the islands. She was in shock and is now being treated here at the hospital."

"Three days? I've been here for three days?" Eric's expression was incredulous.

"Yes, but the police have it all under control." She patted his hand. "You just get better."

"But you don't understand. I have to find Audrey." Eric shook noticeably. "She could be lost or hurt out there."

"A police officer is waiting outside to speak with you, so why don't you just start with what you remember?" "Do you think you're strong enough?" Eric squeezed his eyes tight and nodded.

A nurse breezed in. "So, you're awake. How do you feel?" She handed him a pill for pain.

"Is this going to make me sleep? I need to stay awake." He tried again to sit up. "I just need my clothes so I can get out of here to look for my wife." He touched the bandage on his chest and grimaced.

"The police are doing everything they can." The nurse gently pushed him back down. "What you need to do is follow my directions and not be so contrary if you want to get out of here any time soon." She took the cup of water from Josie.

Josie brought in the constable then sat on a chair in the corner.

"You can only stay for a couple of minutes." The nurse said with her hand on her broad hip. "Then you'll need to let him get some rest. Is that clear?" She handed Eric his water and directed him to swallow the pill.

Constable Weatherman nodded then sat down. He opened a notepad and encouraged Eric to take his time. Eric began by explaining how they went on a sailboat ride around the islands with a college professor. He needed the police to understand that he had lost his wife out in the ocean, and they needed to search for her. Constable Weatherman assured him they were looking on all of the islands, and he was confident they would find her. Claire had given a good description of the sailboat and the men involved. Television and radio news reports also alerted all islanders to be on the lookout for a young female tourist. He referred to his notes.

"We've been watching Mr. Bortnik for several months, and it's believed he's involved in some illegal trade of exotic artifacts. Do you know anything about that?"

"We had our suspicions. You know, the guy has a warehouse full of stuff." Eric adjusted himself and frowned at the pain.

"He's also thought to belong to a Russian Mafia gang operating out of his shop. We have a file of documented complaints from islanders who have been threatened or beaten up. He's a nasty guy." He looked up at Eric. "You do realize you're lucky to be alive? What were you doing out there anyway?"

"We should be home right now, but instead, we missed our flight. That shop owner, Mr. Bortnik, followed us to the airport, so we hid to get away from him, and our plane left without us."

"Why didn't you contact the police?"

"I guess we thought we could handle it. Professor Rodin showed up and invited us on a sailboat ride to see the fireworks."

The constable nodded while continuing to write notes into his notebook. "And the professor teaches at the college?"

"Yes, he teaches Russian History. The lady in the administration office directed us to his class. She said he might be able to help us."

"Uh-huh. Help you with what?"

"Well, we got a matryoshka doll at the Straw Market, and we wanted to find out more about it." Eric's eyelids drooped for a moment then opened wide. "Someone told us the matryoshka wasn't supposed to be sold here in The Bahamas. Is that true?"

"The dolls aren't illegal, but we do try to keep the selling of them to a minimum since many of the locals are superstitious. They believe the dolls have caused some unexplained deaths." He looked over at Josie, not sure how much she already knew. "The islanders have heard stories and are afraid."

"I need to get out of here so I can help you guys find my wife." Eric rubbed his hand across his face.

"We have everything covered, and we'll let you know as soon as we hear anything." He put his notepad into his shirt pocket and stood.

"But, isn't there something I can do to help?"

"If you know what's good for you, you'll stay here in the hospital and listen to the doctor. You won't help your wife by going out and getting yourself killed."

"Please find her. She must be so scared."

"We will. Try not to worry," The constable said. He turned to Josie, "Make sure the station has all your contact information."

When Constable Weatherman returned his focus to Eric for a couple more questions, Eric's eyes were closed, and he snored lightly.

"Can we finish in the hall?" Josie asked.

"Of course." He took Josie's elbow and ushered her out the door.

In the corridor outside Eric's room, Josie looked him in the eye. "Constable, please don't sugarcoat the situation for me. I heard a man was found dead on one of the islands, and everyone thinks his death is somehow related to my granddaughter's disappearance."

He breathed a sigh. "It is true, but we are still investigating the crime. We don't know if there is any link to what happened with your granddaughter and Eric."

"Crime? So, you at least know that much. Was he murdered?"

"I can't disclose any more at this time, but I promise to keep you informed as we go forward."

"Thank you. I'd appreciate that."

The constable shook Josie's hand. "I'll be in touch, but please call me if you need anything. Welcome to the islands." He left the hospital through the side exit, and Josie went to check on Claire.

⌘

Most of the information Eric shared with the police ended up being dead ends. The college informed them that Professor Rodin left for summer break with no forwarding address, and they didn't expect him to return until September. Constable Weatherman knew getting information from Russia would be difficult. He included in his notes to follow up with the college when the students returned for the fall semester. Mr. Bortnik's shop was locked up tight with a chain on the door. The police used bolt cutters to gain entry but found the store deserted. They did, however, seize thousands of dollars in stolen merchandise and artifacts from the warehouse.

Josie traveled back and forth from Claire's room to Eric's waiting for news of Audrey. The police searched the islands for her but had little to go on. Josie prayed for any new information, but she thought it best to take Claire home after a week of no leads.

Eric continued his stay in The Bahamas after being released from the hospital to ensure Audrey's name stayed in the news. He kept up with the police reports and shared her picture with locals and tourists alike. He vowed never to stop looking for her and blamed himself for how it all went down.

One afternoon Eric stood outside the Straw Market showing Audrey's picture to tourists from one of the cruise ships and caught sight of Davie and Buddy boarding a bus. Just as the doors closed, he slipped on at the back and sat where he hoped nobody noticed him. Most everyone disembarked at the last stop, which was the park entrance.

Tourists made their way across the street toward local shops while Davie and Buddy walked down the sidewalk and sat on a bench. Eric casually strolled by, pretending to be unaware of them. Buddy touched Eric's hand with his nose as he neared. Eric reached over to pet him.

"I was wondering when you were going to make your presence known," Davie said. Buddy's tail wagged, and he licked Eric's hand.

"I knew that sooner or later, I would see you around town," Eric said. "What do you know about what's happened to my wife?"

"Only what I already told the police." Davie raised his hand, palm up to Buddy. He returned to Davie's side and sat.

Eric collapsed onto the bench next to Davie and ran his hands through his oily hair. It was long and tangled. His wrinkled clothing hung on his thin frame. Then, he leaned forward with his forearms planted on his thighs. His hands fell between his knees, and he dropped his head.

"I know she isn't dead. Otherwise, I'd feel it." His bloodshot eyes looked up at Davie's reflective sunglasses only to see his own unshaven face. "Why aren't the police doing more to find her?"

"I believe they are doing everything they can." Then, he said, "I'm sorry this has happened." He tilted his head to one side. "Have you considered the notion that she can't make her presence known? Even to you?"

"What're you saying?" Eric sat up straight and grabbed Davie's wrist. "That she's purposely hiding?" Buddy stood.

"What I'm saying is," Davie twisted his wrist out of Eric's hand. "Maybe she's afraid." Davie held up his hand, and Buddy laid down.

"Of me?" Eric looked incredulous.

"Of course not, but if I'm not mistaken, you both are aware of what those guys from Russia are capable of." He leaned in. "Maybe she's trying to protect you."

Eric fell back into the bench once again. "But I don't need protection! I'm capable of taking care of myself."

"Go home, Eric. You won't find her here."

"I will never give up on her. She's alive, and I'm going to bring her home."

Davie grabbed Buddy's leash and stood. "Well, I wish you the best of luck, and I'm glad you're doing better now that they released you from the hospital." He turned and continued down the sidewalk with Buddy leading the way.

⌘

The doorbell rang for the third time.

"I'm coming, don't get your panties in a wad," Jenny called when she walked into the living room. Her Ohio apartment was small but tastefully decorated with colorful wall hangings and overstuffed pillows. She opened the front door to find an old lady standing in the hall. Her hair, so gray it was almost blue, and her eyes hid behind over-sized sunglasses. She wore a pale green polyester pantsuit, and she clutched an over-sized black purse.

"If you're the Avon Lady, I already owe most of my next paycheck for rent, so I'm sorry I can't afford to buy anything." She began to close the door, but the woman stuck her walking cane between the jam and stopped it from closing. Jenny looked back at the woman and put her hands on her thick hips. "Okay then, if not the Avon Lady, who do I owe the pleasure?"

"May I come in?" the old woman asked.

"Well, actually, I was in the middle of something," Jenny said. She tried again to close the door. She had been cleaning her parrot's cage, and he flew to his perch behind the sofa. Music was playing softly, and the bird tweeted along.

"I promise not to take too much of your time," the old woman said. She slipped through the opening and closed the door behind her with her face angled to the floor. Jenny bent over to get a better look. The woman took off the sunglasses, and her head rose slowly.

"Are you selling Scientology? I don't go in for all that space stuff."

The old lady pulled a few bobby pins from her head, then tugged her hair back from her forehead. Beneath the gray was dark hair held up in a tight bun.

"Oh, my God! Audrey? Is that you?" Jenny screamed.

"Oh my God, Audrey. Is that you?" The parrot squawked.

Audrey dropped the cane and wrapped her arms around her best friend. "Yes, it's me." She squeezed Jenny tightly.

Jenny pulled away. "Wait a minute. Everyone said you drowned in The Bahamas. I was so upset. What happened?"

Audrey peered up at her friend's expression and saw only love and concern. Her lip trembled, and her eyes filled with tears. She shook her head. "I don't know how to begin."

She wrapped her arms around Audrey's shoulders and guided her to the couch. "Here, come sit down."

"What happened? What happened?" The parrot mimicked.

"Would you shut up?" Jenny glared at the bird.

Audrey smiled wanly. "I guess I'll start at the beginning." She told Jenny all about her honeymoon, leaving nothing out.

"I'm so sorry to put you into the middle of this, but I had nobody else I could trust."

"There's nothing else to discuss. Of course, you're staying here. This was our plan all along." Jenny smiled and squeezed Audrey into a hug. Audrey looked at her friend with a blank stare. "Remember? We were always going to get a place together. So, you just stop being sorry. What friends are for?"

Izzy turned the page but found it blank, then thumbed through and found nothing more. She peered over at Audrey, whose face had slipped out of the blanket, but she was still asleep. Reaching over to return the diary to the carry-on bag, Izzy froze. Teresa had stopped at their row and said they would be landing soon. She asked that they leave the blankets in their seats. Audrey stirred. Izzy leaned back into her seat and looked through her backpack.

"What are you doing?" Audrey said when she noticed her journal sitting on the seat between them.

CHAPTER TEN

No Turning Back

Izzy slid her backpack beneath the seat in front of her. "Your journal fell on the floor, so I was trying to return it to your carry-on bag." Her eyelids fluttered. "I just didn't want you to forget it on the plane."

Audrey's eyebrow arched up. "Is that so?"

"Okay, I have to be honest. I did take a peek at the journal." Izzy smiled sweetly.

Audrey's eyes flashed, and her nostrils flared. When she found her voice, she said, "What an invasion of privacy." She shook her head and returned the journal to the pocket of her bag. That's all I need is to have some crazy girl snooping into my past, she thought.

"Hey, don't worry. Your secret is safe with me." Izzy touched Audrey's arm lightly to get her attention. "I'm serious. So, what's your plan?"

"What do you mean?" Audrey stared at her travel mate. "What's it to you, anyway?"

"I'm just wondering why after all these years of hiding,

you're flying to Moscow."

Audrey cocked her head. "Well, I'm going to return the thing to where it belongs. Or, at least where it can be cared for and protected."

"So, that should take care of it?" Izzy asked, returning Audrey's stare.

"I think so, yes. It's something I have to do."

"You've got to be kidding!" Izzy raised her voice.

Audrey sat up and scanned the cabin to see if anyone heard. Everyone appeared relaxed and absorbed in their movies, computers, or books. The little boy behind them played with his toys, making airplane noises.

"Would you keep it down? I don't want the whole world to know my little story."

"That wasn't just a little story. If what you wrote is true and I believe you at least think it's true, you should have gone to the police." Izzy shook her head. "Instead, you lived the rest of your life, afraid to go out in public? You even gave up your husband!" Izzy threw up her hands.

"You know nothing about it or what it means to be in fear for your life," Audrey whispered.

"Excuse me? Growing up in Russia isn't exactly the safest place for a woman. I had to learn to be tough. I've been robbed at knifepoint three times and nearly raped. Luckily, that one was a stupid, fat drunk."

"I guess we grew up in different environments." Her face tightened.

"Yes we did, so don't you see, you can't take it back to Moscow."

"Why not? They know how to protect it better than I do."

"But aren't you supposed to keep it safe from them? The bad guys?" Izzy made finger quotation marks. "Weren't those guys originally from Russia?"

"Again, you know nothing about it. You read my private journal without asking."

"Awe, come on. What's the big deal? I guess I should apologize."

"Look, it was just a story, anyway. Forget it."

"Okay, but you can forgive me, right?"

Audrey looked out the window with nothing more to say.

⌘

The plane landed in Moscow as the sun peeked over Red Square. Izzy followed Audrey off the flight but almost lost her while waiting to get her guitar. She wanted to apologize once again for reading the journal, but Audrey remained cool. Neither said much until they were through customs at the airport.

"I can show you to the luggage retrieval area." Izzy fell in step behind Audrey, who pulled her carry-on behind her.

"It's not necessary. I just brought this one case because I have another flight in the morning back home."

"Wow! Quick trip."

Audrey stopped and turned to face Izzy, causing them to collide.

"Oops, sorry," Izzy said, backing up.

"Well, nice meeting you." Audrey stuck out her hand. "Good luck with your recording contract."

Izzy stared at her, then reluctantly shook it. "Would you like a lift? I have my car here in the lot, and I know my way around town."

"That's alright. I'm sure I can find my way. I'll just call a cab."

"They have Uber here," Izzy said, trying to be helpful.

"Never got the hang of all the phone app things. A cab will

work just fine."

She stepped outside into a chilly April morning. A taxi pulled up beside the stand and waited for his next fare.

"See, here's one now." Audrey rolled her luggage to the stand.

The snow from last week's storm lay packed along the edges of the street with an opening cut out where the cabs loaded and unloaded fares. The driver rolled down the passenger side window and leaned over to speak to Audrey.

"Тебе нужна поездка? (You need a ride?)." The driver was a young man, possibly a college student.

"Do you know where the Mother of Our Savior Church is on Krasnogvardejski Boulevard?" Audrey said in English to the driver. He nodded and jumped out, then vaulted over the trunk area and opened the rear passenger side door. "Прямо по этому пути (Right this way), the driver said and used hand gestures to Audrey into the back seat. She turned and waved to Izzy before climbing inside.

Izzy stood on the sidewalk and watched the cab pull away into the early morning traffic. She turned and headed back into the airport, where she noticed an older gentleman fumbling with his luggage. He was tall, wearing a blue suit on his slender frame, and sported a thin gray mustache. His hair looked wet and bottle dyed jet black with a receding hairline. In his hand was a fedora. When their eyes connected, he tipped his hat to her, then put it on his head. She nodded back, then went through the exit doors to the parking garage.

⌘

Over the years, Audrey kept a low profile and worked odd jobs, such as gardening and animal sitting, to support herself. She stayed away from computers, never having any connection to social media. Finally, her curiosity consumed her, and with Jenny's help, she went on the Internet to look for information about the matryoshka. Audrey finally came across an article that included information about maternal nesting dolls after searching for many months. The origin and author were unlisted. The writer included information concerning a special matryoshka bequeathed to the Mother of Our Savior Church around the turn of the 18th century by the wife of an old Russian doll maker from the Abramtsevo estate in Moscow.

The wife claimed mysterious forces within the government found a way to poison her husband. No one believed her because she hadn't any proof. For most of his life, the artist was happy and healthy, never needing to see a doctor. But, after weeks of stomach complications, he hemorrhaged and died a slow and painful death. Before his demise, he told his wife of a secret doll kept hidden in the shop. It held secrets of high power, and if anything happened to him, she would need to keep it safe. During his final days, he made her promise that if she couldn't keep it, she would give it to the church and never allow the Kremlin near it.

At that time, the priest doubted there was truth to the story the wife told but decided to help by placing it in a stone tomb beneath the altar floor. There it stayed until the church burned to the ground five years later. The priest passed the matryoshka off to one of the practicing nuns and told her to hide it at her next convent while they rebuilt, Mother of Our Savior. This nun, being young and curious, figured out how to open the doll. When she realized its power, she left Moscow, taking it with her. The Kremlin learned of the general whereabouts of the matryoshka and dispatched a small army to find it. The nun then handed it off to another relative before the military caught up with her. When interrogated, she claimed to know nothing. Without more to go on, they eventually released her. Years passed without a word. Then, shortly after the Russian Revolution began, a group of fortune hunters stormed the Golitsyn estate, where rumors claimed the doll resided. They were too late. The matryoshka sailed to the United States.

The article listed some of the rumored matryoshka sightings, but its exact whereabouts remained unknown. Many fortune hunters claimed to have found the real doll only to learn all were forgeries. The rebuilt Mother of Our Savior stands today and is in operation on its original site. The priest, Father Matthew, runs charity programs for the poor out of the church. Audrey tracked him down.

Father Matthew had no prior knowledge of the matryoshka but promised to research the church's historical ledger. He called Audrey back a week later and told her he did indeed find where someone donated the special nesting doll to the church, but the records stopped there.

He didn't think it was safe to bring the doll back to Russia because the church was under scrutiny. Some government officials wanted to close it down because it was said to be a haven for homeless immigrants and drug trafficking. But Audrey was persuasive. In the end, he agreed to accept it and would look for a safer, more appropriate location for it. After getting her passport, she made plans to fly to Moscow.

⌘

Audrey rode in the back of the taxi in silence. The heavy traffic gave her time to think. *If I can pass this off to Father Mathew, it will no longer be my problem. I'll never have to worry about hiding again.* After thirty minutes on the meter, the driver pulled the cab to the curb.

She paid him, stepped out, and walked up the sidewalk

avoiding the iced snow piled along the street. The cab pulled away, leaving her alone. She climbed the three wooden steps to the large double doors and pulled on the handle. Someone had locked it from the inside, but a doorbell hung askew on the wall. She pushed it with her index finger several times and heard it buzz within. No answer. Maybe it's too early, she thought. Hmm, I wonder if there is a sign showing hours of operation. She looked around. Without luck, she sat down on the top step and pulled out a map. Maybe I'm not at the right church, she thought.

A small red Renault drove up and parked on the other side of the street. The driver's side door opened, and Izzy stepped out. Audrey's eyes narrowed, then focused more intently on the map. Izzy sauntered up the steps and sat beside her.

"Is this where you are supposed to drop off the matryoshka?" Izzy said.

"Maybe. How did you find me?"

"I heard you tell the cab driver where you wanted to go." Izzy looked up at the building behind them. "You know, this church is only used for the homeless now." Her eyes cut over to Audrey. "The government shut it down last week."

"What? Why?" Audrey folded the map and stood. She tried the door again, then turned and peered at Izzy, who stared out across the street. Her dark hair, now mostly covered with a gray woolen hat.

"Maybe the cab driver was mistaken and dropped me off at the wrong church," Audrey said.

"No, this is the right church."

"Well then, where's Father Matthew? He told me this was his parish, and he would meet me here."

"You mean the old guy who ran this place? They took him to jail. It was on the news and everything."

"But that doesn't make sense. Father Mathew is not a criminal!" Audrey searched for the truth on Izzy's face. "Is he?"

Izzy's head cocked to one side, and her shoulder raised for a moment. "They said it had to do with all the homeless people hanging out here. The junkies were getting their fixes here or something like that." Izzy took out a cigarette and lit it. "I think it's a bunch of nonsense, you know. Trumped up charges so they could close the place down." She blew smoke up into the sky. "Who knows, maybe they'll let us open a club here."

"What? It's a church!" Audrey said.

"You don't think we are a band with good principles? We love God."

Audrey drummed her fingers on the railing. This trip isn't working out the way I planned, she thought. Her eyes scanned the neighborhood for the first time and noticed how run down it appeared. A man slept on a bench about fifty feet further down the sidewalk from them. A woman across the street slowly pushed a cart full of plastic bags and jugs to the corner. There was an old Asian grocery across the street with bars on its windows where Izzy parked her car. Audrey noticed all the buildings had bars on the windows and the doors too.

"I can't believe this. I made this trip for nothing."

"That's possible. Can I give you a lift somewhere?" Izzy stood and wiped the wetness from her bottom and jacket trim.

Audrey sighed, then haltingly moved down the steps. She backed off the curb and into the road. Looking up, she saw the wooden building with its forlorn cross atop a peaked blue roof. Emptiness and neglect were evident. How did I miss that when I first arrived? A car horn honked, startling her. She moved out of the narrow street, allowing the car to pass.

⌘

Audrey's shoulders slumped. "A lift would be nice, I guess. Thank you." She put her hands in her coat pockets and walked back up the steps to grab her carry-on luggage. "He's in jail, you say?"

"That's what I heard on the news, but maybe he's out by now." Izzy walked to her car and opened the driver's side door.

Audrey went around to the passenger side and set her case onto the sidewalk to take off her coat. When she reached for the car door handle, a teenager on a skateboard grabbed her carry-on as he rolled past. Audrey turned to see him continuing down the street. He stopped about thirty feet in front of them and looked closely at its latch to figure out how it opened. A tiny padlock held the zipper.

"Hey! That's my luggage!" Audrey shouted. She ran after him. The kid grinned at her, then shook the case to judge the weight. He began to skateboard once again down the sidewalk, staying just out of her reach. She soon had to stop to catch her breath and leaned forward with her hands on her knees. She looked up to see Izzy running after the kid in a full sprint. He rode at his leisurely pace, not noticing her.

She dove for him, knocking him to the concrete. He wrestled away from her and to his feet. Audrey's carry-on skittered into the road. He ran for it, but Audrey reached it first. She snatched it up and held it to her chest. He lunged at her, but she backed away. Izzy stepped between them with a switchblade knife opened in her hand. She waved it at him and dared him to attack her. He looked like he was going to, but in the end, he grabbed his skateboard and took off skating to the corner.

A taxi with darkened windows waited there with its engine running. The exhaust plumed into the chilly air. As the kid rounded the corner, the cab made a full turn in the middle of the street and followed him out of sight.

Izzy closed the knife and put it back into her pocket. Without a word, she hiked back to her car. Audrey could only watch her. Who is this woman? She thought.

The man who slept on the bench minutes before sat up and rubbed his face. The blinds on the Asian grocery front window snapped shut. Audrey hurried back and got into the passenger seat, relieved to be leaving the neighborhood.

"Where are you staying?" Izzy asked, steering the Red Renault away from the curb.

Twenty minutes later, they pulled up in front of the Marriott in downtown Moscow.

"I can't thank you enough for your help," Audrey said. "You certainly know how to take care of yourself." She gathered her coat and carry-on bag, then grabbed the passenger handle. "That was a horrible part of town, right?"

"You should consider carrying a weapon during your stay in the city. Here, take this." Izzy dug into her purse and pulled out a pink box about the size of a pack of cigarettes and held it out to Audrey.

She stared at it. "Uh, what's that?"

"Look, if anyone comes near you, just push this button." Izzy pushed it, and a thin electrical charge arched between two silver points.

Audrey bit her lip and frowned. "Oh no, I couldn't."

"Are you sure? Ladies can't be too careful here in Moscow."

"I'd end up zapping myself." Audrey opened the door to get out but stopped. "You know, I'm returning to the U.S. tomorrow, but I'll be here all day. How would you feel about joining me for dinner? I hear they have a nice French restaurant right here in the hotel."

Izzy thought for a moment then said, "I'm supposed to meet my boyfriend."

"Oh, I'm sorry. Of course, you have a boyfriend waiting for you. That's okay. You're a very nice girl, and I'm pleased I met you." Audrey climbed out and extended the handle to her bag, then put her coat under her arm. "Oh, and that story?" Audrey smiled. "Just a story." She closed the door and started walking toward the entrance.

"Audrey, wait," Izzy said through the passenger side window. "My boyfriend will enjoy a night with his friends. What time?"

"You're sure?" She came back and leaned in the window. "You've helped enough without having to babysit an old woman."

"It will make Andrew want me more." Izzy laughed and pulled out a piece of paper from her glove box. She wrote her name and number on it and handed it over.

"Get settled in, see a few of the popular sights in town, then call me. I can be here in thirty minutes." She grabbed the Taser and once again held it out. "Here, you'll need this. You can return it to me tonight."

Audrey accepted it this time, turned it over in her hands, and then dropped it into her coat pocket. "Thanks, I will. See you tonight." She backed away from the curb and watched the red Renault slip into traffic.

⌘

Safely checked into her room, Audrey sat on the bed against some pillows. She pulled the matryoshka from her travel case and turned it over in her hands to gaze into the young mother's eyes.

"So, what now?" She asked as if waiting for an answer. "I suppose I'll take you home with me and look for another town to disappear into."

The years had been kind to the matryoshka. It hadn't aged a day. "You win the award for the longest pregnancy." Audrey laughed. "I once thought I looked like you."

She glanced around the room and noticed her reflection in the mirror. Wrinkles around her eyes and mouth appeared as deep shadows across her face. She thought about all she'd lost since taking possession of the nesting doll. Her life with Eric. Grandma Josie. She missed Palm Glade and all of its charm. She even missed her mother.

Audrey did contact her grandmother a few months after she went missing and made her swear not to tell anyone she was alive. Josie was heartbroken to learn Audrey wasn't coming home or that she couldn't let Eric know. She'd keep the secret because she knew Eric well. He'd never stop looking.

"You have to keep this a secret until I can figure out what to do," Audrey said. "I'll be home soon. I promise."

Josie hated to think of her granddaughter scared and alone somewhere in the world. She prayed for Audrey to return home where she belonged. She didn't understand why it was crucial for her granddaughter to stay away but didn't question it.

Eric's dad learned he had a heart condition and needed his son to help out in the auto shop more than ever. After his encounter with David Sanders, Eric returned to Florida. Every couple of weeks, he boarded a plane to The Bahamas and resumed his search of the islands without fail.

One evening when Eric closed the auto shop for the night, he carried two full trash receptacles to the side of the building and dropped the garbage into the cans for pick-up. His mind raced over the conversation he had with Constable Weatherman earlier in the day and mentally ticked off details that he needed to accomplish before catching another flight to Nassau.

"We found a woman's body washed up on one of the smaller islands," Constable Weatherman said. "Maybe it's not Audrey, but I believe it would be worth a trip over to take a look."

Eric frowned as he gripped the telephone receiver. Audrey would never drown, he thought. It can't be her. The constable described the woman as in her early twenties with long dark hair.

I'll just fly over and check it out, but I know it isn't her, he told himself. His brain thought logically, but his stomach was in knots. He slammed the galvanized lid onto the trash can, and it echoed down the mostly quiet street. A few cars passed.

Whoever the woman is, I'm sorry for her family, but it's not Audrey. He shook his head. I just don't understand why she hasn't come home yet. I think the Russians must have kidnapped her to get to that stupid doll. Maybe I should be flying to Russia instead. He pondered this.

Then he sensed someone behind him. The hairs on the back of his neck stood up. When he turned, he almost fell back. A few feet away in the dark stood a frail old lady. She leaned on a cane and watched him from beneath a large oak.

"Oh, I'm sorry." Eric laughed and looked around for more people hiding beneath trees. His gaze returned to the woman who stayed put without speaking a word.

"We're closed, but we'll reopen at 9:00 tomorrow morning." Eric searched his memory without luck for an older person dropping off a car. He leaned closer, not taking a step for fear of making her nervous, but he wanted a better look. Her large sunglasses prevented him from seeing much. Maybe she's blind or something, he thought. He moved slowly toward her, but she backed away again into the shadows.

"Wait. It's okay. Are you lost?" He raised a calming hand to her. "Do you need a ride? Can I call you a cab?"

The old lady turned to hobble down the sidewalk, but he

grabbed her by the arm. She froze, then slowly faced him. She looked up into his eyes and took off the sunglasses. Eric shuddered.

"Oh, my God! You're here!" He wrapped his arms around her and lifted her. He spun her around before returning her to the ground.

"I'm so sorry! I never meant to hurt you."

"Shh, don't talk," Eric said. "Just kiss me."

Audrey dropped the cane, allowing it to clatter onto the sidewalk, and reached up to hold his face in her hands. He leaned into her hungrily, and they kissed long and hard. She rocked back on her heels and lost her balance, but he held her up. Light-headed, she giggled.

He scooped her up like a child and carried her into the shop. He sat her on a chair in the waiting area, then went back and locked the door. He turned out the interior lights so nobody from outside could see them. Only a street light shined in through the window. Then he knelt in front of her, but her attention focused on the floor. He pulled her chin up so he could look into her eyes. Tears rolled down her cheeks.

"Oh, baby, don't cry. You're home now. Everything will be alright. I promise." He pulled the gray wig from her head, exposing her dark hair held in a tight bun. "It must have been terrible for you, having to hide, but you're safe now. Nobody will hurt you ever again."

She gazed into his eyes. "Eric, I can't stay. I just came to ask you to stop looking for me."

"What? Of course, you can stay. Palm Glade is your home. You're my wife. Your life is here with me."

Audrey gently put her fingers to his lips so he would stop and listen. Then she held his face in her hands and directed him to look at her chest. He became very still.

"Eric, listen to me. You mustn't go to The Bahamas to search for me anymore. Now you know, I'm no longer there."

Eric's eyes focused on the bluestone that swirled against Audrey's chest. His mouth was slack, and his face appeared drained. He tried to pull away, but she held him firmly in her hands.

"You must forget me. Do you hear?" Audrey sobbed harder. "Don't come looking for me anymore. You need to go on with your life without me."

"No."

"Yes." She put her hands on his chest. "Eric, I'm leaving now. Don't follow me."

"No!"

"I love you, baby." Audrey slid out of the chair while he stayed on his knees, looking at the empty seat. She covered her dark hair once again with the gray wig and went out the door. She grabbed the cane and hurried to the cab waiting for her at the end of the street.

Eric stopped traveling to the islands, but he never stopped waiting for Audrey to walk in the door. Every time the phone rang, he thought it could be her or information about her.

After high school, Tabitha, Eric's life-long friend, trained to be a nurse and returned to Palm Glade to work at the hospital. She never made it to the New York Philharmonic, but she played with the local orchestra.

Audrey asked Grandma Josie to legally declare her dead to help Eric move on with his life. Eric's father died in January 1982, and Tabitha was there to comfort him. They eventually married and had two beautiful daughters. Josie sent Audrey pictures of the children.

Claire was never quite herself after her trip to The Bahamas. She continued to drink and eventually lost her home. Most of the time, she could be found at the Highway Inn retelling her story of how her daughter was at the bottom of the Atlantic Ocean. Many took pity on her and bought her drinks or a meal. She refused to move in with Grandma Josie but would stop by from time to time to ask for money or stay the night. The local police arrested her in 2000 for public indecency. Grandma Josie eventually convinced her to go to Green Briar, an assisted living facility. Grandma Josie died in 2004 and willed her house to Audrey in the event she returned from the dead. Josie's estate continued to pay the taxes on the property and Claire's stay at Green Briar.

⌘

Audrey set the matryoshka on the bed beside her, then rubbed her temples. I must have a mean case of jet lag, she thought. After hiding the nesting doll, she took the elevator down to the hotel's front desk. An elderly gentleman stood at the counter, peering at a computer screen. Audrey crossed the lobby and stood in front of him. When he looked up, she asked, "Is there a pharmacy close to the hotel?"

The man gazed at her over reading glasses and said, "English?"

"Oh, yes. I apologize." It looks like I'm not any different than all the other Americans who think everyone speaks English, she chastised herself.

He held a finger in the air, then turned on his heel. Thirty seconds later, he reappeared with a young girl of maybe fourteen in tow. He pushed her to the counter then gestured for Audrey to speak. The girl reminded her of Tabitha with a face covered in freckles and short red hair. The girl rolled her blue eyes at the man, then smiled at Audrey.

"Can I help you?" She asked.

"You speak English." Audrey's eyes crinkled at the corners into a smile.

"I do!" She pointed her thumb over her shoulder. "My grandfather doesn't, though." She tried to brush his hand off her shoulder as she spoke, but every time she succeeded, it returned. She glared at him, then whispered in Russian over her shoulder. He responded by backing away.

"Let's move down a little." The girl pointed to a spot at the other end of the counter and beckoned Audrey to join her. Her grandfather returned to his computer.

"I'm looking for a pharmacy, but I don't want to stray too far from the hotel," Audrey said.

"Sure. Turn left when you go out the door, and it's three blocks down. You can't miss it. You don't even have to cross the street." The girl turned and took a few steps back toward the room she was summoned from but stopped and returned. "If you pass a restaurant with a lobster on the roof, you've gone too far."

"Thanks. I'll keep that in mind." Audrey laughed at the visual image. "You speak English very well." She realized the girl was older than she first thought, maybe eighteen or nineteen.

"I grew up in New York with my mom." She smiled with a mouth full of braces. "I visit my grandparents for a few weeks a year, usually during Spring Break. Papa likes me to help out with the customers who don't speak the language."

"You get a lot of English speakers here?"

"Not really, but I speak seven languages."

"That's impressive. Your family must be proud of you. Well, thanks for your help." Audrey turned and strolled to the door.

"You're welcome. Ask for Shirley if you need anything else, and I'll come out. I'm studying for finals, but I'm glad to help."

⌘

The pharmacy sign illuminated with a green cross, and a picture of a bowl and pestle made it easy for Audrey to locate. With the pharmacy clerk's assistance, she managed to buy a pain reliever and took two right away. Instead of leaving the store immediately, she perused the aisles, realizing it would be her only chance to learn anything about Russian culture. The products lining the shelves resembled drugstore merchandise in America, except for the names. Row upon row of products displayed the language of Moscow. Audrey considered learning to speak Russian at one time. Now she wished she did. Her stomach rumbled, and Audrey realized her last meal consisted of snacks the previous day. This little trip has been more than enough culture for me, she thought. I better head back to the hotel and see if I need to make reservations for dinner.

A brisk wind blew through the door when Audrey stepped outside, causing her to shiver. The sun moved toward the horizon, and she recalled Izzy's warning about being alone in the downtown area after dark. The dwindling light made the streets and buildings grow shadows in darkened corners. Everything looked different, and she became unsure which way to go. An uncomfortable tension set into her neck, and she raised her shoulders to loosen the stiffness. I'll just look for familiar things, she thought. I know I didn't cross the main street, so if I don't see anything I recognize, I'll turn around. After walking for another five minutes, she noticed the restaurant with the lobster and remembered what the girl at the hotel said.

"My brain certainly isn't what it used to be." She chuckled to herself out loud. A young man in a crisp suit and tie looked at her as if she were crazy, then continued, keeping his brisk pace. Well, the younger generation seems to be the same everywhere, she thought.

She turned around to retrace her steps. Then, her eyes caught the tail of a blue jacket flitting behind the corner of one of the taller buildings. She stopped. People milled about while she stood anchored to the sidewalk. The streets bustled with Muscovites leaving work. Some gave her stern glances, but most continued on their way. Audrey's mind raced but refused to allow confusion to absorb her sanity. Taking another glimpse behind to collect her wits, she steeled herself to put one foot in front of the other. When the corner lay two steps before her, she stopped and leaned forward to peek around the side. There in the shadows, a lone man offloaded crates from a delivery truck. With nobody in a blue suit in sight, she hurried across the alleyway.

Reaching the pharmacy once again, she slipped inside. The teenage clerk who helped her before wasn't in any hurry to break away from his phone. She stood back from the window and searched the people passing in both directions—no blue jacket. After several minutes, she shook her head. I need to stop imagining things. When I get home, I'll write my memoirs. 'Lost in Moscow.' Even if Bortnik followed me here, he isn't going to attack me with other people around. Get a grip, old lady. She waited another five minutes to be sure and allowed herself to breathe when he didn't appear. I'm just hyper-vigilant because I'm so far from home, she thought. Still, in case I didn't imagine it, I need a plan.

Jenny tried unsuccessfully to convince Audrey to take karate or at least a self-defense course not long after moving in. After killing the man in The Bahamas, Audrey knew she wouldn't be any good at it. Just the thought of hurting another person, even in self-defense, made her sick. The years she spent in hiding taught her to look for ways out of any situation because the day she let down her guard would be the day they'd catch her.

The pharmacy occupied a corner, so she decided on a

different route back to the hotel. Surmising that most downtown areas consist of city blocks, she'd walk down that road to the next corner behind the pharmacy. If she's correct, she will approach the hotel from behind. Standing at the intersection, she peered in all directions. The Moscow evening came to life with people carrying on conversations and heading to dinner destinations. She darted down the sidewalk.

Still feeling vulnerable, she turned several times to see if anyone followed. After two city blocks, she spied the hotel over the rooftops of the lower buildings. Mixed relief coursed through her. She turned left at the next intersection to find herself on the backside of the hotel. A couple of kitchen workers smoked cigarettes on the loading docks. Yes! She thought. I made it.

She rushed around to the front, but someone grabbed her wrist before she dashed to the entrance. She was jerked back around to the side of the building and pushed against the wall. Her head hit the red brick, blurring her vision. Pinning her shoulders with his hands, he leaned in close to her ear. When the barrette holding her hair broke, strands fell into her face. She looked up into Mr. Bortnik's furious glare. He held her stiffly, and although he appeared much older, he was quite forceful. Terror penetrated her brain, and she felt her knees crumbling.

"Little Miss Audrey dares to come to Russia. How dumb are we?" His voice sounded raspy, and he smelled of stale cologne mixed with cigarettes. "Did you think you could come here and escape us?"

"You're hurting me!" Audrey's chin trembled. She struggled against his hands and cringed when his tongue licked her cheek. "Ugh! Please, let me go." Her voice rose barely above a whisper. He laughed. Do something, Audrey, or you'll die here far from home, she thought. Her chin came up, and her nostrils flared. "I'm going to scream!"

An older couple walked toward them, deep in conversation. Audrey called out to them. "Help! Please help me! Call the police."

The woman gasped, covering her mouth with her hand when she realized the situation playing out in front of them was more than a lover's spat. The man grabbed the woman's arm and pulled her back in the opposite direction, and they hurried across the street.

"See? No one will help you." Mr. Bortnik's face turned to the sky, and he laughed again out loud. He didn't seem to care if anyone heard him. "Are you that naive? You aren't in America anymore!" He squeezed her chin between his fingers and yanked it up so she would look into his eyes. "You are in Russia!" Spittle shot from his mouth onto her face, and she squeezed her eyes shut. "We do things differently here." He pulled out a knife with a curved blade and held it to her neck. "Now. I need the matryoshka." Audrey's head hit the wall again as he shook her. "You've held onto it for too long." He pressed the knife to her neck, and she felt it slice into her flesh. Her face turned ashen, and her vision was darkening. Her eyes rolled to the corner of the building.

Bortnik noticed a shadow on the wall next to him, but too late. His bladder emptied before he felt the bolt of electricity flow through him. His teeth clacked together while dropping to his knees on the sidewalk, then his body jerked and spasmed at odd angles. He fell forward, hitting his jaw on the concrete. He attempted to get up once but fell back down and floundered like a fish out of water. His head bounced rhythmically, and blood dripped from his mouth where he'd bit his tongue. Audrey bent forward to calm her upset stomach and watched him writhe in agony. She shuddered violently then looked into Shirley's eyes.

Shirley, from the hotel desk, shook a silver taser at Audrey and smiled. "I watched this creep follow you, and when you didn't come right back, I thought I would take a quick look around." She wrapped her arm around Audrey's waist and walked her to the front of the hotel. "I was afraid you might've gotten lost, but I knew you couldn't be too far."

"I don't know how to thank you," Audrey said once they were inside the safety of the lobby. She reached into her coat pocket and pulled out the pink taser Izzy let her borrow.

"They only work if you use them." Shirley chuckled. "Hey, we American girls got to stick together, right?" She assisted Audrey up to her room.

⌘

After getting a few more pain pills in her, Audrey called Izzy then took a shower. A heavy knock on the hotel room door caught her off guard. She quickly toweled dry and wrapped herself in the hotel terry cloth bathrobe. At the door, she looked through the peephole.

Izzy wore a violet form-fitting cocktail dress. The over-sized bomber jacket she had on that morning was draped over her shoulder, held by two fingers.

"Come in." Audrey stepped aside so that Izzy could enter.

Izzy paused a moment then sidestepped Audrey while keeping an eye on her. She noticed Audrey's eyes were red. "When I stopped at the hotel desk, they said someone attacked you." Izzy looked closely at Audrey's face. "Are you alright?"

"I'm fine."

"Was it that stupid kid again?"

"No. It seems I was followed from the United States by Mr. Bortnik." Audrey rubbed her hair dry with a towel. "You remember reading about him in my journal?"

"I do. Now that I think about it, I did see a strange man watching us this morning at the airport. I didn't think much of it because I get old men flirting with me all the time." She stood a little straighter. "It comes with being famous." She winked. "Hey, if you don't feel like having dinner, we can cancel. I'd understand."

"Actually, I'm pretty hungry. But there are a few things I want to discuss with you first." She grabbed a pair of black slacks and a gray sweater from the closet. "See if there's something on T.V., and I'll be out in a few minutes." Audrey closed herself in the bathroom.

"No rush, we can head down when you're ready. At least we don't have to leave the hotel." Izzy's hair was loose, and the soft waves curled around her face. Opened toed high-heels made her appear inches taller. While Audrey dressed, Izzy looked around the room. Nothing under the bed or in the closet. She opened each drawer. Empty.

When Audrey came out, Izzy was sitting in a chair and sipping from a bottle of water with her legs crossed. Audrey walked to the closet and grabbed a pair of low black heels while Izzy followed her with her eyes. Audrey's ears wore soft white pearls, and although her hair had thinned some over the years, it was still quite beautiful. The gray streaks made it appear to shimmer in the muted light from the nightstand lamp. When she turned, Izzy noticed there a trace of blood.

"Is your head bleeding? I think you have blood on the back of your head."

"A lump too. It only hurts when I touch it." Audrey smiled wanly.

"You look nice, anyway."

"Ha! Thanks, I'll take the compliment." Audrey sat down on the bed to slip on the heels, and her mind drifted.

Izzy stood and moved to the vanity mirror. She tugged the hem of her dress down, then took a tube of lipstick out, applying it to her lips. "You okay?" Izzy asked. "You look a million miles away."

"Sorry, I didn't mean to stare. It's just that." She thought for a moment. "You know what? We have time." Audrey went to the closet and pushed her coat to one side to reveal a small safe. She keyed in a set of numbers, and the door popped open. She took out the matryoshka and held it in her hands.

"So, that's where you hid it."

Audrey cocked her head to one side. "Were you snooping?"

"I can't lie, yes I was. I wanted to get a look at the thing that would bring you halfway across the world only to be attacked not once, but twice."

Audrey sighed. She was so tired of running and hiding. It's time for this to end, she thought. "I want to show you something, but I just don't know if I can trust you."

"You know, I could've taken it from you today at the church, but I didn't."

"That's true." Audrey stared at Izzy. "Just who are you?"

"Would it make a difference?" She smiled. "It's just the two of us here. I could take it from you now if I wanted to."

"I've kept it safe for so long. I owe it to those who came before me to keep it out of the wrong hands. I would fight you."

Izzy laughed. "You mean the way you fought off Mr. Bortnik?" She shook her head. Then she said, "What if I told you I am aware of a claim of ownership of the matryoshka. If it's authentic, of course."

"Oh? Who?"

"Remember how I told you that I work in insurance? Let's just say, I work in stolen antiquities."

"What does that even mean? Who do you work for?"

"Does it matter?"

"Absolutely! The one thing that everyone drilled into my brain was that I had to keep it out of the wrong hands of,"

"Those who would use it for evil." Izzy completed the statement. Yes, yes. I know all that from your story." Izzy returned to the chair. "Okay, listen. I'm going to be straight with you. About a year ago, someone discretely hired me to follow the doll, not to take it. Just follow it. The only information I received about you was your name. I didn't even know where you were until you applied for a passport. But, after reading what you wrote in your journal, I became curious."

"You need proof." Audrey dropped the hand with the matryoshka to her side. Her shoulders sagged. "Does your employer work for the Russian government?"

"Not at all. If it makes you feel any better, I work for a little insurance company hired by the Abramtsevo estate."

"The estate of the original doll maker?"

Izzy nodded. "Not the government."

Audrey thought for a moment, then returned to sit on the bed. She used her thumb to release the catch. The doll's pregnant belly flipped open with ease. She pulled on the tiny red silk blanket, and the baby emerged. Then she opened it to reveal the stone attached to the gold chain and held it up for Izzy to see. Izzy sat across from her and held out her hand. Audrey moved it out of reach.

"This thing contains some sort of power." Audrey held it out to Izzy again and let the stone land on Izzy's open palm. The brown swirls appeared to shimmer deep within the stone.

"So, you kept it all these years?" Izzy stared down at it. "Did you ever use it to get something you wanted?"

"Like?"

"I don't know, like a new car?"

Audrey laughed, "I was too afraid even to take it out. It's been decades since I last opened it. Luckily, the doll has a very tight seal."

"I find it hard to believe that you never used it." Izzy narrowed her eyes.

"Okay, I did use it once. I needed Eric to stop looking for me." Audrey swallowed hard and looked away.

Izzy went to the vanity, held it up to her chest, and admired herself with it in the mirror. "You could have used it to do good things." Her eyes met Audrey's through the mirror's reflection.

"I had already lost my husband and family because of it." Anger seeped into her voice. The last thing she needed was someone second-guessing her decision to do nothing other than to hide it. She glared at Izzy, then her eyes softened. She stepped over and stood next to her. "But for curiosity's sake, what kind of good things?"

"I don't know. Maybe be a superhero or something." Izzy laughed nervously.

"Yeah?" Audrey smiled. She wiggled her eyebrows. "Someone like Wonder Woman?"

"Maybe." Izzy's posture became rigid.

"Maybe the next Keeper could use it to do good things." Audrey turned and looked into Izzy's eyes. "Heaven knows, the world needs a real superhero."

"That someone would need to be brave."

"Yes, someone who can take care of herself," Audrey added.

"Maybe use it to help people who are just trying to find a place where they can live their lives in peace and safety." Izzy's voice became a whisper. "They could use a superhero."

"Here, try it on." Audrey took the necklace and clasped it around Izzy's neck from behind.

"There, let's see it."

Izzy turned to face her. They held hands as the brown swirls began to circulate within the stone. They looked into each other's eyes as it did its magic.

"I promise to guard it with my life and only use it for good." Tears formed in her eyes.

"That's all I needed to hear." She squeezed Izzy's hands. "Bless you, Isabella."

⌘

Audrey giggled to herself as she leaned across the seat and tipped the Uber driver. *Imagine me using Uber.* She stepped onto the sidewalk and into the bright morning. The confederate jasmine in bloom invited her to breathe in deeply. It felt good to be home again. She opened the glass door, and a bell chimed softly. A gray Persian cat perched high on a shelf stared at her and flicked his tail curiously—a new human.

Audrey lingered at the door a moment to gather her courage. *He must hate me. If he does, I'll be able to see it in his eyes. Then I'll leave and not bother him again.* She made her way to the counter, where a young man focused on a computer screen. He looked up when she approached.

"Can I help you?" The young man asked. Embroidered letters above a pocket protector on his crisply ironed shirt revealed his identity.

"Hi, Theodore. Is the owner here?" She glanced around the lobby. It hadn't changed much.

"Everyone calls me Teddy. What kind of car do you have?"

"Oh, I'm not picking up a car. I'd just like to speak to the owner." The glass door behind Teddy exposed cars parked in rows in the large garage area. Every time someone moved while working on them, she'd glance up to see who it was. Teddy's brow wrinkled, and his mouth twisted. His hesitation was evident. He picked up the phone.

"Hey, is Gramps back there?" He looked up at Audrey while he listened. "I know, but he needs to come up to the front desk." Teddy's eyes met Audrey's. "Yep. Uh-huh. Yep, right now."

"Maybe I should come back at another time." Audrey stepped away from the counter, and her eyes darted to the door.

Teddy held up one finger and, in his best James Cagney accent, said, "There's a beautiful dame here, see. Tell him to come up and see. See?" He listened again, then said, "Okay, tell him it's his last chance to hook up with a classy broad." He smiled brightly at Audrey. She backed away from the counter toward the cat and massaged him behind his ears.

"I don't mean any disrespect, Ma'am," Teddy said after he hung up. "I'll never get him up here unless he thinks it's for a good reason. If he hits on you, tell him you're married."

Audrey smiled. "I will."

On the opposite wall hung a poster of a man sitting in a chair playing guitar. It called on all fans to join Michael Reynolds for an exclusive engagement. He would be sharing his new rhythm and blues recordings. With gray hair cut short beneath a denim newsboy cap, the image captured a comfortable smile with a twinkle in his eye. His expression was self-assured and brought back memories of when he played at her wedding. A lifetime ago. A time when she and Eric made so many plans for the future.

The door opened, and music streamed in along with the whining of lug wrench drills and the clang of tools. Audrey felt the urge to slip out the door but kept her feet planted.

"What is it, Teddy? You know I need to get this tune-up finished before 10:00," a gruff voice said. He wiped his hands on a towel.

Not able to wait, Audrey stole a peek. His once wavy blond

locks were now mostly gray and his face red from the heat of the shop. Her heart pounded in her chest. She'd know that face anywhere. He looked older with thick creases on his forehead and laugh lines around his eyes and mouth.

Teddy pointed to Audrey. "Mac was supposed to tell you. You have a customer who wants to speak to you."

Audrey turned slowly to face him. His blue eyes looked at her the same way they had when they first met. As recognition set in, he froze. The towel he was holding fell to the floor.

"Audrey?" He rushed around the counter and stood in front of her.

"It's me." Her breath caught in her throat.

"Oh, my God!" Eric pulled her into him and held her tight. She melted into his chest. His body felt the same, and he smelled of home. She instinctively wrapped her arms around him.

Teddy looked on with opened mouth. "Grandpa? Is everything okay?"

Eric held Audrey at arm's length. "Is it you?"

"Eric, I'm so sorry." She broke free of him, and tears fell down her cheeks.

He stared at her silently. He couldn't wrap his brain around what was in front of him. Unable to handle his scrutiny, she lowered her head.

"Everyone said you were dead." He shook his head. "But I knew you weren't. I would've felt it if you were." He waited for her to look at him. "What happened to you?"

Audrey turned away, and the tears came harder. "I thought you died on that boat." She sobbed, then turned back to face him. He needs to hear it from me, she thought. "When I found out you were alive, I thanked God. I could never allow anyone to hurt you again. I'm sorry, but I didn't feel I had a choice."

"I looked for you. For months."

"Grandpa? What's going on?" Teddy asked.

Eric searched for the answers in Audrey's face. After a few beats, his stare broke away. He looked at Teddy and smiled. Eric's strange expression made his grandson uncomfortable. Teddy ran his hand through his auburn locks, and his mouth turned down. A gesture Audrey saw Eric do many times so long ago.

"It's okay." Eric motioned for him to come around the counter. He put his arm around Teddy and squeezed. "I want you to meet someone."

"You okay?" Eric said to Audrey. She nodded and wiped her eyes with a tissue.

"Theodore, I want you to meet Audrey," Eric said and smiled at her. "We knew each other before I married your grandmother."

"It's nice to meet you." Teddy held out his hand. Audrey hesitated for a moment, then took it into hers.

"It's nice to meet you too."

"This is my youngest grandson. He's studying to be a pilot and going into the Air Force in September." Eric couldn't conceal the pride he had in Teddy.

"Wow! You already graduated from high school?" Audrey eyed him skeptically. He looked so young and so like Eric.

"I'm getting my degree in Aeronautical Engineering in June," Teddy said.

"He takes after his mother. Who takes after her mother."

"Sounds like it runs in the family," Audrey said.

"Where are you staying? I would like to see you tonight after we close up."

"I'm at Grandma Josie's place. I can make dinner for you and Tabitha; I'd love to see her again."

"Granny died last year. She had cancer," Teddy said.

"Oh, I'm so sorry. I didn't know." Audrey's mouth turned down. The phone started to ring.

"It's okay," Eric said. "Tabby was sick a long time. It was skin cancer." He shook his head and remembered something that made him smile. Audrey waited. She'd missed so much over the years and was hungry to hear details of Eric's life.

"Her dad always said her freckles were stars waiting to be born so they could fly up to the Heavens to live out their days." He smiled sadly. "Now she lives among them." Then added, "But, we were together for thirty-six years and had two beautiful girls. Now we're blessed with five grandchildren."

"All as smart as Theodore, I bet." Audrey glanced at Teddy. Eric grabbed her hand. "How long are you in town?"

The phone continued to ring. Eric turned and scowled at Teddy, then tilted his head toward the phone. Teddy hurried back to the counter and answered it. He took down information from the caller while attempting to listen in on his grandfather's conversation. He wanted to know more about the mysterious woman.

"Well, I plan to check on Claire, and then we'll see."

"Let me take you to dinner." He rubbed her hand with his thumb as he held it. "They've opened a few restaurants since you were home." Then, "Oh, and Michael's playing at The Crab Shack." He grinned at her. "He'd get a kick out of seeing you."

"Michael looks like he did okay for himself." Audrey pointed to the poster.

"Yes, yes, he did. He never married, though." Eric's shoulders inched toward his ears, and he shook his head. "He hasn't found anyone willing to put up with his *unique* personality. He keeps trying to find the perfect girl on those dating websites."

"Did you tell him there is no such thing as a perfect girl?"

Audrey giggled in her familiar way.

Eric's breath caught, and his face flushed. "I told him to be patient because his perfect girl is out there, and when he finds her, he should never let her go." He looked into her eyes, and although her face had aged with time, her eyes hadn't. Except, they seemed sadder. She turned away from him. "I'm so sorry," Eric said.

"You have nothing to be sorry about."

He stepped closer and took her cheeks into his hands, then found the familiar scar he came to love so long ago. He guessed she no longer had the matryoshka. Otherwise, she wouldn't be standing in front of him. Many questions ran through his head. Is she still in danger? Where has she been all these years? Where is the matryoshka? He sensed her hesitancy and hoped she would be able to trust him again. He stared at her a moment, then shook his head. He laughed, then cleared his throat.

"I'm afraid to let you walk out that door." He dropped his hands to his sides.

Audrey smiled weakly and shrugged her shoulders. "Don't worry. I'm here to stay."

Epilogue

On the other side of the world, unexpected snow silently fell as spring brought blooms to the cherry blossoms in south St. Petersburg. In the wee hours of the morning, a little cafe hosted The Smoking Guns. Their final tune was a song by The Pixies, called 'Where is my Mind.' Tables interspersed with groups of late-night customers applauded as the last notes rang out. After a few minutes, they gradually made their way out into the street.

A lone man sat at a darkened corner table and watched the band members make small talk with the cafe owner. When it was nearly empty inside, he got up and walked out.

"Andy, wait for me." Izzy jumped down from the stage and hurried to the door.

"Where are you going?" Andrew, Izzy's boyfriend, called after her. "We need to pack up and be on the road in thirty." His British accent rang out, alerting the rest of the band members of a possible snag in their tight schedule. They stopped packing instruments to gaze at her going out the door.

"Don't worry. I won't be long," Izzy called over her

shoulder.

She stood on the sidewalk and assessed her surroundings. The streets were quiet except for a few couples chatting outside the café. Also, patrons of the theatre milled about before leaving on foot or by car. Electric lights glowed dimly with rings of fog floating around them. She looked in both directions and caught a glimpse of him to her left at the corner. She jogged to catch up, following him around the building.

"Wait!" She yelled, but he ignored her and continued. He picked up his pace.

"Stop!" She shouted. At a full run, she caught up in the middle of the next block.

He stopped abruptly and turned to face her. With arms stiff at his sides and chin held high, he challenged her, "Why are you following me?"

"Hey, no big deal. I just thought I knew you from somewhere." She held her palms up. A breeze blew through her dark rhinestone tank top and stretchy Capri pants. On her feet were black Doc Martin boots, laced halfway. A new tattoo, still red around the edges, burned above her left breast when goose pimples appeared there. The man took one look at it and shook his head, then turned away.

"Wait. Hold up." She took a step toward him. "Do you know of us? Are you a talent scout? You were in the café. I saw you there sitting alone in the dark." Her long dark hair, held on top of her head with a scrunchy, fell loosely around her face. "I noticed you were just looking at my chest. You like my new tattoo?" It was a Russian nesting doll.

"I just wondered why you'd put that on your tit, but no matter. I know." He said. "Now, if you don't mind, I have a train to catch." He started walking again.

"Hey! I remember you now. At the airport last week. You

were watching me. I thought you might've been a talent scout or something." Realization spread across Izzy's face, and she poked her chest out and pulled her top away to give him a better view. "Does your interest in my tattoo have something to do with a special artifact?" He started walking again, but Izzy grabbed his sleeve. "It does, doesn't it. Aren't you, Mr. Bortnik?"

This time he turned and hissed. "You're in over your head, girlie." His eyes flashed anger, and his rage caught Izzy off guard. She stepped back.

Andrew walked up to them and put his arm around Izzy's waist. "Izzy, what's going on? Is this guy bothering you?"

"Don't worry. The creep was just leaving." She looked Bortnik in the eye. "I'm not like Audrey, you know. You can't push me around."

Andrew stepped closer to the man until they were nose to nose. "You got that, buddy? Get lost!"

Mr. Bortnik stood his ground for a moment, then turned away. He continued down the sidewalk.

"Are you alright?" Andrew asked. "What was that about?"

"I'm fine." She wrapped her arm around his waist. "Let's go pack up."

"I'll see you around, Izzy from Smoking Gun," Bortnik mumbled to himself. Izzy looked back at him without breaking her stride, but she frowned, biting her lip. When they were out of earshot, he pulled out his phone and punched in a number. He put it to his ear and waited.

"She has it. Yes. I am certain. Of course not." He turned to watch Izzy and Andrew turn the corner to the café. "Don't worry about me. I got this. They are traveling back to Moscow tonight for another show tomorrow. I will be there ahead of them." His mustache twitched, and his lips peeled back into a sneer.

ACKNOWLEDGMENTS

First and foremost, I'd like to thank my husband, George, for reading my first drafts without saying how terrible they were. Your patience and belief in my success helped me grow and pushed me to finish the story.

Next, I'd like to thank my darling sister-in-law, Merrilie, who tirelessly edited the drafts several times without a single gripe. Your eagle-eye managed to find errors no one else noticed, and your insights into the plot were invaluable. You helped me to see the story from the reader's perspective.

Finally, I want to thank my very creative and talented brother, Daniel, who designed the beautiful cover. With your artistic ability, you created something original that is crisp and pops.

ABOUT THE AUTHOR

Jessica May Broyles is the author of, The Nested Charmer, A Matryoshka's Hidden Legacy. As a certified high school counselor, she spent most of her career working with teens. As a result, her characters bring to light some of the social and family issues plaguing today's society. Jessica has written several short stories and nonfiction. She lives with her husband, George, and golden-doodle, Charlie a few miles outside Kennedy Space Center.